Advance praise for
i know how this ends

"Your destiny can be a person. Your destiny can be an event. But sometimes, your destiny is a question so old that you can't remember a time when it wasn't part of you. Until its stunning conclusion, you won't know how I KNOW HOW THIS ENDS does, in fact, end. Once you know, you'll never forget it."

— **Jacquelyn Mitchard, NYT #1 bestselling author,** *The Deep End of the Ocean*

"A magical and moving tale of love and loss, hope and re-demption, *I Know How This Ends* explores the winding and complex journeys we take to find where we ultimately belong. In this time-bending and totally unique story, Amy Impellizzeri once again proves herself a true standout voice in the fiction world."

— **Kristy Woodson Harvey, bestselling author of** *Slightly South of Simple*

"Mind blown. Amy Impellizzeri's first novel, Lemongrass Hope, has always lingered in my mind, in the way that only some stories can. *I Know How This Ends* is no exception. It will make you contemplate your life, wonder about the choices you've made, and think again."

— **Barbara Bos, Women Writers, Women's Books**

"With this compelling follow-up to her bestselling book *Lemongrass Hope*, Impellizzeri stretches the boundaries of time, love, and family with an imaginative premise that leads the reader to think...what if? We all wonder how life might have turned out if we'd made different choices and *I Know How This Ends* explores this possibility for Kate, Ian, Rob, and Dee. It was a delight to return to these characters, but readers new to Impellizzeri can just as easily be captivated by this standalone story. Be prepared to tell yourself, "Just one more chapter..."

— **Camille Di Maio, bestselling author of *The Beautiful Strangers***

i know how this ends

i know how this ends

amy impellizzeri

Wyatt-MacKenzie Publishing
DEADWOOD, OREGON

I KNOW HOW THIS ENDS

Amy Impellizzeri

ISBN: 978-1-948018-64-7

Library of Congress Control Number:2019956858

Wyatt-MacKenzie Publishing
DEADWOOD, OREGON

Wyatt-MacKenzie Publishing, Inc.
www.WyattMacKenzie.com
Contact us: info@wyattmackenzie.com

dedication

To the earliest readers of *Lemongrass Hope*.
You embraced me on this journey with open arms and
I will never stop being grateful to you.

i know how this ends
A Paraquel to **Lemongrass Hope**

IN THE SPRING OF 2020, a very special class is graduating from high school. This class of students has just one thing in common. The class is composed completely of 37 survivors—of children whose pregnant mothers were in and around the World Trade Center on 9/11, but whose mothers survived, and gave birth within the next few months. These 37 students are part of a longitudinal study known as "Operation Steel Survivors" and their very public commencement is now scheduled for Carnegie Hall in Manhattan.

Hope Campton is the Valedictorian and graduation speaker of Operation Steel Survivors Class of 2020, getting ready to deliver five to seven minutes of inspiration to a class full of young adults who were born in the aftermath of the greatest tragedy of a generation. Press and public are awaiting the start of the ceremony, but it's beginning to look like the only two people who Hope wants to see in the audience are not going to make it.

Meanwhile, Kate Monroe and Ian Campton are battling more than just New York City traffic to get to their destination. It seems a lifetime of choices are catching up with each of them, and the detours and traffic stops aren't helping anything.

Enter Rory Garcia, a young and hungry journalist who gets detoured on her way to cover an immigration rights protest at City Hall. When her cab is involved in a collision outside Carnegie Hall, she decides instead to cover the commencement of Operation Steel Survivors, and the highly anticipated Valedictorian speech of the day.

Rory arrives at Carnegie Hall on the heels of a bitter argument with her Cuban-American husband. Frustrated and flustered, Rory unwittingly uncovers a story that threatens to dwarf Hope Campton's graduation speech. While waiting for the commencement ceremony to start, a mysterious stranger tells Rory a time-bending story about epic love, loss, and sacrifice, and suddenly the story Rory thinks she is covering only as an outsider looking in— becomes so much more.

It's The Life of Pi meets Sliding Doors meets Sophie's Choice.

It's neither a prequel, nor a sequel, but rather another chapter altogether of the award-winning novel, *Lemongrass Hope.*

Welcome to: *I Know How This Ends.*

FEBRUARY 11, 2001.

AGAIN.

prologue

THERE'S A MOMENT before I drown that I know the truth.

Just before my head goes under the water is a moment in which I feel such clarity that I think I must be dying. No one should know so certainly all the things I suddenly know, and still go about their life as before. Even this—the acknowledgement of my clarity is a thought that as it forms, I fear is just too clear and too focused to be trusted.

Ian and I have come on this trip to get away. But I know that in reality he is trying to help me. I suspect that he would like to start a family, but when I bring it up, he keeps telling me to focus only on myself.

Ian wants so badly to cure me. He can't of course. No one has been able to. No therapist, no psychiatrist, and certainly not Ian. Drugs have been powerless. Behavioral therapy has been fruitless. I've read articles about electro-convulsive therapy from the 1940s, shoddily referred to by the mainstream media as "shock therapy" and dismissed summarily as well, and I've wondered if I should beg for that. It seems cruel that this method went out of vogue for reasons that seem to pertain to politics and the power of the pharmaceutical companies, rather than efficacy. I'm worried about Ian's reaction, so I don't bring it up to him. I keep my research to myself. I long for something that might work, but I can't find the words to ask Ian to go to any extremes for me. I am certain that if I ask him to find a doctor who still performs ECT, he will do so. And this fear of being indulged, rather than a fear of being dismissed, is why I don't ask. I understand even in my compromised state that I need to put less pressure on him, not more. Ian wants to help me so much that he will do anything for me. I know this and the little girl in me who still believes in unicorns and fairy tales also believes this sort of love alone should cure me. But the woman who has been struggling for a decade now, knows it doesn't work this way.

Sigh. *A decade.*

Has it really been that long? Has it really been *only* that long?

A decade ago, I chose Ian. I chose Ian fully and completely because I believed—no at that time, I *knew*—that I could not have a whole and happy life without him.

And yet ever since I made that choice, I've been on a downward spiral toward madness.

I can't explain it. I can only feel it. And I'm taking Ian down with me. This is my greatest sadness.

I've begged him to go.

"I can't leave you, Kate," he says.

"Leave me and create a life that you want. You deserve that," I have cried night after night. I can't get well, and I hate myself for that.

There are nights I wonder if my life has any worth at all. But still I persist. I cling to that small fact. Every morning I wake and move forward. I am not suicidal. For all my isms and osises, I am *not* suicidal. My therapists and doctors emphasize this fact almost to remind me lest I forget at any time. They share it with each other with a glee that seems misplaced to me. *Yes, I want to keep living,* I concede. And yet, I don't have the faintest idea why.

"Hope. That's why," Ian says in response. He says this every single time I question.

"What is that? What is hope?" I ask him often, and with despair. I am losing bits of myself and I don't know how to find them again. "What is hope?" I asked him just before we came on this trip. I don't even remember what that word means anymore. I've tried to remember the emotion it denotes, but my memory fails me.

We are on a cruise ship named The Beatrice II. We came on board in 2011, but we're leaving in 2001, after traveling through the Bermuda Triangle, and the shock of that realization is the reason I landed here in the water. It's the reason I'm drowning.

But the miracle is not that we've gone back in time. The miracle is that suddenly, just before I drown, with a clarity I fear I cannot trust, I finally realize what Ian has meant all along.

Hope is not a what.

She's a who.

COMMENCEMENT DAY, MAY 5, 2020

chapter one

Rory

RORY GARCIA GLANCED at the time on her oversized wrist watch: *9:30 am.*

She'd been up for two hours and all she'd managed to do so far was get dressed and pick through the half-used cups littering every surface of the closet-sized Manhattan apartment she shared with Marcos, as she tried to find one cup that was not too gross to wash out. She sniffed each cup tentatively, until she found one that turned her stomach only a little bit. Marcos had decimated all their drinking cups with that foul-smelling kombucha he loved to drink while he was working, letting it seep into the cheap plastic rather than washing them out as she'd asked him—no *begged* him—a thousand times. Now she'd have to venture out to the suburbs to find a Target or a Walmart just to find affordable replacements for the ruined plastic cups. She shuddered at the thought. Rory abandoned the sniffing and picking to rummage through the only cabinet in the kitchen (more like kitchen "area") of the studio apartment to find a coffee mug to fill with diet coke as per her morning ritual.

Outside the kitchen window Rory caught a glimpse of new scaffolding going up on the apartment building across the street. Lately, everywhere she turned, something or someone was getting a new facelift in New York City. It was disconcerting and oddly rejuvenating at the same time.

Rory plucked a mug from the sparse cabinet and sank into the only chair in the only room of the only apartment she'd ever lived in. Before the apartment was a house. A house the right size for Rory and her mother. Which is all it had ever been before it became Rory and Marcos.

Her mother had been reluctant at first, before finally giving Rory her blessing to move in with Marcos. Though her blessing was unsolicited, it was nevertheless appreciated. As it turned out, it was also short-lived.

"Go on. Move in together. I get it. It's time for me to spread my wings anyway."

An odd phrasing, Rory had thought briefly as she kissed her mother's cheek and headed to the mutually agreed-upon place where she was meeting the rental broker with Marcos. Wasn't it Rory who was meant to be spreading *her* wings?

Rory headed to the first of many meetings with an impatient and ambitious broker who ended up showing them fourteen apartments the same week she showed them this one.

Marcos said he knew it was the one because it had a certain charm the others lacked. Rory said she knew it was the one because it was the only apartment they could actually afford. With Marcos's erratic art-related and warehouse income and Rory's low-paying position as digital content writer for *The Manhattan Street*, an online journal with a cult following, they couldn't even afford this one. They couldn't afford lunch in SoHo, or their monthly Metro pass, or the high prices of the Union Square green market that came alive every Saturday morning. They couldn't afford Manhattan, but both of them agreed they'd do whatever was necessary to keep on living there, because they couldn't imagine a life anywhere else.

These were all the things they agreed upon. Without exception and without compromise. It felt like enough. Rory and Marcos and New York. From the moment they met, it felt like this was all they'd ever need.

That is, until Marcos got an offer to leave and go somewhere else. After that happened, suddenly everything was upside down and Rory wasn't at all sure how to turn it right side up again.

Miami.

It was like the opposite of New York City. Miami was a colorful paint-splattered town. New York was sleek and monochrome. Just a little more than two weeks ago, Marcos told Rory he wanted to move to Miami, and he was still shocked that she couldn't get on board.

"You just need more time," he said often.

"I don't think I do," Rory replied just as often.

Marcos argued that Rory's reluctance was simply that New York was known. Miami was not. Rory exclaimed—"Yes! Exactly!"—trying to show Marcos that he'd actually made her point for her. They wouldn't have their grounding in Miami. No friends. No social calendar. No history. No memories together. They wouldn't be able to smile as their taxi sped past the art gallery where they first met. They wouldn't be able to go to the breakfast nook around the corner and ask for "just a dash" of cinnamon on their French toast. They wouldn't cross paths with the same pit mix named Lulu on the first leg of their daily morning run, and the English lab named Buster on the second leg. Nothing would be familiar and everything would be like starting over. How could he be thinking of taking such a leap? Rory felt her legs give out with the thought. Even though she was sitting, she knew her legs were too weak to hold her. She stayed in her seat, with her chipped coffee mug of diet coke as Marcos slept nearby, letting her resentment and fear bubble up inside of her like an angry volcano. Rory listened to the distant signs of construction and newness taking shape right outside their apartment while she sat stewing in her own emotions.

Of course, this thing with Marcos? It was itself new.

They'd met less than eight months ago, and here they were. *Eight months.* The significance seemed both random and daunting. After all, it was less than the length of human gestation, less than the time needed to grow and birth a human child but much more than the time needed to grow and birth a kangaroo, lion, or a pig. (Rory had researched gestation periods for an article. Yes, elephants had the longest, as most people knew, but sperm whales were a close second, and giraffes and alpacas had gestation periods of +1 years, which was irrelevant to the article she was writing, but still an interesting surprise).

Marcos had gently pointed out that while eight months was long enough to have fallen in love, and to have created some wonderful memories in New York, it was hardly a lifetime. And so, he said, their history together in New York wasn't a compelling reason not to create new memories somewhere else. Rory couldn't argue her point logically with him, but that didn't keep her from trying.

Rory thought about alpacas instead of Miami as she traced the broken edge of the coffee mug, distractedly drinking from the opposite side so she wouldn't cut her lip. She was relieved when she realized what she was doing. It was a relief that self-preservation was still flowing in her veins and in her self-conscious. She'd have to make do with this chipped coffee mug. There weren't any more. This apartment, unlike the apartment of nearly every other human they knew, had a scarcity of coffee mugs on any given day. This one was probably left behind from the former resident, in fact. Rory could not remember buying it. As she twisted it in her hand, careful to keep the broken edge away from her lips, she read the logo—Two Valley Coffee Shop. Rory was certain she'd never been to such a place, let alone bought a mug there to commemorate the visit.

Rory and Marcos had hardly any coffee mugs because neither of them drank coffee. And truthfully, in a world that seemed dominated by mocha cappuccinos on every street corner, the fact that these two non-coffee-drinking New Yorkers had found each other at all seemed some kind of crazy karmic connection at the start.

At the start.

The start of what?

Rory looked at her watch again. *9:45 am.*

Over the top of her broken mug, Rory looked at Marcos sleeping on top of the too-small sofa in the living room (more like, living "area") of the small apartment, snoring and dreaming. She stared at him as if she could decipher his dreams, but lately, she was having trouble doing that even when Marcos was awake.

When Rory and Marcos had moved in together in the fall, this apartment had felt like all they needed. Would ever need. But it wasn't long before Marcos made the apartment smaller and smaller.

He did this with his kombucha and art supplies strewn everywhere. He did this with his long limbs barely contained by the West Elm hand-me-down sofa that Rory had bought from a friend. Rory brought the sofa to the apartment and nothing else, because she knew there wasn't room for a lot of her old things from the house she'd shared with her mother in a small seaside neighborhood in Queens since birth. There wasn't room for her things, but she didn't care. She just wanted to be in the apartment with Marcos. That was enough.

Until Marcos made the apartment too small even for her sofa.

The thing was—Marcos made everything small. It was an art form for him. Literally.

Marcos had not shared his art with her until after they moved in together. He'd made it clear that it was something he shared with very few. Rory felt honored and humbled when he shared it with her, not spending too much time to think about how an artist who didn't share his work, actually survived.

Rory loved his secret passion, and loved being in on it. But now all that had changed. Marcos was going to share his passion with everyone. And maybe, if she was being honest with herself, that was what was eating her alive: the fact that she'd no longer be special. Maybe the real problem was that he would be off in Miami sharing his art, and maybe learning to love coffee, and who knows what else.

Who knows what else?

Maybe she wasn't worried about being left behind in New York City. Maybe she was worried that if she went with Marcos to Miami, she would *still* be left behind.

"I'm leaving early tomorrow morning for an assignment." Rory had said these words to Marcos the night before without even looking up from her laptop, as she tapped out notes and questions in preparation for the next day.

He'd walked over to her and tipped her chin away from the screen up at him.

"Which assignment, *Bella*?"

He's trying to hypnotize me, Rory had thought briefly with her chin pointed up toward his dark eyes. She couldn't look away.

(Early on in the relationship she'd asked him, "Do you call all your girlfriends, *Bella*?" He looked hurt as he responded, "No, it's actually a very old-fashioned Spanish word. I never used it with a woman before. My father, though, he called my mother, *Bella*, on occasion, and I always thought it was so endearing. I stored it away thinking I'd use it for the right someone. Someday.")

Marcos had been attentive and interested as he tried to talk to her about her assignment. Rory felt a little bit guilty for dismissing him. But she'd dismissed him nonetheless. "The immigration protest. At city hall."

"Are you not working on the other story, then?" He smiled as he said it. But still she'd been annoyed. "I'm not giving up that story, Marcos. Don't ask me to. This is just another angle of it."

He nodded and walked away from her, letting her get back to work.

The "other story" that Marcos had been referring to, was a different kind of immigration story. She was covering a murder trial of a man who had immigrated and never became a legal citizen. Rory was writing installment pieces for the ongoing trial, twice a week. Her editor was happy with her work, and encouraged her to pursue the trial to its natural conclusion.

But Marcos made her feel the piece was beneath her. Marcos kept saying, "But that's not the right story. You're making it a story of an immigrant accused of crimes, but it's just the story of a man on trial. Maybe you're making this bigger than it needs to be. Bigger than it *wants* to be."

Rory did not accept Marcos's judgment. "First of all, stories don't *want* to be. They just are. This is the difference between fiction writing and journalism. And you want me to write this piece as if it's a story about yet another man in New York City on trial? Well, I'm sorry, but that's not a story that anyone wants to read. And it isn't a story that sells online ad clicks, Marcos."

Rory knew her explanations were falling on deaf ears; Marcos just shook his head.

"*Bella*, don't go out there looking for a story that doesn't exist. Try telling the story that finds you instead."

It made her angry—his exuberant dose of optimism. She feared the thing she first fell in love with about Marcos, was starting to overtake their relationship and swallow her whole.

Rory wanted to bounce that fear off someone, but she was hiding the growing tension between Marcos and herself from everyone. She was hiding it from one person in particular: her mother. This wasn't too hard to do, as Rory's usually pragmatic and calm homebody of a mother had up and left town. Up and left the country, actually.

Hidden away at a yoga retreat out of the country for the last month with nothing but strangers, (if the Instagram pictures were to be believed), Rory's mother was too far away to observe and question the tension herself. Rory hoped it would dissipate before her mother got home to see it, and before anyone had to make any rash decisions about Miami.

Rory flipped through her mother's most recent Instagram story on her phone as she sipped diet coke out of a chipped coffee mug reflectively. Was her mother old enough to be having a midlife crisis? She thought not, but the pictures hinted otherwise. One after another showed her mother twisted and bent in various yoga poses while a yogi surveyed the class from the perimeter.

And what about me? Am I too young to be having a midlife crisis?

The unasked and unanswered question lingered in the space between the sleeping Marcos and the long wakened Rory.

Rory noticed then that the construction had stopped. Or at least she couldn't hear it any longer. What she heard in its place was the sound of raindrops hitting the sidewalk below their apartment. When she was finished with her soda, Rory looked at her watch again and got up to leave without so much as a half-hearted goodbye kiss to the sleeping, dreaming Marcos with limbs overflowing from the West Elm sofa in the middle of their tiny apartment.

Rory closed the door quickly and loudly behind her.

The truth was, the problem between them—the one she wasn't saying out loud to her mother or anyone else for that matter—wasn't the kombucha or Marcos's belongings or his limbs jutting off the edges of their worn-out secondhand furniture.

Marcos had made the only apartment they had—the only apartment they could afford—too small with his big dreams and optimism and right now, Rory hated him for that.

Kate

KATE MONROE GLARED at her watch, willing it to stop. She stared out the window through driving rain at the brutal traffic on the George Washington Bridge leading them from New Jersey to New York. It was barely moving.

"There's an accident up ahead," the cab driver shook his head, apparently dismayed at having to share the news, but not too dismayed to forego sharing it altogether.

"We're never going to make it in time." Kate pulled up a Google map on her phone and tried mapping out the walking distance. "Even if we walked, we couldn't make it in time." She leaned back into the seat despairing.

The driver laughed, a little too menacingly, Kate noted, before delivering the punchline. "Ma'am, with this weather, you're not going to be walking anywhere right now."

In the adjacent lane, a mud-splashed, grey-blue minivan inched alongside Kate's cab in a race no one could win. Through the rain and dirty windows, Kate could make out two small, sleeping humans buckled into rear-facing seats in the back of the minivan. Kate stared at the children, wondering if they were twins or just siblings too close in age to allow their parents to rest. In the front seats, she could see the silhouettes of a man and a woman who were staring straight ahead at the traffic, seemingly oblivious to the other. Kate nodded knowingly on their behalf.

She looked out the window, mentally counting the miles that stood in the way. As they moved forward and were pushed back, the trip became a perfect metaphor. Even she could see that.

It will mean everything if we make it there in time.

If we aren't all there, she'll be so disappointed—

Kate tried not to finish the thought and sighed instead.

In answer to her sigh, and maybe also to the words she didn't think she'd said out loud, the driver addressed her gently. "Have faith, lady. Have faith. I haven't given up yet."

Kate watched him reach into a pocket on the driver side door and pull out something she hadn't seen in years: an actual map.

Kate thought back to when she was a little girl. A memory sprang up of running errands with her father. They ended up at the local travel agency, asking for a Northeastern road map. Her dad said he wanted to keep one in the glove box, in case they ever just felt like going on a road trip, then they'd know some places to go—some highways to travel.

Kate's dad unfolded the map immediately, and with all its new creases and bends, it never really went back into its original position. He kept it in the glove box, and rarely pulled it out. When they traded in that car for a shinier model around the time Kate got her driver's license, she assumed the map went along with the car. She never thought to ask her dad to take the map out of the glove box before they handed over the keys to the dealer.

Watching the cab driver study the creased and folded map while they were stuck on the George Washington Bridge brought about a kind of nostalgia in Kate.

My life feels like that map, Kate thought.

Sometimes, it's exciting and an adventure, all wrapped up as one.

But other times, it's a little crinkled and folded along the wrong lines.

Truth be told, that map my dad bought was never as beautiful as it was that day we removed it from its plastic wrapping at the desk of the travel agency.

Some things do lose their shine, after all.

Ian

ALTHOUGH IAN COULD see only her profile as she looked out the cab window, Kate looked nervous. Pretty but nervous.

He'd missed her so much. He tried not to let his heart go there but still it did. Things were breaking inside of him anew that he thought were already long broken. The fact that there were still pieces of him left to break came as a relief in spite of that pain.

In pain there can still be joy. A mystic had told Ian this a long time ago. Ian never really understood the words until he'd experienced their meaning firsthand again and again over the years that followed.

The outskirts of Central Park came into focus as they moved through the streets like an obstacle course. There were unexpected road closures on the Upper West side that necessitated a new route. Ian didn't mind the delay but he could tell Kate did. He distracted himself by imagining what lay beyond the perimeter of Central Park—a zoo in the middle of Manhattan. He'd always found it an exhilarating prospect. Kate had called it irony, but he'd corrected her and told her it was a redundancy.

Always a writer, Kate had laughed. How he'd loved the days when it was still so easy to make her laugh.

In New York, Ian had been a writer, but really, New York had been a stopping off point between bigger stories. He traveled to India and Africa routinely, and wrote about what he saw and experienced there. Before Kate, he had only came back to New York to pitch his next story to his editor. But meeting Kate changed everything. New York became much more than a stopping off point.

Their last August together, Ian and Kate had won a family membership to the zoo at a benefit gala for the Wildlife Conservation Society. Ian had gotten tickets to the gala from his editor and he'd insisted that Kate and he get dressed up and go.

"We won't have a chance to do things like this much longer," he argued persuasively. Kate didn't want to bid on anything, but Ian put raffle tickets into a few bags in the silent auction room. He was thrilled when his name was called out as the winner for the zoo membership.

They'd walked the paths of the zoo one day in early September to christen their new membership, after Kate had come home from teaching, and Ian had finished writing for the day. Deadlines met, and editors and students appeased, they walked hand-in-hand past the yelping sea lions, under a canopy of flowers, past the monkeys, and circling the reptile house to close the loop in front of the sea lions again.

"So, it's not a real zoo?" Kate had asked as they walked along the path the first time, the leaves just starting to change color around the outer edges, the golden corners devouring the green innards of the leaves hovering above.

"Well, I don't know about that. What do you call a real zoo?" Ian had asked.

"One with lions, tigers, a giraffe or two maybe."

Her hand had been linked comfortably in his. He could remember the feel of her fingers wrapped around his. She had never been in the zoo before that night. All those years of living in and around the city, and she'd never even been to the Central Park Zoo. Ian had been surprised to learn that. He'd been surprised to discover every little thing about Kate. Those discoveries had been the things he held onto later on. When it all went away.

Ian knew even then that his hold on everything was tenuous. Kate was well for the first time in a decade. Maybe more. But at what cost? Only Ian knew for sure and lived his life alternately fearful and overjoyed. He tried not to stay in either place too long.

"If you want to see lions and giraffes, you don't go to a zoo," he explained to her. "You go to Africa."

"Fair enough," she said.

"We'll go there together one day," Ian promised as he shared tales of the Okavango Delta in Botswana with her. He'd fallen in love with that place and he wanted her to fall in love with it, too: the elephant sanctuary, the sunsets, the healing marula trees and their shade. Botswana was a very special place for Ian, and he wanted to take Kate there, to have her experience its magic firsthand.

Kate had smiled indulgently as if she didn't know whether or not he meant it. But he did mean it. There was a healing magic in the Okavango Delta that Ian had begun daydreaming about. Perhaps the answers were there—the answers to the questions Ian was too nervous to ask Kate out loud. When he talked about the Delta and the marula trees, Kate would rub her belly absent-mindedly. The doctor had told them to walk nightly. He'd told Kate to make sure and get plenty of exercise. To listen to her body. To rest when she needed it, and to stretch when she needed it. Ian had listened to the doctor reverently. He wanted nothing other than to take care of Kate, and to be there for her. Despite all his conflict and fear and guilt, still he was grateful to the universe for giving him Kate, and this life, and this gift.

He whispered a silent thank you to the universe every day that summer and into September.

The universe had responded by flipping him off.

In the cab, a block past Central Park Zoo, Kate turned to him. "Does the city look familiar? Different?"

Ian nodded. "All those things."

"What are you thinking of?" Kate squeezed Ian's arm, gently releasing the answer from him unwittingly. He intended to keep his thoughts to himself on this trip.

Nevertheless, he blurted out, "I was just thinking about Central Park Zoo."

"Central Park Zoo? Ah, funny. I haven't been there in so long." Kate turned her head to look behind them at the place where the hidden zoo might have been.

Ian didn't ask if the last time she'd been there had been with him that warm September evening or not. He didn't want to know. What he knew as he rode through the city and let the memories flow over him, was that he shouldn't have come back to New York City. What good could it possibly do to come back here and re-open everything he had put behind him?

"I'm sorry. I'm not letting you go again this time. The last time, I stood by and let you go. But not this time," Kate had promised as she pulled him off that Mexican beach three days ago and practically pushed him all the way to the airport. "You're coming to see and hear Hope deliver her commencement address. You're coming home. Where you belong."

Home. Where you belong.

Those words. They gutted him. He didn't believe them, but God, how he wanted to.

The driver plodded along through the streets of Manhattan, dodging puddles and potholes, and the rain slowed down and then started back up again. Kate was trying to hurry him and give him detour directions. But Ian hoped the driver would ignore them. He was in no hurry to get there. He was in no hurry to start the rest of their lives. He knew the cost. He'd known the cost all along. That was why he left in the first place all those years ago.

He hoped leaving would alter the course of things.

And he had the audacity to believe it *had* changed things. All these years, while he'd been away, and even when he'd been in Mexico, haunted by memories and loneliness, he still believed that his decision to leave was a noble one. The right one.

I was a fool. It was all a lie, Ian thought unhappily as he watched Kate's profile in the cab.

Ian had left believing that it was the only way to help Kate. He believed if he stayed, Kate would continue to be his. And that would ruin everything.

The truth came to him like an unwelcome guest only recently, of course. Kate didn't belong to Ian. And probably never had.

chapter two

Rory

OUTSIDE THEIR APARTMENT, the rain was falling in pelting drops. Rory ducked the rain and jumped into a cab outside the now-too-small apartment while Marcos slept.

"City Hall," she told the driver and then leaned back heavily into the leather upholstery. A Cuban flag hung from the rearview mirror and darted in and out of her line of vision as she stared straight ahead.

Of course, he's from Cuba.

Rory nodded to herself. The universe had been sending her these crazy signs lately. She was never quite sure what they meant, of course. That's what made them all the more unwanted. The first time she'd ever taken notice—really taken notice—of the Cuban flag was seven months earlier, not long after they'd met, when she and Marcos sat on his late parents' living room floor sorting through their things. There were Cuban flags everywhere among their belongings. Rory stared at the Cuban flag hanging on the taxi rearview mirror like a pendulum and remembered her conversation with Marcos that night.

"This living room is bigger than most Manhattan apartments, Marcos." He laughed. She wasn't joking, though.

He was sorting through one of the last boxes of his parents' possessions, when he blurted out, "I guess I always thought more of my family would come here from Cuba, you know?"

Rory nodded, narrowing her attention away from the huge apartment to the task at hand: cleaning out the apartment and finding Marcos a new place to live. "And now they can't even try?"

"The Wet Feet, Dry Feet policy remained the law until Obama ended it in 2017. Don't get me wrong, I love me some Barack, but he did make things more complicated for my family."

Rory assessed Marcos carefully. It felt like she could say something all wrong here. Something unwittingly political, or insensitive. She was neither, and she didn't want to mislead or disappoint him this early in the relationship.

Some would argue that it was hardly a relationship. They'd only just met at that point.

Three weeks, four days, five hours and forty-six minutes ago.

Rory remembered chuckling to herself as the thought presented itself in the big apartment decorated with Cuban flags. Because the truth was, she didn't really know how many hours and minutes. But she wouldn't have been surprised if her brain was right without her knowing it. The connection with Marcos was strong and it had been instantaneous.

Marcos and Rory had met nearly a month before they sat together on the floor in his late parents' apartment, and the whirlwind had commenced immediately upon their meeting. And now Marcos needed a place to stay. Rory was trying to figure out a way to say the words she was thinking: "Let's find a place together."

She'd tried out the sentiment first to her mother to dismal results. Her mother was a feminist and an outlaw unless either conflicted with her stern mothering, in which case she was tyrannical and provincial.

"You can't move in with a boy you just met."

"Mom. Not to shock you or anything, but I'm almost 22. And he's 23. And that doesn't qualify for the term 'boy.' It also means I don't need permission from you. I'm just telling you. Not asking."

Her mother ignored her logic.

"But honey, what are his plans? Listen, I hate to say this out loud, but you're my daughter, and I have to. Is he here legally? Are you absolutely sure he's not using you? The political climate such that it is, I wouldn't blame him, really, I wouldn't. But you're my daughter, and it's my job to protect you. Not him."

"Mom. I'm going to refrain from walking out of the room right now. But you are so out of line. His parents came here in 1996, and his mom was pregnant with him. They made it here free and clear. Clinton's Dry Feet Policy with Cuba and all that. So, he's a citizen and his parents became citizens through all the proper channels. And this part of the conversation is now officially over."

"I know. You told me all this. It's just—"

"What, Mom? It's just what?"

Rory's mother had looked at her defiantly and Rory had wilted a little under her gaze, as she was prone to do. Her mother was strong. She'd earned her strength, and Rory respected it; she just wished she'd inherited a little more of it.

Rory tried pushing back. "What are you trying to say, Mom? Just say it, already."

"Honey, how can you be sure he's telling you the truth? Have you seen any, you know, *proof* yet? Love is a funny thing, believe me. It feels like enough, but it's really not. I don't say this lightly, really, I don't. But his mom just died in her late 60s. You said so yourself. She was receiving Medicare assistance on her deathbed. That means, she would have had to be in her 40s when she came here pregnant with him. Does that make sense to you? Think about it."

"Yes, mom. I've already told you. He was a late-in-life baby. A miracle baby according to his parents. He was, in fact, the catalyst that helped them decide it was time to leave Cuba. They did it all for him. It makes perfect sense. Unlike this conversation."

A sigh came in unison from both the women. And then from only one of them came a warning: "Oh Rory, please just be careful. I don't know what else to say."

Rory dismissed her mother's cynicism, but gently. She knew the place it came from. Rory's mother had been in love once and he had left her mother behind for dreams of something bigger. When she'd leveled with Rory about her origin story, but still only in the vaguest of terms, Rory's mother had been quick to tell her that her father didn't know about Rory when he left. Neither of them had. "He didn't leave *because of you*," she said again and again as if that was supposed to make everything ok.

"But did he ever find out about me?" Rory got up the nerve to ask. Rory's mother had looked down at the ground with sad eyes, and Rory guessed at an answer without her saying it.

He might not have left because of Rory.

But he hadn't come back for her either.

Rory knew her mother had come by her skepticism and distrust honestly.

And so, as Marcos and Rory were sitting on the floor of his parents' apartment, going through boxes of photos and memorabilia, Rory was thinking about looking for proof of legal citizenship in spite of herself, with her mother's admonitions ringing unwelcome in her head.

Love is a funny thing you know. It feels like enough, but it's really not.

Unfortunately, there wasn't a single legal document among the morass. Just memories and smiling faces and Cuban flags.

Marcos distracted Rory from her internal fight against

her mother's warnings by handing her a photo. It was a picture of a woman with a round belly and a joyful smile. The photograph was faded to a brown-orange sepia tone, but still Marcos held it gently between two fingers as if he could manage to preserve it forever.

"*Mi mama,*" he said simply.

"She looks happy."

"I'm sure she was. She had just made it to America. That was no small thing."

"No, I'm sure it wasn't."

"It was a very big thing."

"A very big thing, Marcos."

He looked up at her. Little moments like this right from the beginning were what connected them. When she let him know that she understood. And he let her know how grateful he was.

Marcos' parents had died just before Rory and Marcos met, one after another, the way people who truly love each other often did. Their life savings, not insignificant, were eaten up in medical bills and rent. The apartment floor where Marcos and Rory were sitting, as well as its walls and every other part of it, had long ago ceased to belong to Marcos or any of his family—legally, that is. The landlord had been kind enough to let Marcos live there to care for his mother who outlived his father from sheer will and determination by two months, even though the rent hadn't been—and indeed couldn't be—paid in nearly a year.

After the funeral, the landlord had asked that Marcos pay the back rent and sign a new two-year lease commitment, or vacate the apartment within two months. He had been kind, but still firm. Marcos agreed to vacate. The apartment, rented by his parents soon after they arrived in America, was nothing Marcos could afford on his combined artist and under-the-table warehouse income. He had helped his parents as much as he could with expenses when they were alive. They'd gotten by and even had some extra to send back to family in Cuba. But now all the money was gone.

"Maybe your family in Cuba could help you out?" Rory asked the question tentatively, and was immediately sorry she did.

"I would never ask that kind of help. They are barely surviving as it is. This apartment is much too big for me. How could I justify it, now that it's clear no one is coming? My parents—they rented it to make room for family, and they always kept this place hoping others would come, but now, well, it's just impossible."

"Because of the end of Wet Foot, Dry Foot policy," Rory repeated, putting the dots together in the conversation as she looked around the enormous apartment—enormous by any standards, not just New York's.

Cuban immigration policy, like all immigration policy, had changed dramatically in the last several years. And Marcos had lost two parents—his only American family, in the midst of the change. He and Rory had found each other soon after.

Too soon to make any big decisions. But still—

"They want me to come back to Cuba now." Marcos picked up a black and white photograph of men and women and small children. He pointed to them one by one. A tall tree with wide leaves half covered one of the faces, but still Rory recognized the partially hidden face as Marcos's mother who would soon become the big-bellied and happy woman in brownish-orange color in the other photo by its side.

"They want me to come back, but New York is my home."

Rory nodded, afraid to use her voice.

"And now I have to choose. Between two lives. They say I don't even really have a home here. So, you know, they think it should be a no-brainer."

"But it's not, of course," Rory responded with understanding and reached across the photos and the boxes to put her hands on Marcos' hand.

"No, it's not."

"My husband is Cuban," Rory blurted out to the cab driver.

He looked at her through the rearview mirror with the Cuban flag dangling down like a hypnotic pendulum.

"Your husband?"

Rory nodded.

"But not you?" She could see the driver's dark eyes in the rearview mirror.

Rory looked down at the floor mats in the back of the cab. They were full of dog hair and dirt and someone had discarded a crumpled candy bar wrapper. The tip of a forgotten umbrella peeked out from under the driver's seat. Rory was tempted to ask who had been there last and was there a way to get their lost umbrella back to them? But she remained silent, not really wanting to know. And not trusting her voice through the wave of emotions crashing over her.

Rory looked out the window at the rain that was not letting up, and reached under the seat to yank the forgotten umbrella free, whispering a little "thank you" to the universe who had sent her a rainy day, and a Cuban cab driver, but also a left-behind umbrella.

Kate

THE LIGHT TURNED green but still they remained motionless in their cab parallel to the Manhattan Cruise Terminal. Traffic and clogged streets prevented them from moving forward. Adele crooned though the car radio and Kate craned her neck trying to see what the new cause of the stopped traffic was, knowing even as she did so that she'd never be able to see. It could be a broken-down car two blocks away or a collision between two delivery bikes three miles away.

That was the thing about this city, Kate thought.

The chain reactions were constantly happening almost out of sight. Equal opposite reactions. Each one acting on the next until you found yourself sitting in a stopped car fighting city traffic, trying to make it to a moment that even a few short years ago, you wouldn't have believed was possible.

Benton's number lit up on Kate's screen and she pushed decline. She didn't want to discuss how very far away they still were. She didn't want to hear Benton's gentle disappointment on the other side of the line.

"Oh, Benton." Kate rubbed her closed eyes and thought back to those early years when she thought everything was so complicated but really it was so very simple. She just hadn't known it yet.

"You can thank me for introducing you to the great love of your life." This was Benton's refrain always and her joyous wedding toast too.

Benton and Kate had first met as young women at the beginning of their adult journeys—falling in and out of love and carving their paths toward independence. In their 20s,

Benton was a young lawyer at one of Manhattan's biggest law firms and Kate was a grad student heading toward the world of academia. After Kate broke up with a musician boyfriend named Ted, or rather after he'd broken up with Kate, Benton had been adamant that Kate should meet one of her law firm colleagues: Rob Sutton.

Of course, on the same day Kate met Rob Sutton, she'd also met Ian Campton. Quite by accident, but also because of Benton. They'd all been at one of Benton's famous Cinco de Mayo parties—the ones she threw annually in Tribeca. In 1997, just weeks before finishing up grad school, Kate was summoned to the party by Benton to meet Rob Sutton, but at the bar, Kate actually met Ian while waiting for Rob. She ended up leaving the party with Rob as planned. But when Ian called her the next day, unplanned, Kate started seeing him instead. Something about their brief meeting at the Tribeca bar captured her. The realist and pragmatist in her hated to admit it, but there it was. Their whirlwind six-week relationship had an end date from the minute it started, however, as Ian was on his way to Botswana for six months, to study mystics and time travel and while Kate was crazy about him, she wasn't crazy. Kate told herself it would indeed be nuts to wait for a man who actually believed in time travel.

Even though he'd made her believe in it too.

As it turned out, Ian boarded a plane to Botswana and Kate let him go, and she got together with Rob Sutton soon after Ian left. Like all good whirlwind love affairs, Ian haunted her thoughts occasionally. But Kate really believed she'd made the right decision, choosing Rob over Ian ... until a getaway trip years later.

Benton had invited everyone on a trip—a cruise to the Bahamas, and directly through the mystical Bermuda Triangle, also called the Devil's Triangle. Kate jumped at the chance to get away. Truth be told, Rob and Kate were struggling fiercely at the time and Kate was anxious for a vacation. She found herself reconnecting with Ian on the trip—again thanks to Benton's invitation, because as she had come to learn, all roads always led back to Benton.

By the end of that trip, Kate had become certain that her relationship with Rob Sutton had run its course; there was little left to it, and it was time to move on. There was a future with Ian, Kate was sure of it. And then something completely incredible happened at the end of that cruise. And it changed *everything*.

Kate and Ian disembarked from that fateful trip in 2001. Benton continued scheduling trips through the Bermuda Triangle regularly, sometimes inviting Kate, sometimes not. Over the last 19 years, their relationship had become a very on-again off-again one, and Kate had deep regrets about that fact.

But recently Benton and Kate had been bonding over something completely different than a cruise to the Bahamas or a trip through the Bermuda Triangle. With this momentous occasion coming up, it seemed it would be bringing them all together again.

"Wouldn't it be amazing if we could all be there filling up the room in a show of support for her?" Benton asked just days ago.

"Yes." Kate agreed without pause.

But now?

Now Kate was stuck in a cab with little hope of getting to see this thing through. And she couldn't help wondering if she'd get a chance to close out this seemingly never-ending loop of regret or not.

Ian

WITH THE QUIET in the cab, Ian could think. And what he was thinking about was his journal.

He didn't remember packing it and wondered if his landlord would find it while cleaning up the Mexican cottage she'd let him squat in for the last few years. Would she read it? Would she read his secrets? What would she think if she did?

He'd written it in Spanish thinking that if Kate or Hope ever found it, they wouldn't be able to read it. Which was silly, or course. They could learn Spanish. They could have it translated. But Ian hadn't been thinking that clearly when he'd written everything down. He'd just needed to get the thoughts out of his head and a journal seemed a safer place to store his memories and emotions than with a therapist or a confidant.

Ian didn't have a therapist *or* a confidant, and he questioned whether either one could have helped with the oppressive loneliness over the last decade or two.

Probably not.

After all, he hadn't been lonely in Mexico or elsewhere because there was no one with him all these years. He had been surrounded by people, most of whom had been incredibly kind. Some of whom had loved him and asked very little in return. But still, he stayed unattached to anyone because he knew he couldn't give anyone—especially another woman—what she would want from him.

Rosa had told him once to stop listening to the voice in his head about what women want, and listen to women instead. Rosa had shared a lot of wisdom with him. And then she left.

On the day she left, Rosa stood across the cottage from him with her hands on her hips.

She wasn't crying. At first he was glad she wasn't crying. *It makes it easier that she's not crying*, he thought.

And then instantly he dismissed the thought. *Tears don't make things harder. I do.*

He would have liked to love this woman. She was beautiful and hard-working and she loved him. He would have liked to return the favor if only as an act of kindness. But he couldn't, of course, so he was trying to end it the way he ended every relationship—cleanly and wholly. Like a thick slice down the middle severing all the loose ends between them.

"I don't love you back, the way you want, Rosa. I wish I did. But I can't."

"Why can't you? And how do you know what I want?" she was asking, staring at him like he was curiosity.

In that moment, Ian thought that maybe he was.

With his heart stuck in another place and time, he constantly felt lost in the world. How could he explain to this fierce woman that he couldn't let go of something that was wrong and long over?

He didn't want to explain it to her, because he didn't want her to see the hypocrisy.

After all, he was telling Rosa not to stay fixated on something that was wrong and over, according to him.

She didn't get a say in this, but that's how love worked. Or didn't.

You only got to stay if both people decided it was right. Otherwise someone would have to leave.

No matter if the leaving broke your heart or not.

The bombshell happened on the last full day of a cruise they had been on together years earlier. How many years earlier was sort of irrelevant because the cruise had gone through the Bermuda Triangle and time had bent during their trip. They had started the trip in 2011 as friends who just so happened to both be separated from their significant others back on land. Kate was unhappy with her relationship with Rob Sutton and Ian was unraveling his relationship with Stella Jordan—a woman he'd grown up with. Their parents had practically arranged their marriage from birth.

Sad as they both were about the turmoil in their respective lives, Ian and Kate were happy to see each other after a long absence. They reconnected quickly. They ended the cruise as lovers, resolved to start a new life together.

And then it happened.

Ian found notes from a trip—notes that had been shredded long before he and Kate had reconnected. At least he *thought they had.* The realization both scared and energized him. What if the time-bending travel he'd come to believe in through his work with mystics in Africa and India had changed the path for him and Kate? If time had truly bent to accommodate them, and to erase the times they had walked away from each other, Ian realized it would mean very different things for both Ian and Kate. That knowledge scared the hell out of him.

Ian had been seeing signs all throughout the trip that made him believe time had sent them back a decade. He had studied with mystics in Botswana and believed in such things, but he also knew this wasn't exactly mainstream thought. He knew Kate would think he was crazy if he voiced any of this to her. He was afraid he might doubt his own sanity if he said any of it out loud, so he ignored the signs and tried keeping Kate cocooned in their own world throughout the trip through the Triangle.

Until that last day when he could no longer deny the truth.

Ian wasn't sure how Kate would react to the news. He

walked her out to the pool deck early in the morning after they dressed.

"Do you think Benton had fun?" Kate asked nonsensically and Ian let himself be momentarily distracted by the question. Benton had invited them both on that trip, and yet neither of them had seen much of Benton on the trip.

"How would we know if she enjoyed herself?" Ian asked practically.

Yes, Benton had invited them on the trip. She set up these get-togethers every few years.

"It beats me why she chooses The Beatrice every time," Kate said, noting that The Beatrice was a cruise ship that headed straight through the Bermuda Triangle. But Ian pointed out the fact that Benton believed the Bermuda Triangle was romantic and tragic, and Kate responded, truthfully, "Like us."

Ian could tell that while Benton made a point to invite them both onto The Beatrice, she didn't seem too crazy about the fact that they reconnected. After all, Benton was the one who set Kate up on that blind date with Rob Sutton all those years ago. But Benton was also the reason Kate and Ian even met in the first place.

Benton was Ian's friend first. His good friend. The kind of friend that helps you nurse broken hearts and the kind who is your default date on New Year's Eve or Saturday night when no one else is around.

She was Ian's friend before she was Kate's. She was Rob's friend before he was Kate's as well, but she didn't seem to mind sharing Rob. That was clear from the beginning. She minded sharing Ian, and that made their friendship awkward.

So, after Kate asked whether Ian thought Benton had a good time on The Beatrice, he was reminded of a few things. First, that his priority was to Kate and not Benton. And second, that he was going to have to tell Kate the truth about them going back in time. And third, that he wasn't at all sure how she would take the news this go around.

Ian had taken her hands in his and tried to say the words. His heart had pounded in his chest as he watched her slowly understand what this trip and their reconnection had meant.

"The thing is, Kate. I think we were meant to be together. I think we were always meant to be together. And I believe the universe has tilted and shifted to make that possible."

"Ian, I don't understand. What are you saying?"

"We're back, Kate. We're right where we should be. All those years of missteps, of walking away from each other. Where has it all led? To unhappiness? Sure. But ultimately, to right now and to where we should be. Where we were meant to be all along."

Ian held her hands while he talked. But Kate jerked away quickly. Ian saw fear in her eyes. And something worse. Mistrust. He saw that she no longer trusted him, and that realization nearly broke him.

"Where are we, Ian? How did this happen?"

They had come on board in 2011. They were leaving in 2001.

Ian told her specific details about his six months in Botswana studying marula fruit and time travel with the mystics. It began the summer they first met. Indeed, that trip to Botswana was the reason he'd first left her. A pre-planned and pre-paid trip by the editors of his journal, Time Travel, Inc. had provided the end date for their summer love affair from the day they met. It was agreed from the start. He was going. He would go.

Kate had let him go to Botswana for a six-month trip, understanding, she said, why he needed to see the trip through. Ian always meant to come back to Kate. It was unspoken but Ian thought she understood. By the time Ian did come back, however, Kate was with Rob, and Ian thought her heart was full. It wasn't until later—after reconnecting with her in the middle of the Bermuda Triangle, that Ian learned Kate's heart had always been waiting for him to find her. And now that he had, he didn't want a thing like time travel to take her away from him.

"I learned things that summer in Botswana after I left you, Kate. Things that I believe are true. The mystic taught me about the universe's energy, about harnessing it. There are places where the energy is unique. Places like the Botswanan marula forests and other places, too."

Places like the Bermuda Triangle.

The trip had been organized by Ian and Kate's mutual friend, Benton, and attended by others who took that same trip through the Triangle repeatedly, including a decade earlier. Ian explained that nuance to Kate.

"I think that being here on this ship with people who were on this very ship 10 years ago, somehow allowed time to shift for us."

Kate jerked her hands away from Ian's again. This time for good.

But he kept on.

"Another thing I learned that summer in Botswana is that there are people who have a special energy—people who together have a special symbiotic energy. I believe that, Kate. I really do. And I know you do, too. I know you felt it from the moment we first met."

There had been an electric current running through Kate to Ian since the day they met. Maybe even before. Certainly long after. It held them together. Even through the years they were apart, it kept them together. It was a blessing and a curse.

Ian looked at Kate's profile in the cab as she watched the city move past them in present day and he thought: *I had good reasons for doing all that I did.*

He pushed aside the nagging reminder: *But that doesn't mean it was right.*

chapter three

Rory

"CITY HALL, you said, right?" Only the cab driver's eyes were visible to Rory in the rear-view mirror above the Cuban flag.

"Yes."

"You joining the protest?"

Rory pulled her press lanyard out of her bag and held it up high for the driver to see in the mirror. "Not exactly. I'm with the press."

"Ah." He braked a little too quickly and Rory dropped the lanyard. It splayed out on the taxi floor half hidden under the front seat. Rory reached down to pick it up and while she was bent down, she felt her head hit the soft seat in front of her and a few expletives flew from the driver.

Rory shot back up, lanyard retrieved, rubbing her head. "What happened?"

"We got hit from behind. You ok?"

Rory kept on rubbing her head and looked behind her to try to make out the car and/or its driver that had rear-ended them. She couldn't see much.

Rory's cab driver got out and slammed his door, jarring Rory more than the collision had done. Was her driver a loose cannon? The slammed door seemed an undue response to a city fender bender. Certainly, he'd been in this situation before? Rory imagined you couldn't drive a taxi in New York City without being rear-ended a time or two. She leaned back in her seat and waited for what seemed an extraordinarily long time for the driver to return.

He never did.

A few minutes later, Rory was still waiting in the cab alone, so she opened her door and got out. The rain had stopped so she left her borrowed umbrella on the floor for the next passenger. She was about to walk back to the car that had rear-ended them, but she was instantly captivated by a sign on the sidewalk near the site of the collision.

Road Closed. Commencement Day. Carnegie Hall. Private Event.

Rory walked toward the sign and away from her taxi and the collision scene. She was still holding her press lanyard, so she wrapped it around her neck.

"What's going on in here?" Rory asked a security guard near the sidewalk sign.

"It's a high school commencement ceremony."

"Do they always close down roads and stop traffic for graduation ceremonies?" Rory was impressed by the setting, as she wondered: *Which city high school reserved Carnegie Hall for their graduation ceremonies?* That seemed rather posh, even by New York City standards.

Next to Rory, a small woman with silver blonde hair was rifling through her bag for something. It turned out to be a ticket which she showed to the security guard. Rory flashed her press lanyard which had the same effect on him as the woman's ticket. He let them both past.

"It's for 'Operation Steel Survivors.'"

The small blonde woman was walking quickly, and Rory sped up to catch up with her. "I'm sorry?"

"You're with the media? And you've never heard of Operation Steel Survivors? Well, I guess that's not all that surprising. We kept them under wraps mostly. I'm Tanya Corbin." The silvery woman reached out her hand to Rory and Rory took it.

"Rory Garcia. Nice to meet you."

"I'm a teacher with the program. Been working with these kids on and off for five years, but I've been watching them since 9/11, really. Thirty-seven graduating seniors and they all have one thing in common."

"What's that?"

"Their moms were all pregnant with them on 9/11. Each mother survived the tragedy, and gave birth that day or shortly thereafter. It's the first class of students to graduate who have known nothing but a life post-9/11. The commencement speaker, and Valedictorian, Hope Campton, was born on 9/11 in the midst of the tragedy itself. She is due to give her opening speech at noon. You're early. Which is good. That means you can still get a seat."

"Oh wow." Rory rubbed her lanyard self-consciously. *What an interesting story.*

"Here, take one of these. I'll try to circle back to you later and see if I can answer any questions for you." Tanya handed Rory a commencement program and headed up front, and Rory said a quick goodbye. She looked toward the stage and tried to find a good place to settle in for the proceedings. If she wasn't going to make it to the immigration rights protest at City Hall, she was anxious to have something even better to give her editor.

From the back of the auditorium, the seats looked mostly full. Rory fiddled with her press badge and stood up on tiptoe, trying to see if there was a section reserved for press. She saw some people with more impressive credentials lining the walls close to the stage where an empty podium stood. She wondered if she should take a spot up front. She was tempted to demand some sort of respect just by jumping in front of the other eager journalists who'd staked out a spot and gotten there before her, but she wasn't sure she belonged up there.

Rory turned her watch around on her wrist. 10:10. According to Tanya, the ceremony wasn't even due to start until noon. What were all these people doing here so early? She mentally judged them for their eagerness as a means of trying to assuage her own guilt for not arriving earlier. And for not even knowing about the event until just then.

Rory imagined telling this story to Marcos later, the way she often did, before remembering that at home, nothing was the same anymore.

Ven aca. Come here.

A man near Rory beckoned to a woman who may have been his wife across the auditorium. Rory was distracted by his voice and his accent. He sounded like Marcos.

Marcos was always telling Rory to *come here.*

She loved when *ven aca* meant *come sit with me. Come be with me.* Not when it meant, as it did lately: *Come to Miami. Leave New York. Leave your life. Leave everything you know.*

Ven aca. Come here.

The first day they moved in together, Rory caught him working as she walked in the door after work. Marcos reached out his hand across the room to Rory who was still standing in the door like a voyeur. She felt his words and his outstretched hand pull her to him. What was he working on? What was he huddled over?

She resisted a moment longer. He looked like he was hiding something, and she wasn't sure she wanted to see it. There was a mystique to his art that she hadn't uncovered just yet. Everything was still so new. They'd just moved in together. They'd just met seven weeks earlier.

Seven weeks, five days, two hours and thirty-three minutes.

Alongside the mystery of the moment, there was something else that kept Rory standing there in the doorway. Later, she'd be embarrassed to recall it: the perception that he hadn't really accomplished very much.

After all, whatever he was covering wasn't much bigger

than a postage stamp under his hands. He was hiding what he worked on all day, she believed, because he'd not made much progress. Standing in the doorway, Rory started to feel discouraged and resentful. While she was out trying to dig up big stories, trying to make a name for herself, he was at home lounging. Lazing.

Lazing. She rolled the word over in her mind's eye. She was tempted to use it out loud, but she didn't dare. She was mad at Marcos but she didn't want him to know. He was looking at her with a child-like innocence, and he was happy.

How could he be so happy about having done nothing all day?

Rory thought to herself that even given the chance, she wouldn't like to do nothing all day. She'd rather do *something.*

She thought Marcos shared her ambition and intention, but maybe she was wrong. Rory walked slowly and purposefully to the postage stamp Marcos was working on across the room, wondering for a moment if her mother had been right. Maybe it *was* premature to move in with a boy she had, for all intents and purposes, just met.

Rory steeled herself as she made her way across the small space to Marcos. How could she even feign enjoyment that would match his? How could she dumb down her own level of ambition to match his right now? The answer was simple. She couldn't. She resigned herself to a concession of defeat before she reached Marcos. But then suddenly she was there. And there was … *more.*

Rory couldn't be sure of what she was looking at, but it was so much more than she expected. It was indeed a postage stamp size piece of art, but it wasn't a scribble or a color or even two or three colors splashed on a small canvas. There was a swirl of color. There were details. There were— *oh God, were those faces?* Rory leaned all the way in.

The images before her came together in a mess of color that went in and out of focus as she bent over it.

"Marcos. What am I looking at?" Her voice sounded breathless to her own ears. Marcos looked even more pleased.

"Here." He held up an instrument triumphantly.

"A magnifying glass?"

Rory held it up to the art and suddenly the colors became blends and the blends became ....

Yes, they were indeed faces.

But how?

"Marcos, how on earth did you do this?"

He nodded exuberantly. She was starting to feel his joy and his wonder. She waved the glass slowly over the small canvas like a magic wand. And indeed, like magic, the painting came to life under her hand. There was a city scene coming into view. Her hand shook with awe, and she tried to steady it with the other hand. Men and women connected—hard to tell where one ended and another began. Not because of carelessness, but rather because of artistry.

"Marcos, how?"

More nodding.

"How did you do this?"

He pointed to instruments on the small table beside him. No thicker than human hairs, attached to thin rods.

"Can you show me?"

"Not on this one. This one is done."

Rory adjusted the magnifying glass again and held it over the canvas. A woman's light brown breasts overflowed from a coral dress with a yellow piping all around the border. A man with black spectacles and blacker hair wrapped around her in mid-dance. Behind them were others, in varying states of blurriness that made them look—not unfinished, but rather closer or farther than the stars of the scene.

He was right. He was done.

No one had been lazing around here.

While Rory had been out there trying to make small

stories big, Marcos had been home making a big scene small.

Rory put the magnifying glass down.

"Marcos, it's spectacular. How long does this take you to create?"

"This one took two months. But it's special. I need to make them faster if I'm going to make a show of them. I've never shown my art in public. I think I might try that next."

"You haven't shared this publicly?"

Marcos shook his head.

"And no one has seen this piece yet except for me?"

He nodded. "And now it is finished. Be happy for me, *Bella*." Marcos wrapped Rory in a hug and she felt like the woman in the coral dress—beautiful and brought to vibrant life in Marcos' hands.

"I am. I can't be anything else *but* happy right now, Marcos."

Rory pulled her glance away from the man calling out *ven aca* to his wife or lover in Carnegie Hall. The woman joined him and together they walked past Rory to find a seat. Rory looked again at the front of the auditorium trying to make out an empty space among the crowd of press to stand in. She thought about trying to find Tanya Corbin again and asking her to help find a seat. But Tanya was nowhere to be found. From her perch on tiptoes at the back of the auditorium, Rory saw a striking woman close to the front waving toward her. Rory looked around, over her shoulder, and to her left and right, trying to understand who the woman was waving to.

But there was no one else around her. It could only be Rory who the woman was gesturing wildly at. Rory pointed to her own self with a questioning look, and the woman flipped her head back easily and laughed. Then she nodded a grand exaggerated gesture that made Rory feel foolish for doubting for even a moment that this woman had meant to summon *her*.

Rory walked toward the woman and took the empty seat next to her as if it was saved just for her. *Maybe it was,* Rory thought boldly. *Maybe the universe has sent me here. Right here. Right now.*

She felt her confidence kick in. "Hello, I'm Rory Garcia." Rory held her hand out and introduced herself. The woman took her hand and nodded. "Hello, Rory." Despite the woman waving her forward and despite the woman's palpable warmth, Rory still was certain they didn't know each other.

The stranger was tall. Rory could see that even as she was sitting. Her legs stretched underneath the seat in front of her and were hidden. Her back was tall and straight and her sheer height gave her a regal air. As did her headpiece, a colorful cloth wrapped around her head tucking away her hair as if it was indeed a crown. The fabric allowed dark braids to escape toward her shoulders and revealed the unlined skin of her face. Her age was unclear. She could have been Rory's age, or considerably older—it was hard to tell. And Rory felt child-like next to her, so she doubted they were true peers.

Rory held up her press credentials. "Thanks for the seat. I'm legit and everything." The woman chuckled but she didn't continue the conversation right away, so Rory continued on to fill the ensuing silence.

"I started out this day on my way to cover the immigration rights protest at City Hall. But my taxi got in an accident right outside Carnegie Hall, and I took it as a sign that maybe there was a story for me here instead."

The woman nodded and made an expression like she was feigning being impressed. It made Rory feel even younger and less mature.

"City Hall, did you say? There is a protest scheduled today?"

Rory nodded.

"Ah, well, there will be delays today for everyone then."

Rory wondered who everyone was. But the woman interrupted her thoughts.

"Forgive me. Are you all right? You say you were just in an accident?"

"Oh yes, it was nothing. A little fender bender. I'm perfectly fine. Thanks for asking. But it brought me here, and now I'm trying to figure out if it's a sign or not."

"So, are you covering the commencement as an official order of business or will you remain just a passerby?" The woman looked genuinely confused.

Rory straightened herself up trying to match the woman's regal and straight posture. "A little of both, I guess. I think it's fascinating. The first graduating class of true 9/11 survivors in a sense. I'm wondering if there's any angle to give it a little more teeth, you know?"

More nodding.

"I'm curious to hear from the Valedictorian. How about you? Are you press?"

"A writer? Me? Like you?" The woman pointed to Rory's press lanyard and laughed. "No, I'm not like you."

"What do you do?" Rory pressed on.

"Do?"

Rory suddenly felt as though she'd asked a very personal question by accident. She kept on nonetheless.

"What do you do for a living?" And then sensing that maybe there was a language barrier at play, she added, "You know, for money?"

"What do I do to live or for money? These are two different questions." Rory felt the woman was playing with her a bit, but she realized this was going to be a long two hours until the ceremony began if she didn't strike up some sort of conversation with this woman.

"For money. To pay the bills. The way I'm a journalist."

"Ah. I see. I have a restaurant. And it helps me live as well."

There was more nodding between the two women, followed by a long uncomfortable silence.

"It's sort of a cheesy name, no?" Rory spoke finally.

"Which one?"

"The Valedictorian. Hope?"

The stranger looked confused, so Rory nodded enthusiastically to make her point.

"Oh, don't get me wrong. I'm all about the cheesy elements of this story. It's just, you know, as I mentioned, I'm trying to draw out some more teeth."

The woman shook her head and turned back to face the front of the auditorium as though she might be done with Rory.

Rory panicked. "Are you family to any of the graduates?"

"Yes. Of course. To Hope."

Rory looked down at the graduation program sheepishly. The key players were listed by name. Class advisors, Class President. Valedictorian, Hope Campton. Rory read through the program. There was little information contained in its pages. She had a feeling the story wasn't going to be in the program.

She'd have to draw more information out of this woman who was apparently family. "How lovely. You're a relative to Hope? On which side?"

The woman threw her head back with a long laugh. "You're so small."

"Excuse me." Rory puffed herself up with indignance.

The woman persisted. "Your experience. What you know. About family and life. It's so small. It's ok, though. I won't hold it against you. So, what is it you want to write about Hope and her family? Tell me, what do you think you know already?"

Rory shook off the missteps. "Just what I learned on the way in here today. That this is a class of survivors of 9/11. Perhaps the very first survivors. Maybe they can provide a little inspiration in a world gone mad. At least—that's how I will pitch it to my editor. He likes cheesy. He's corny like that."

The woman turned her head again toward the stage and away from Rory. Rory took a deep breath and tried a different approach. "Ok. I'm in over my head. I get it. It's just that I need a good and important story. Like make-my-rent-and-food-bill-this-month kind of important. Whatever you can give me on Hope and her classmates, I promise I will be eternally grateful and I'll tell all my readers to come to your restaurant—wherever it is. Where *did* you say it was?"

The woman smiled warmly and familiarly. "It's not here or now. Come, we'll take a walk. And I'll tell you a story you can sell to your boss. One that will help you eat and live this month. And maybe for a few more months after that."

The woman stood up from her folding chair and started walking toward the door. Rory began following her and then looked over her shoulder at the empty chairs.

"Should we save them in some way?"

"Save the seats?" The woman looked confused.

Rory pointed to them as if there was some confusion over what they were talking about. "In case someone tries to take them?"

"Why would someone try to take *our* seats?" The woman shook her head at Rory, and Rory followed her outside, suddenly reassured that the seats would be safe, but with no idea why.

Outside Carnegie Hall, there was no more hint of rain and the sun was pulling out from behind the wispy post-storm clouds. The mysterious woman walked over to the curb where a coffee truck was parked and was re-opening his side window following the storm. She ordered two coffees. There was a chill in the air still from the storm, and

Rory took the coffee offered to her without mentioning that she didn't drink coffee. She glanced around for a glimpse of her taxi, but he seemed to have left. She wondered vaguely if he'd be able to get restitution from the guy who had rear-ended him.

Rory shielded her eyes and looked at her companion. No longer a profile view, she could study her new friend, although it appeared that Rory was actually the one being studied. She tugged on her press lanyard with her name emblazoned on it in bold letters. "We have not properly met, I don't think," Rory suggested.

The woman looked her up and down with warm dark-colored eyes and then rubbed one long finger on her high check, while her dark lips pursed in a circle. "I am Dee." Rory took Dee's outstretched hand and felt her own collapse in a warm grip. She was surprised by Dee who then pulled Rory in, and wrapped her in a close hug where Rory could feel the woman's long and thin frame. Then Dee held Rory out in front of her and studied her some more. "Nice to see you," she said.

And Rory, dismissing the confusing syntax as a language barrier, said only, "So, you said something about a story?"

Kate

AS THEY PASSED slowly by Manhattan Cruise Terminal, a large docked boat came into view through the taxi's windshield and Kate shuddered in spite of herself. There were places in the city that still had that effect on her—even all these years later.

That was the reason she preferred her New Jersey suburban home with its dress boutiques and cafes. Her good friends, Pam and Lex, never seemed to understand why she shunned girls' trips into the city and impromptu shopping or lunch dates a train ride away on the other side of the bridges and tunnels.

How could they understand that even though Kate had long ago said goodbye to Ian, the ghost of that love affair traveled the city streets even today, making it difficult to fully let go?

Long after he left her, memories of her time with Ian hid in all the coffee shops and restaurants they'd frequented. From Bryant Park's carousel to the corner outside Rocco's on Restaurant Row, Kate had trouble steering clear of those long-ago memories whenever she came into New York City.

She had avoided telling him how much she loved him that first summer they got together. After all, their affair had a time stamp on it from the moment they met. He was leaving for Botswana and it was all terribly romantic, but also doomed. Then again, she'd let him leave much too easily. She regretted it deeply and often afterward.

But they'd reconnected on a cruise ship years later. Oh, how they'd reconnected. Ian taught her how to play blackjack, and he introduced her to Dee. He showed her the places he'd fallen in love with while they'd been apart, and introduced her to the people he respected. And it all happened in a short week-long cruise through the Devil's

Triangle. The collision at sea was just as powerful as it had been the first time around during those six summer weeks on land in New York City.

From her taxi window, Kate glanced again longingly at the docked ship. A ship not unlike the one where Ian and Kate had found each other and finally stopped keeping their love a well-kept secret.

It was easy to remember Ian's hands in her hair and his lips in her ear on that fateful trip through the Devil's Triangle. His words had been powerful.

"Here's what I know, Kate. I know that you are so strong but also so, so vulnerable. I know the claws that you use mercilessly to take care of yourself, and the soft touch you use to take care of those you love. I know that you fall in love completely, deeply. Even if you don't say the words? The ones you fall in love with can feel it."

Those fuzzy Manhattan days, in which Kate avoided telling Ian how much she loved him, gradually came into sharp focus with the memory of Ian's words.

"I know that you like to think you are practical. Maybe you are practical. In some ways. Like when it comes to money and blackjack. But not when it comes to love. You are just so damn reckless when it comes to love. You will throw away perfectly good love just because it doesn't make sense. To you.

"But I know, too, that you are a devoted friend. You will never let go of your true friends. And you are open to so many ideas. So many philosophies. Time travel and mystical serums. You entertain them. You listen. You have the most open heart of anyone I know. You give me hope like no one I have ever met in all of my travels."

There was more, too. Kate was having trouble remembering it all as she watched the pier and the water pass them by as they headed down the West Side Highway alongside the cruise ships. But the crescendo she remembered clearly:

"I know that you laugh readily and beautifully. And when you wake in the morning, unretouched, I know that you are, in fact, the most beautiful woman I have ever known. I know you, Kate, and I do love you."

She had always loved Ian. And probably always would.

As she stared out the taxi window at the Hudson River leading out to the vast and deep ocean, Kate thought: *But it is time now to finally let him go.*

Ian

THE CAB DRIVER had decided to take the West Side Highway around the outskirts of the city. The roadblocks and detours inland were difficult to navigate. Kate was understandably impatient. Ian watched her try to tap out texts to Hope, but everything came back undelivered.

Ian couldn't find the words to reassure her, so he stared out the window as they passed the Manhattan Cruise Terminal. He could make out the rear section of a cruise ship docked at the pier, and he wondered briefly if it was coming or going. He let himself daydream about the adventures the passengers either had or would have shortly.

A familiar sense of déjà vu settled over Ian. He glanced at Kate and wondered if she noticed where they were passing. If she did, she didn't mention it. She was so focused on the destination at hand, she seemed unable to see anything else around her.

But Ian did. In the cruise ship's silhouette, he saw 2001. Just like always. He saw 2001 again and again. In his dreams. In a drunken haze. In the blue Mexican waters Kate had just made him leave. In the bottom of every bottle he'd drunk, and on the edge of every ledge he'd stepped onto since then. He'd seen it again and again. He rethought it and relived it. He felt guilt and hysteria and relief and loss and happiness. All of it. And none of it.

Again and again.

Kate thought she'd help him escape by making him come back here. But she didn't seem to know that 2001 was the thing he couldn't escape. No matter how hard he tried.

Ian had a sense that he and Kate had found their way back to 2001 many, many times. But he didn't remember how many and he didn't remember what happened every single time.

Maybe there were times that different decisions were

made. Maybe there were times that circumstances turned out very differently. But Ian couldn't speak to those times.

What he knew of 2001 was that it was the year that found Kate Monroe choosing Ian Campton over Rob Sutton. Again and again, it found her making that exact same decision.

And that decision—though it should have made Ian whole—had broken him in ways he had never quite recovered from.

Ian knew in his heart that he and Kate had boarded a cruise ship several, maybe even many, times at the Manhattan Cruise Terminal over the years. It was hard to know how many times for certain, as time had bent and shifted around them and over them and through them. Kate and Ian had traveled back in time to 2001 many times. He was certain of it although he really couldn't remember each time very clearly. What Ian remembered clearly instead was the *last time.*

The last time Kate and Ian boarded a ship at that terminal, they hadn't come there separated. And they hadn't come there married to or connected to other people. They had come there together as a couple. They had come there as Kate and Ian.

The calendar read 2011 at the start of that last trip. They weren't in other relationships and there were no children to leave behind or return to. On that last cruise, Kate and Ian had been together for an entire decade—ever since 2001, but those hadn't been easy years.

It should have been enough. It should have been enough that they were together and in love, but it wasn't. And that's why they boarded the ship that last time when the calendar read 2011. It was *because of the shadow.*

Kate swore there had been a shadow she'd seen rising up on the brick buildings in Manhattan as she walked by them.

"A shadow that both is and isn't me and I feel certain that things are not as they should be. The shadow walks a little in front of or a little behind me. Never beside me. Never in sync." Kate tried to explain it to Ian over and over again but he had trouble grasping it.

She's afraid of her own shadow, he thought.

He knew too that this phrase likely littered her therapist's notes at that time as well. According to what Kate had told Ian, she spoke the shadow-on-the-bricks anxiety out loud to her therapist so often she feared that her therapist's notes resembled school yard taunts.

Ian tried to assure Kate that couldn't possibly be true. That her therapist couldn't possibly be thinking that or writing that. But his words were disingenuous. After all, he thought it too.

She's afraid of her own shadow.

And so, as much to take her mind off the shadows and the therapist notes, as to get away, Ian booked them a trip leaving from New York City and headed to the Bahamas.

Kate tried to protest. She tried to say she couldn't leave. That she wasn't up to it. That she'd ruin the beauty and the calm, not just for Ian, but for the rest of the passengers too—just with her transparent anxiety.

Ian held her and wiped away her tears and consoled her.

"Kate, this trip? It's a *one more thing.*"

It was not so much a last-ditch argument as a go-to argument by that point.

Despite Kate's admonitions, Ian was always sure there was still one more thing out there that would help her.

"There's one more thing we can try," he would say to her every time he convinced her to try a new therapy or a new therapist.

About the cruise ship being the *one more thing*, Kate had said, "You always say that with such enthusiasm and lightness, one more thing doesn't seem to mean 'only one more thing' to you, even though it definitely has that connotation when I hear it in my own head."

She was right. That was not how Ian heard it in his head at all.

Boarding the ship that last time was a "one more thing," like all the "one more things" they'd tried for the decade *before* they boarded the ship that last time. And maybe that was the reason Ian felt such déjà vu as they boarded the ship. He told himself it was just that. Just harmless déjà vu, and he ignored it. He boarded the ship with Kate that last time and set everything else in motion.

Something he was both eternally grateful for and regretful for ever since.

As the traffic broke and let them pass the Manhattan Cruise Terminal finally, Ian glanced back and forth between Kate and the driver, letting his mind go to the place it hadn't in years.

What had they done?

What had they given up?

The choices they'd made felt so real and true in the moments they'd made them, but Ian had spent the rest of his life with regrets that consumed him.

Now, with Hope 18 and about to graduate, Kate seemed untethered by the same regrets and that seemed impossible. After all, given what she'd disclosed in Mexico, the choices they'd made all those years ago were even *more* tragic for *her*, weren't they?

While he was drowning his sorrows in Mexico, he chose to believe she'd found her way back to the destiny that had been waiting for her all along. But now, it seemed she had not.

Ian studied her with curiosity from across the cab seat.

These thoughts didn't seem to be eating Kate alive the way they were with Ian.

Kate looked beautiful and hopeful. She talked only of getting to Hope. Of seeing her walk across the stage, and making her speech. While Ian was broken and remorseful, Kate seemed genuinely whole and happy.

There was no mention of grief or loss—other than losing Ian for all those years.

Unlike Ian, Kate seemed light and happy. There was no dark cloud over her very existence, and the shadows certainly seemed gone. She kept saying "We're all going to be together now. Finally." She seemed focused singularly on seeing Hope up on that stage, and on bringing Ian with her to do so.

It was almost, Ian thought as he stared at Kate's profile against the window, *as if she didn't remember what she'd given up to get there.*

Or whom.

chapter four

Rory

DEE AND RORY found an empty bench near the coffee truck and sat down. Dee blew on her coffee and looked Rory up and down solemnly. "Tell me what this commencement story means to you."

"Well, for one thing, I need to understand the meaning of the survival story behind these kids' paths. These kids are about to experience a level of fame I probably never will—just for being born."

Dee nodded. "Yes, for being born. No 'just' about it. It is a miracle anyone is born at all what with the way we are, all of us, constantly trying to change the future."

Rory shook her head with frustration and Dee seemed to read it in her movements. "What is it, Rory? What are you moving around trying to change in your own life?"

Rory blew the steam over her unwanted coffee and reached up to massage her neck. "That's exactly it. I don't know."

The day after Marcos told her he wanted to move to Miami—that he wanted *them both* to move to Miami—he woke up like it was just another ordinary day in their lives since they met.

31 weeks, 4 days, 16 hours and 45 minutes.

"Well look at you. It's 9:45 and you're attacking your diet coke and yogurt. Breakfast of champions." There was a laugh in his voice that had become so familiar to her—but still she resented his voice cutting through the angry silence she was trying to drape the apartment in.

"You startled me," Rory said more grumpily than she intended.

Marcos had two speeds. Awake and sleep. And when he was awake—it was instant. He was engaged and living alive. Hence no need for coffee. Rory, on the other hand, transitioned to awake. She savored the caffeine in her morning diet cokes like a fine roast and savored her morning silence like an aged wine. She could be found trying to soak in the morning before Marcos awoke, knowing that when he did, he would arrive more easily than she did. She didn't resent him for his gift of waking easily. She envied it. But she couldn't emulate it no matter how hard she had tried these last nearly six months of living together. So, she woke before him. She rummaged for clean dishes. She savored her diet coke in the moments of silence that separated them both in the morning routine.

"Did you forget I was here?" Marcos folded his long legs up into his body and used them to propel himself as he climbed off the couch and headed toward her.

He tripped over a stack of books on the floor between them and she watched unmoving as his long body started to fall toward her. She didn't even have time to be nervous, duck, or get out of the way as he recovered quickly.

"Holy sh—where did that come from?" He caught his breath as he steadied again on the other side of the books.

"Oh! I'm so sorry." Most of the clutter in the small apartment was Marcos's. But this pile was all her own. Rory suddenly became mobile and swooped over to pick up the stack of used books she'd dug out of the shelves of a used bookstore just the day before. She'd stumbled in there after Marcos and she had their fight.

A fight? I'd hardly call it a fight, Rory. Marcos had chided when she'd come home demanding an apology. *We're allowed to disagree, and hash out the disagreement without anyone needing to apologize.*

His rightness frustrated her. Of course, they could talk and disagree. Of course, they could even debate issues for hours until one of them had to leave the apartment to catch her breath, to steel her arguments, and sort through her logic to answer the points made by the other that were so frustratingly correct.

She had walked for hours in the city on a Sunday morning until it turned into an afternoon, along sparsely crowded streets, past rows of coffee shops with disheveled patrons and giddy Tinder dates that had lasted into the morning. She had walked past shops and window displays, fighting for space on the sidewalk with tourists and shoppers who had arrived by bus and every other means of transportation. They had come in droves to a city Marcos was so desperate to leave.

That was what they had been arguing about. The city, and Marcos's plans to leave, and his request that Rory go with him.

"I got it," he said with no sense of irony—the words setting off a chain reaction that had led her out into the city streets on that Sunday.

"Got it? It's not like it fell from the sky, Marcos. You pursued it. You hunted it like a dog, and it succumbed to you. It's not like fate has intervened to tell you which road to choose here. You tricked fate by doggedly going after this. You didn't 'get' this art showing in Miami. You chose it."

Without giving a second thought about how I would feel about it.

She thought the last words without saying them, because they were heavy in her mouth. They didn't feel right. Even as they stuck in her throat, she knew she shouldn't utter them aloud—because, of course not. Why would he give it a second thought? Why should he?

They had met seven months earlier—at an art opening for a mutual friend—an event both of them had planned *not* to attend. It turned out to be an event neither of them even enjoyed very much. They ended up at the same time in front of the same piece, and puzzling over it the same way, holding flutes of pink champagne. The piece was a photograph of a large woman's bare, pale belly, spray painted with a dark yellow circle, the paint bleeding through the canvas to create something that resembled street art or a tag, but not as pretty.

They'd laughed about it afterward—about the art, not their meeting. They found it hysterical that they had responded to the piece in the same way—with stifled, and immature, giddy laughter.

"We better get out of here," Marcos had whispered when they both came up for air in front of the large photograph. Rory had nodded with her hand still clasped over her mouth, and they ran out together like they were both escaping from and toward the same thing, which is how they ended up next door for cappuccinos. They sat over untouched mugs of frothy liquid amazed when they both admitted that no, neither one of them actually drank the stuff.

Over cold cappuccinos, they'd laughed about karma and fate and how they both ended up somewhere they didn't intend to be, yet mesmerized all the same, and how they both hated coffee but had ended up at this cappuccino bar anyway. If this didn't mean they were supposed to meet despite all the odds, despite all the people passing each other on the New York City streets every day, then really what did?

Rory had smiled coyly at Marcos over the high-top table. She wondered if he was lying about the coffee thing. She wondered whether he had in fact downed three espressos before the art gallery opening like every other New Yorker.

She wondered whether he was saying all of this just to make her believe in something that wasn't really true. She wondered for a moment if maybe he was even thinking the same things about her.

And while she was sitting and smiling and flirting, Marcos leaned across the table hungrily and kissed her and she kissed him right back, devouring the taste of champagne and mints without even a hint of coffee.

They moved in together about eight weeks later. She said "I need to find my own place, anyway. My mom and I are outgrowing each other. Why don't you just move in with me until you figure out what you want to do next? I mean, it's not like we're getting married or anything. I just want to help."

She immediately regretted the words as sounding too desperate, too stalker-y, but Marcos had looked at her so sweetly, absolving her instantly.

It felt like fate again. Like things were working out exactly as they were supposed to. That she could have met this man in a city of eight million at the exact moment that he was single and needing a place to stay—

Rory was breathless by the coincidence—no, by the *meaning* of all of it.

On the day she signed the lease, she declared "Thank goodness, you're moving in with me. Because I have *all this room.*"

Yes, indeed, all this room. Marcos had swept his arm around the space that could barely contain Rory and now would contain them both somehow.

Less than six months later, he wanted to leave *all this room* behind, and he wanted her to go with him. She had probably bought all those used books as a silent means of rebelling against the plan. Planting that pile of books right in his tripping path was likely subconscious, she thought, as she watched him recover.

She'd stood in front of the racks and rows of books, studying titles of household names whose labors of love had ended up in a used bookstore, marked down to a buck or two. She thought about the rooms that no longer had space for these very books—books, who had been abandoned by their owners. She thought about owners who were willing to forfeit the prices spent to read them once, twice, maybe five times before sending them off discarded. She tried not to be morose about the whole thing, but found herself unable to stop.

She wiped tears from her eyes in front of the book-shelves, and embarrassed, dripped tears on the mass market paperbacks on a table in the back of the store next to a sign that read: *fill a bag for $5*. She filled two bags before she remembered she'd have to cart these all back to the space she still shared with Marcos for a short time at least. She paid the woman at the register $10 for the discarded treasures and headed back to the apartment.

At home, Rory found Marcos on the West Elm sofa with his laptop in his lap. He hadn't changed his mind. He was seemingly even more sure.

"I have an idea. I sprang this on you too abruptly. Come with me, *Bella*. A little vacation of sorts. We'll check it out, and see if you could see yourself living there."

He turned his laptop around to face Rory with photos of Miami littering the screen. "Let's go. Let's just go."

"When?"

"Tomorrow."

"That's crazy. We need to get ready."

"What do you mean, get ready?"

"Deal with work. Pack, plan."

"*Bella*, do you pack and plan for every single day?"

"No, I—"

"Exactly—you live. You wake and you live. And you write. And you email your editor. So, we'll do the same thing in Miami. We'll put a change of clothes in a bag. We'll wake up and go to the airport and we'll see. We'll just see."

"But I don't live there. So, it's different."

"It doesn't have to be."

Rory let herself be pulled in by Marcos—but mostly by his words. She let herself be pulled across the room. Then she stopped as she reached him. "You don't have a passport, Marcos. How are we going anywhere?"

He looked at her blankly. He started to say something, but she interrupted him. "And by the way, I'm not going anywhere until I get an apology from you for starting this entire fight."

Marcos shook his head, and refused to apologize, and she started to question fate and destiny for the first time since she'd met and fallen in love with a stranger standing in front of a piece of art with a giant yellow circle on its raw belly.

At a bench outside the majestic Carnegie Hall, Rory held onto her coffee sadly and even sipped it gently. Rory wanted to tell this woman how very much she hated coffee but she didn't want to ruin the spell. Dee's presence itself was captivating. Rory swallowed the coffee in delicate sips that softened the taste while she waited. After a long silence, she ventured in again, "You said something about a story?"

"I've known Hope's parents for a very long time," Dee began. "Actually, I met Ian first, but it feels like her mother has been in my life so much longer. They came to visit me many times in the Bahamas."

"Are you from there? The Bahamas?" Rory wanted to take notes, but something told her she'd be able to remember every word just by listening.

Dee shook her head. "No, I'm from Botswana. A beautiful country. And if you've never been there, I highly recommend it."

Rory smiled and nodded a silent promise that she'd visit Botswana one day soon. Botswana and The Bahamas and anywhere else Dee recommended.

"I've lived in the Bahamas for many years. I run a restaurant there—something I've done ever since my mother died. And I lost other people too. Dee's eyes looked sad for a brief moment. Rory felt uncomfortable watching this stranger's personal grief, but Dee recovered quickly. "It's the most peaceful place on the planet, I believe. Not that I've been everywhere on the planet, but I've been to a lot of places so I feel I can say that with some confidence."

"Well, no wonder Hope's parents loved it there and came back so often."

"Each time they came to me they were stuck in a certain place, and a certain time. But still, each visit they were a bit changed."

"Changed?"

"Different. We're not the same every single time. None of us are."

"Every single time what?" Rory felt like a toddler trying to understand a grown-up conversation.

"Every single time we pass through a certain moment of our lives. We bring with us different experiences, different memories. Everything is not the same."

Rory changed her mind about being able to remember everything merely by listening. This woman's story was starting to unravel. It didn't make complete sense. Rory put her barely-touched coffee down, and reached into her bag and pulled out her notepad and a pen. She sat across from Dee with her pen hovering over her notepad, trying to decide a way to write this that would make sense. Maybe there was a way that would make it a compelling story and help her editor understand why she had decided to skip the immigration protest, but words evaded her. They didn't seem to evade, Dee, however.

"I'm sorry. I see you're trying to understand. They are special—Hope's parents—they travel back and forth through time. They've done it for as long as I can remember. Ian is the one who figured out it was possible while he was visiting Botswana. That's where he and I first met and became instant friends."

Rory rested her pen on her notepad without writing any more. She smiled at this pleasant woman wondering if she should give up or give in. Dee really seemed to believe the tall tale she was spinning.

"Time travel? Really? Is it just that easy then? To hop on a space ship and travel back and forth to different times and places?" A laugh escaped Rory. She didn't want to mock this lovely woman, but she couldn't help herself.

Dee laughed too—a laugh that seemed to come from a deep place within. Deeper than her belly even, this laugh came from within her soul. "Well, of course it's not easy. But they found their way back to me again and again. Still, they were lost. Ian would tell me every time they came that they were looking for something. Something that was missing. They could feel its loss, but they couldn't quite remember. So, they were stuck. And they came back decade after decade, at all different points in time, trying to find it again and again."

Decades of time travel?

Rory looked at Dee skeptically. "And each time they were a little different?"

"Well, yes, but the one constant in all those visits was their love."

Rory felt something creeping into the story. It was both unsettling and reassuring. Rory remembered then a story her mother had read to her often as a little girl.

"I will love you even then." Rory said it out loud before

she could stop the memory from coming out of her mouth. Dee looked at her quizzically.

"Oh, I'm sorry. It's a bedtime story my mother used to read to me when I was a little girl. I haven't thought about it in a long time. It's about a little bunny and a mother rabbit, and the bunny keeps asking if her mother will love her until the end of lunch, until tomorrow, until next week, and finally until the end of time, and the mother rabbit keeps saying "I will love you even then." My mother used to love that story. Even if she was bone tired, if I wanted her to read to me, and I picked that one, I could get her to agree. I dog-eared its pages until it was tattered and torn. I'm sure my mother still has that book somewhere, although I'm not sure why I just thought of that after so long."

"Because it's the same thing."

"Sorry?"

"Love that transcends time. It's the thing that connects us all. It's what I'm talking about."

Rory shrugged. She didn't understand and she didn't believe in time travel. But she wanted to. How else would she explain to her editor how utterly captivating this woman had been? Rory picked up her pen and started writing again.

"Were you able to help them?" Rory asked.

"They found what they were looking for if that's what you're asking."

Rory waited patiently a few seconds and then impatiently asked, "And then what?"

"Ah. Then they lost it again."

Rory felt her heart sink. She was interested already in these two strangers in Dee's story. What kind of ending would it be for them? She glanced over her shoulder at the doors to Carnegie Hall.

"Are Hope's parents here?"

Dee sighed. "Sadly, no. I didn't want Hope to be alone today, so here I am. I thought maybe, but, oh, life is complicated, don't you know? And then you showed up! So, it's just turning out to be a fascinating day."

Oh, no.

Alone on Graduation Day?

She's the commencement speaker and her parents aren't going to make it?

Although she didn't know this young woman named Hope, Rory could imagine her disappointment. At 23, Rory was still tied by an invisible thread to her mother's approval and presence. It was a relief and frustration at the same time. Her mother could affect her in many ways, not the least of which was to throw gasoline on the fires of insecurity Rory herself was starting to feel about Marcos.

"Honey, I just worry he's using you without even realizing it. I mean he's caught between worlds right now. And you're so young. How do you know what you're going to want in three or five or twenty years? Spoiler alert—you don't."

After accepting their decision to live together, Rory's mother had done an about face, and spent an inordinate amount of time over the next few months trying to talk Rory out of Marcos. Especially when the marriage discussions started.

Rory agreed that they had jumped quickly into a discussion of marriage, but there were reasons to do so, of course.

"Mom, please, you're being unfair. Marriage isn't really that important after all. Isn't that what you always said?"

"No. That's not what I said at all. I have always said marriage isn't necessary. Marriage is such an important step when you take it, and very difficult to unravel from if you choose it. It's because of those things that I *didn't* choose it. Not because it isn't important, but because it is *so* important."

Rory's mother always made her single motherhood sound like a decision she'd made for herself rather than one that had been thrust upon her. Rory's father had been little more than a donor, a transient traveling gypsy, with a firm stance against parenthood. He swept up her mother in a brief romance and then left her with bittersweet memories and a positive pregnancy test.

Rory's mother had decided in short order to have the baby and had spent a lifetime insisting she was living life on her own terms, but Rory was always unsure just how much of that was fact and how much was fiction. Recently, now that she was talking her only daughter out of living her life on her own terms, Rory was concerned that she had somehow overlooked just how hypocritical her mother was.

"This is a very confusing time in your life. And I remember, Rory. Please understand where this is coming from. *I remember.* Love him. Spend time with him. Learn from him. But for God's sake—don't marry him and ruin the rest of your life. You have no idea how this will end."

There was a silence between them and then her mother asked a conciliatory question. "Can you at least tell me how he asked you to marry him?"

Rory smiled. "I'll keep the details to myself, thank you very much."

"Oh, Rory." Rory heard a softening in her mother's voice, perhaps toward Marcos, and perhaps toward marriage as well.

Rory and Marcos sat on the floor of their apartment a few months after they moved in together, practicing yoga poses. Marcos's parents' urn was sitting in the middle of the floor. The final resting place of his parents' ashes continued to be an unresolved topic in Marcos's life.

"Do you have a picture of your mother?" Marcos asked out of the blue while Rory worked on a warrior pose. They hadn't met. They knew all about each other. But they hadn't met. Rory had moved in with a man who had yet to meet her mother. She had complicated emotions about that fact.

Rory pulled up a photo on her phone.

"She's beautiful."

"Yes." Rory stared at her mother on the screen. Her face was unlined, and so beautiful. She was approaching 50 and had stopped dying her shoulder length hair years ago. It was almost completely grey but against her unlined face, her sleek hair looked fashionable and timeless. Her mother often joked that she'd stayed beautiful and preserved by never marrying. It was a badge of honor and Rory had often wondered if it was a lie created to help her feel better about certain sacrifices and decisions. Sitting there with Marcos in an apartment filled with promises and new memories, it was easy to believe the latter.

"My family wants me to bring my parents home to Cuba."

Rory groaned audibly. "How can they ask that of you?"

He leaned to her and tipped her chin gently. "*Bella*, I want to go. I want to honor them. I think my parents would want it too. Even though we never talked about it, I still believe it's what they would want. How odd that we were always so busy living and surviving we never really talked about death and dying, and the plan for what would come next."

"You want to go?" Rory asked with surprise. Marcos had been adamant about not returning to Cuba. He saw no point. But then again, she hadn't known him long enough to know if this was truly a life-long stance at that point. Was *sixteen weeks, five days, one hour and twenty-three minutes* really long enough to know anyone? Her mother was constantly arguing that it was definitely *not*.

"I do. I want to take them to Cuba, but then I want to

come home. Back home to you. But my family, they're convinced that if I go, there will be complications. That I won't be able to just come back."

"Ah yes. No passport. No license."

"*Bella*—it's just—"

"It's just, what? You're American. You're a legal citizen. Get a passport. You're never too old to get your first passport, you know." Rory felt the defensiveness creep into her voice. She closed out of the screen with her mother's photo. She didn't want the image of her mother invading this uncomfortable discussion.

"Yes, yes. I will figure it out. My parents—they became citizens—but how do I prove my citizenship? I didn't go to classes or take a test or get a certificate. I've simply existed here."

"What do you do about filing taxes? Your paycheck?"

"There's never been much money. It's always been cash for my art and cash under the table at the warehouse. I keep it up here." Marcos walked over to a closet and pulled down a shoebox from the top shelf with stacks of bills.

"Health insurance?"

Marcos shook his head sadly. "My parents never had it until the years just before they died. They had Medicare, thank goodness. But even still, the money flew out the door and I didn't want to spend any of it on insurance for myself."

"And your birth certificate? Social security card?"

"All these things I have, of course." Marcos nodded vigorously as if they were finally getting somewhere. "They're just not easily accessible. I need to finish going through my parents' things in storage."

Rory nodded less vigorously. She tried not to let the doubt settle over her. What she hadn't admitted to her mother as she defended Marcos was that Rory actually couldn't believe how unsubstantiated Marcos was. He'd lived off the grid so long he didn't think it was odd. Until it was time to prove who he was in the world. In order to crowd out the unspeakable doubts this off-the-grid living created, Rory directed her focus on the unfairness. With her alabaster skin, would she ever have to prove who she was? Would she ever have to dig out long forgotten birth documents to prove who she was?

"How did you never get your driver's license? It would have obviated all this."

"I never needed it. New York City public transportation is second to none. You know that."

Rory rolled her eyes. She had doubts about that. But of course, city living made car licenses moot for many of its residents. There was nothing suspicious about that. Still, most New Yorkers got a license just for identification purposes, not to actually use it. There was no doubt, however, that Marcos was not like most New Yorkers.

"So, no license and no birth certificate and no social security card," Rory said.

"Well, I'm sure I *have* a birth certificate and social security card. Somewhere. My parents didn't seem to understand the importance of these documents. They believed they were citizens and that was enough."

"Yes, it was, in theory. But now, you need documents. To prove who you are. To prove you belong here."

Marcos looked a little gutted by her words and guilt propelled her forward.

"What hospital do you think you were born in? Surely someone must have a record of your birth that would help us sort this out."

"Well, my mother used to tell the story of the midwife on the 9th floor delivering me right there in the living room. Honestly, I'm not even sure I went to the hospital after I was born." Rory looked at the floor she was sitting on with renewed wonder.

Her mother's warnings rang in her ear. Was she crazy to believe this man?

Was *sixteen weeks, five days, one hour and thirty-eight minutes* long enough to form the feelings and beliefs she seemed to have formed?

That answer was easy of course. It was enough time, because she *had* formed them.

"It's ok. We'll figure this out. I'll help you." Rory reached across the yoga mats and took his hands.

"Before you came into my life, *Bella*, I often wondered if I was making a mistake clinging to this country so badly—but now—I'm starting to think I was meant to be here after all. That the journey my parents made, the sacrifices—the timing—all of it was for something. For this moment."

Marcos moved toward her and laid Rory down on the floor. He moved her hair out of her eyes and stared at her intently. "Marry me, *Bella*. Let's start our life now. Then if I go to Cuba, I'll have a reason to come back. My family will understand and accept my decision. They will see how much I love you in my eyes."

Caution and reservation whispered in Rory's ear but she ignored it.

Marcos slipped her shirt over her shoulder, and slid her pants down and off her legs. He kissed her bare shoulder quietly and tenderly. Rory tried not to let the way her heart turned around in her body matter. But it did. How could she deny the way he made her feel? Safe, and cherished, and loved.

And yet it was a prison, this thing called love. It was what her mother had warned her about. And she knew why. It changed the chemistry of your brain and it made you act in ways you would never act otherwise. Marcos stood up to pull his shirt and shorts and boxers off and Rory followed his lead stripping the last barriers between them. He lay back down and lined his body alongside hers, kissing her and enveloping her. Skin on skin. Breath on breath.

"Yes," she said into his mouth.

He pulled his head away slightly. She wanted it back, but she wanted him to see her when she said it. So, she endured the agony of being separated at the mouth only for a moment.

"Yes, I'll marry you."

As he brought his mouth in closer in a soft cascade of rhythm with his hips, she raised up to meet him entirely.

He made her feel whole. He loved her with everything he was. The universe had brought them together against all odds.

Why wouldn't she marry this amazing man?

Kate

KATE LEANED FORWARD to look at the traffic ahead of the taxi she felt hostage in, as they plodded along the New York City streets. In doing so, she caught a glimpse of herself in the driver's rearview mirror.

Her reflection, and particularly the reddish tint of her formerly brown hair, startled her anew.

Lately the changes in her life had been spiraling quickly, and she had decided to make the outside reflect her inner transition. She'd gotten a tattoo in Mexico, a move that had surprised even herself. After looking through the tattoo artist's book for only a short time, she had pointed to one particular design with enthusiasm.

Que significa? What does it mean?

"Crazy monkey," the artist had replied matter-of-factly.

"Hunh." Kate had turned the page around and around trying to make out a monkey in the design. She didn't see it. She saw a warrior. Then she noticed the design on the same page but below it—a monkey. A crazy one, at that.

"Oh! No, not that one. *This* one." She pointed again to the warrior and steered the artist away from the abstract monkey design further down on the page.

Que significa? What does it mean? She asked again.

The tattoo artist nodded enthusiastically, and then replied. "*Nada.* Nothing. Just a design, *Senorita.*"

But Kate had been insistent. "Can we pretend it means Mayan Goddess Warrior or Mayan female Head of State or something like that?"

The tattoo artist had smirked, his English much better than Kate's Spanish. "You sure you don't want crazy monkey, *Senorita*?"

Kate had laughed first and then grimaced as he proceeded to sketch the Mayan Goddess Warrior on her forearm. In the taxicab days later, she traced the finished product. She loved it. She also loved her new hair. She'd used a red color wash. Although, unlike the tattoo, it was temporary. She wasn't sure why she'd been more wary about committing to a hair color than forearm ink, but there it was. She finished tracing the Mayan Goddess Warrior on her arm, and then ran her fingers through her reddish hair. She looked different, not like her former self at all.

Which was exactly right for this brand-new day.

She'd stand with a room full of people, including Ian, and she'd witness a brand-new beginning, and then she'd say goodbye.

This she could do. She had been going over it again and again in her head for days. She had come to understand that the only way to move forward now was to let go of the past. The same past that had been haunting her for too long now.

The time was *now*.

It was finally *time*.

Ian

"SIR, CAN YOU lower the window?" Ian asked the driver. He needed air.

"*Si, Senor.*" The cab driver nodded and released the window at Ian's request.

Ian leaned his head into the late spring breeze. The air was so different here in New York City than in Mexico. How had he forgotten that? He'd gotten so used to the oppressive memories squeezing and suffocating him that he'd forgotten that here in New York, it was the smog and car fumes doing all the squeezing and suffocating. At least the air in Mexico had been clean. The beach breezes had done their best to lull him to sleep each night for all these years.

He'd done what he could to put the past behind him. And the future.

"Dee."

They spoke about once a month when they could. Sometimes a little more, sometimes a little less.

Dee was his connection to another place and another time, and Ian sought solace in those conversations. He spoke to his own parents only briefly. Enough to keep the most modest of relationships. His connection to them was tenuous, at best, and he acknowledged that it was of his own doing. His parents made arrangements to see Hope and Kate occasionally, and they seemed to all make peace with their limited relationships. In recent years, Ian's parents had moved to Florida and were becoming significantly less mobile and aware. They wouldn't make it to Hope's graduation, a fact that seemed a little lost on them the few times they'd spoken recently. Ian was both saddened and relieved that their seemingly age-related confusion prevented them from remembering Hope's big day.

But while Ian welcomed their relationship with their granddaughter, Ian kept his parents at arm's length from him. He kept them out of his emotions. He kept them out of his heart. He didn't want anyone to see the blackness that was there.

But Dee knew him too well to be kept at arms' length.

When they spoke, she always opened the call in the same way.

"How are you, Ian? Have you found happiness yet?"

Yet.

Ian was intrigued that Dee still believed happiness was a thing that could be found. That *would* be found.

She had suffered profound losses in her own life, but still she moved forward with optimism and a love for life. He always found her so inspirational.

He loved her dearly and had been so grateful for her place in his life.

Until now.

His connection to Dee had turned from solace to an albatross around his neck in just a matter of a few days.

Because when Kate came to find him in Mexico, he came to understand that everything Dee had told him over the years since he left was nothing but lies.

chapter five

Rory

"DO YOU THINK her parents will make it in time?"

Dee chuckled softly. "*In time?* I don't know. Time has been a confusing and complicated thing for this family.

Ah, the time travel thing again. Rory wished Dee would stop sprinkling eerie time travel references into their conversation.

"How did they lose it?"

"What do you mean?"

"You said they found something and then lost it again. What did you mean?"

"Well, Hope's parents traveled back and forth many times until they actually found her. The story of today has its roots in each of those trips."

"They lost Hope?"

"You could say that." Dee glanced over her coffee cup toward the doors of Carnegie Hall. She was waiting for someone. Hope's parents? Or someone else?

"Are you married?" Rory suddenly asked Dee.

"I am not."

"Do you believe in marriage?"

"Believe? Like a religion?" Dee's wide smile reached the corners of face.

"I know, that's a silly choice of words."

"Actually, no. It's not. Marriage is consuming, if true. Much like a religion. But I don't believe two people have to go through certain steps or formalities just to be "married" if that's what you're asking."

It wasn't, but Rory continued on.

"Do you think there's a period of time people have to be together before they can decide whether marriage is right for them?"

Dee shook her head.

"Well, do you think there's an age that's too young to know whether marriage is an appropriate next step or not? Hope's parents—how old were they when they met?"

Dee looked at Rory coolly. "They were 26 when they found each other for the first time."

Rory nodded. "Do you think they were too young to know what would happen next?"

"Too young? Because of their age? No, not necessarily. But too early on in their journey. They didn't know and they couldn't know. So much happened to them."

"As they got older?"

Dee shook her head with an expression that seemed to imply that Rory was acting so much younger than 22.

"So much happened to them as they continued on their journey. I mean nothing more than that. Anyway, marriage isn't necessary. But if chosen, it is indeed important."

"You sound like my mother." Rory tried to keep her eyes from rolling as she said it.

Dee laughed. "Your mother sounds like a wise woman."

"I just can't help but wonder if two people end up together, if they are meant to be together, does it matter how soon they jump in? I mean, does time even matter? Does it change anything?"

Dee paused; a smile curled on her lips as if she held secrets she would not be revealing. "Why, Rory, time is the *only* thing that can change love. That is why love that survives time is the most powerful thing of all."

Rory turned her finger around and around on the rim of her still full, now cold coffee cup. Then she twisted her press lanyard in her hands, the one that recently had been printed with her new married name, Garcia, after a quick courthouse marriage, with vows said before anyone could change their minds. Marcos had somehow secured a NYC ID card. He'd apparently cobbled together letters and verifications that had convinced the issuing agency that he was who he said he was.

"They are used to sorting through gaps," Marcos had kissed Rory as he held up his ID card, the one that would allow them to get married now. "They help victims of domestic abuse and the homeless receive ID cards. They were kind and accommodating with me." Rory had decided not to question it or delve too deeply. She just wanted to be with Marcos and she wanted him to feel safe. Getting married seemed to check both of those boxes. Better yet, after they got married, there was no more talk about Marcos leaving for Cuba. He seemed to let go of that idea which relieved Rory.

But then he came home with a new idea. The one about moving to Miami. And this one he didn't seem ready to let go of.

Her mother had come to the courthouse to be at the wedding. Rory had told her she didn't need to, but she'd come and she'd smiled and she'd kissed them both on the cheek and wished them joy. After the courthouse wedding, she stayed a polite distance away from the newlyweds, coming to visit occasionally, and only when invited. Then a month ago, she showed Rory her one-way plane ticket and told her about the upcoming yoga retreat.

"But when will you be back?"

"I'm not sure, darling. I'll be away a few weeks at least. I'm feeling like I need a little time away. A little quiet time. Consider it my wedding gift to you. Take this time to get settled with your new husband without your mother underfoot. I never imagined myself being an intrusive mother-in-law. Let me do this to prove it to you.

From the day they got married, Rory was grateful to her mother for stifling her judgment and never letting it show, even though Rory was certain it must have been coursing through her veins. She'd looked nothing more than brave, Rory thought, as she watched her mother witnessing her wedding to Marcos.

It had been a miracle, really. Her mother's ability to show up and be present in a way that Rory needed, had been extraordinary. And it made Rory understand, not for the first time, that incredible things truly were possible, if you kept your eyes open to them.

Rory turned back to Dee on the bench outside Carnegie Hall. "Ok. So, help me understand the time travel component of your story. Hope's parents, they really traveled back and forth in time?"

Dee nodded. "Rory, darling, I know you're not sure you believe me. But try. Just try."

And Rory nodded a promise in return.

Rory looked around at the crowd milling about outside Carnegie Hall. More road blocks were being set up for the event. There was even some police presence monitoring the crowds now. A few more food trucks and coffee trucks like the one they were sitting outside of had been allowed to set up for the long day. Rory thought briefly as she looked around at all the people, that they would have certainly lost their seats inside by now. But she wasn't ready to go back inside. She wanted to hear more of Dee's story. And Hope's. While she was debating what to ask next, Dee interrupted her thoughts:

"Have you ever been to the Bahamas?

"I haven't. My mom—she has a little wanderlust. She liked to talk about traveling to far off places when I was little. But she was a single mother and we didn't get to travel too much. She's making good on overdue promises to see the world, however. She just bought herself a one-way plane ticket and I'm not sure when she'll be back."

"How nice for her."

"Yes. I'd like to start traveling myself, soon. I'll add Bahamas to my list." Rory chided herself silently on giving away so much personal information, and making a childish promise to go somewhere just because this woman was from there.

Dee seemed unfazed. She continued on.

"The water is striking in the Bahamas. It is so blue and so full of fish; you don't have to go very far to find fresh dinner. We eat fish for every meal when we can. It's quite delicious and healthy. I live and work on that water and it is my lifeblood. You become lulled into a sense of security by the sea. You forget it's actually quite dangerous. When a storm comes through, it will churn up those waters and the waters that sustain you can actually become a murderous traitor. And it takes you by surprise. No matter how long I've been living on that water, when the storm comes through, it still shocks me. I'm awestruck by it. Sometimes the water is so changed afterward that the fish leave and it takes weeks, even months, for them to come back. It can be devastating to our little community."

Rory was thinking about Marcos. She wanted to say, "I'd like to travel there with my husband." But she was afraid to say the words out loud. She was afraid they weren't true anymore. That soon Marcos wouldn't be her husband anymore, and that they wouldn't be traveling anywhere together. She was afraid that he'd move to Miami and reclaim something he thought was lost. Something that didn't involve Rory at all.

Instead Rory said sadly, "Storms take me by surprise each time too."

Dee nodded. "But I've come to understand that even the storm has a purpose. It has beauty in it. It draws us together. In my little town, we pool together whatever we have to make it through those times. We shift. We turn. We become different."

Rory nodded. This was a lovely ecological lesson but seemed completely unrelated to Hope and her lost and found parents until Dee said, "It was a storm that finally helped Hope's parents find their way."

"A storm helped them figure out what they were missing?"

"Not what. Who. It was in the storm that they found Hope."

Kate

KATE'S PHONE WAS sitting in her lap and started to buzz softly.

She looked down at it and hit decline. Another call she wasn't quite ready to take. Not here in this cab with listening ears at least.

But she couldn't deny something. That number lighting up on her phone made her heart feel something it hadn't felt in quite some time.

It was too soon to call it love. She knew that.

But it was something that could turn into love. Given the right nurturing and the right conditions.

Sure, this feeling was different than her feelings for Ian. That's why she had mistrusted it at first. Kate believed unless she felt about another man what she felt for Ian, it wasn't meant to last. This misbelief had caused her to make a great many mistakes over the last decades. But she was wiser now. Age and life and time had made her wiser.

Her newly-found wisdom would guide her from here on out. And when it was all over, would Ian understand why she had agreed to this day? Or would he believe it was a reconciliation of sorts? Was it narcissistic to even believe he was giving it the same amount of thought she was?

The long cab ride and unexpected traffic meant she had time to dwell on these and other thoughts.

Her phone buzzed again—this time with a text.

Just tried calling. Miss you. Boarding soon. Have a wonderful day. We'll talk later.

No, it was too soon to call it love. But it was something even more powerful.

It was hope.

Ian

WHAT WOULD DEE say about his coming back home? Ian wondered as they sat in stand-still traffic only a few miles from their destination. Kate seemed to think she'd be there, waiting. A thought that made Ian even more nervous. He wasn't sure he trusted himself to see Dee today. He didn't want to get into her reasons for lying. He knew what she'd say. Surely, she'd tell him that she *had* to do it. But he didn't want to hear it.

Dee had told him that Kate was happy. That while Ian was gone, Kate had found her way back to Rob Sutton. That she'd had her boys too. That the universe had found a way to complete Kate's path and destiny by giving her Hope *and* the boys.

But now that Kate had come to Mexico to literally pull Ian off the beach and drag him home to see Hope, Ian had learned from Kate that there were no other children.

There was only Hope.

Dee was wrong.

No, worse than being wrong. It was clear that Dee had lied.

2001 haunted Ian again and again for so many reasons. He remembered going back in time with Kate on The Beatrice and trying to explain it to her. When he found the notes from his trip to India—notes he'd shredded years earlier, he became bold. And hopeful. He told Kate they'd gone back in time.

"Ian, I don't understand. Where exactly do you think we are?"

Kate's eyes had darted back and forth when she realized it was true; that Kate and Ian had gone back to 2001 together.

"There have been clues all along of course. But I think I ignored them. Deliberately. And then this morning, I found notes in my bag. The notes I made in preparation for a trip to India to live among local artisans in 2001. I hadn't seen or thought about those notes since that trip. I shredded those notes in India in late 2001 after I wrote the article."

Ian watched as Kate put the pieces of the puzzle together. The completed picture would look so differently for her than from him.

She had looked panicked. Like she was choking even. Her hands went to her throat and she backed away from him toward the ship's pool. He lunged toward her but it was too late. She was in the water, sinking, drowning, with the weight of a new reality pushing her under water faster than Ian could save her.

After Ian dragged her out of the pool, it felt like hours before Kate opened her eyes, but it was only minutes, of course. Ian had done her breathing for her. As she came to, he was still huddled over her, harried and distressed. He was exhaling hard. Kate coughed repeatedly, and then she choked out a word: "Ian."

"I'm here, Kate."

"Ian, please. You saved my life. Take me home."

And so he had. It was 2001, and they had a brand-new start. She had chosen him. Thoughts of a different life seemed just that: mere thoughts.

But, they'd both come out of that water confused. Had they traveled back in time or had they simply imagined the whole thing? Ian worried whether he could make Kate truly whole or truly fulfilled. No matter, Ian couldn't imagine Kate anywhere but in his arms. So, he would certainly do his best.

The next decade, however, proved to be a trying one. There were terrorist attacks and shifts in the world that rocked Kate and Ian to their core. While the rest of the New York City was trying to come to terms with new fears and new insecurities, Kate seemed to be feeling fear and insecurity even more acutely, and her decision weighed on her. She worried she'd lost her mind. She had dreams at night of another life. Of children. Of motherhood. Something that seemed to be eluding her in real life but haunting her in her dreams.

Ian spent the next decade caring for her. Trying to get her the right medical care. Trying to help her. Trying to convince her to have hope, and trying to figure out if they'd done something wrong just by choosing each other. It seemed incomprehensible to him that they'd made a mistake. But when Kate started talking about the shadows, he grew worried that he was losing her to a madness she might not ever escape from.

He'd suggested the only thing he could think of. He'd taken her aboard his friend Captain Mauricio's ship again and headed directly into the Bermuda Triangle. The Beatrice had been decommissioned, which is why, *that time*, they boarded her successor, The Beatrice II.

"It's *one more thing*, Kate," Ian promised with confidence. Maybe all they really needed was a do-over—a return to 2001 yet again—and if so, he'd get her there.

chapter six

Rory

DEE GESTURED TOWARD the building behind them where the graduates would soon be taking the stage inside. "It's getting closer to start time now."

Rory tried to sort through her feelings. This woman seemed a little crazy. Was there really a story here or just the ramblings of a madwoman? What would Marcos say if he were sitting here?

Rory didn't have to think about that too hard. He was just crazy enough that he might believe this.

Rory sighed with the realization, and with some jealousy at the thought of how easy it would be for Marcos to just *believe*.

Dee tilted her head to Rory. And Rory realized her sigh and maybe even some of her thoughts had been audible. "Who were you thinking about just then?" Dee asked.

"My husband."

"You're married. Of course." Dee pointed down to Rory's press lanyard swinging like a pendulum around her neck. "Garcia is your married name?"

Rory nodded.

"So, tell me about him."

"Marcos? What do you want to know?" Rory narrowed her eyes defensively.

"Everything."

Rory didn't even pause. "Marcos is a painter."

She was surprised with herself that was the first thing to come out.

"What does he paint, your Marcos?"

"Small paintings."

"Small? What do you mean?"

"They are the tiniest pieces of art you've ever seen. And yet incredibly detailed. Paintings of entire city blocks covered in people of all shapes and colors doing various activities contained on a canvas only a few inches wide. It's astounding, really."

"Small paintings of life?"

"Yes. It's a big statement. He arranges them on a wall, and you think you're looking at an installation of a single word—like hope, or love, or freedom, or bondage. But really, when you get closer, you can see the canvases are an entire world in and of themselves."

"You seem quite proud of his work."

"I am. I'm no art critic. But I can recognize art that tells both a personal and a universal story and his does. But it's not—"

Long pause.

"It's not what?"

"It's not practical for commercial success. Each piece can take days or weeks to work on. You can't appreciate the exhibit without spending hours, or even days, to fully examine each square under a magnifying glass."

"That sounds exquisite."

"Well, it is. It's just that the experience is not, you know, practical."

"You worry he'll never make money with his art?"

"Well, I used to worry more. Now I worry differently. There is a Cuban-American gallery in Miami that wants to display it but they're not even sure people will give it the time required to appreciate it. It's so unlike any of the flamboyant, sort of larger-than-life Cuban art they are used to displaying. His parents came here from Cuba while his mother was pregnant with him, so you see, Cuba is in his blood and he wants to try to connect to others with his art. He wants to take the chance in Miami. Marcos is always erring on the side of hope."

"What a wonderful way to live life."

"It's a wonderful way to life your life when someone else is paying the bills and chasing down steady employment." Rory was surprised by the edge to her voice and the sharp response.

"You resent his freedom."

"I envy it. I think it's naïve in many ways."

"You mentioned his parents?"

"Yes. They came here under very challenging circumstances.

"They risked life and limb to be here?"

"Indeed. Under the immigration policy in effect at the time—Wet Feet, Dry Feet."

Dee nodded knowingly.

"They knew if they made it to land, they'd be granted asylum. It was a calculated risk, and they succeeded. They lived out the rest of their lives here."

"They died here in this country?"

"Yes, Marcos says it was a great disappointment to them that they weren't able to go back home. But he fears that he is somehow disappointing them in death because he doesn't want to go back to Cuba in their stead. He doesn't consider it "home." How could he? He was never there. He didn't live there. He wasn't born there. And yet—"

"Yet?"

"His art. It is entirely about Cuban life. About the Cuban landscape and cities that he's never seen with his own eyes."

"He's searching for his own authenticity, yes?"

"Yes." Rory was embarrassed that it took saying all this out loud to a stranger named Dee to really put it in perspective for the first time.

Of course, this was why Marcos's art both inspired him

and tortured him. He once told her he felt he'd appropri-
ated art from his own culture. He felt he'd betrayed his
parents and his culture by simply not feeling connected to
it while they were still alive to see it. This was nothing Rory
could empathize with and so she hadn't even tried. She was
ashamed sitting there with Dee.

But still.

She didn't want to move to Miami.

Rory spun her oversized watch on her thin wrist.

"He wants us to move to Miami. But I don't have a life
there. I have a life and work here. And it seems so risky to
give all that up. The museum in Miami is in a lot of turmoil
and turnover, and they aren't even sure they can draw an
audience for Marcos's art. And yet, I can't tell him not to
go."

Dee held Rory's eyes in her own. "Why not?"

"Because I'd be signaling something pathetic to him."

"What?"

"That I couldn't, oh God, I don't know, that I couldn't
live without him or something."

"Do you want to live without him?"

"Well, no. I mean, I don't *want* to. But I *could*. Of course,
I could. I'm stronger than I look."

"I have no doubt you are strong. Also, you *look* strong
to me. On the record."

Rory laughed at Dee's phrase and delivery.

"For the record." Rory corrected Dee before she could
stop herself.

"If you prefer."

Rory felt embarrassed. She covered it up quickly. "Yes,
and so obviously I could live without him."

"Right. If that was your only choice."

"Yes, I'd live without him if that was my only choice."

"But you'd also live with him if you had to. If that was
your only choice."

Rory nodded slowly, as if she was stepping into a trap. Which she was.

"If I beg him to stay, he wouldn't want me then. I'd be weak to him."

"Ah," Dee said. "That vulnerability—it's what makes us all human—the thing that connects us in our humanity. And yet it's also what threatens to keep us from connecting at our core."

Rory looked at Dee with an open mouth. She had put her finger on the exact conflict Rory had been feeling. She didn't want to beg Marcos to stay. She wanted him to stay but she didn't want to beg him to do so. Maybe this was the result of being her mother's daughter.

Or maybe it was the result of the being her father's daughter.

Rory stared at Dee. She didn't even know this woman and suddenly she felt closer to her than she'd felt to anyone in a long time.

Even her mother.

Even Marcos.

"Vulnerability is a complicated thing. Troubling. Yes?"

Rory nodded and looked down at the twisting turning watch on her wrist. It was a gift from her mother who valued punctuality the way other women valued a quality handbag or a pair of Louboutin shoes. Her mother thought punctuality—the keeping of real time—was exquisite and rare. She handed down that belief to Rory, who arrived everywhere well before the starting time. She laughed wryly with the realization she was early even for this graduation event she hadn't planned on attending.

"Why are they not here yet?"

Dee looked over her shoulder.

"Who?"

"Hope's parents. Why are they not here yet? They're cutting it a little close, no?"

Dee shook her head. "Yes. Well, a lot has happened to them. I haven't seen Ian in quite a long time, in fact. I'm hoping, well—we'll see ...."

"You said they visited you often in the Bahamas?"

"Yes, for many decades, until the last time."

"When was that?"

"Well, it was in 2011."

"It's so odd," Rory interrupted.

"What is?"

"Your sense of timing. It can't possibly be right. I mean, are Hope's parents approaching 70 or 80? How can you have seen them decade after decade after decade, but not for about 9 years? I feel like your numbers are off."

Dee just laughed and continued on, with confidence, ignoring Rory's timeline, much to her dismay.

"That last time in the Bahamas, it showed on Hope's mother's face. The struggle and the difficulties of the decade before. She was greatly changed. She was thinner and paler. It was heartbreaking to see. She wasn't at all sure she was ready for motherhood."

"So, they were still childless on that last trip?"

Dee nodded.

Rory shook her head in confusion. "But, if that was only 9 years ago, then how can they be Hope's parents?"

Dee seemingly ignored her. "They were afraid of having children at that time. And I knew they wanted some words of wisdom and encouragement from me. Ian had kept me up to speed in their absence. He didn't know yet what the real source of her sadness was. I knew, but I couldn't tell them. Some things you just have to find out yourself, you know what I mean?"

Rory nodded and shook her head at the same time. She had no idea what Dee was talking about actually.

"I remember what Hope's mother said to me as soon as we saw each other at the restaurant on that visit. As soon as we embraced. She said, 'I realized when I got off the Beatrice

II and headed here to see you. I am supposed to be here. Right here. The thought came to me as we headed here and was as surprising as it was calming.'" She was starting feel better. Things were already in motion by that point. The storm was brewing. The direction was changing. I was relieved for them both.

"We spent some time together on that trip. I let Ian talk to other friends at the restaurant, and I took Hope's mother alone with me for the afternoon.

"We headed into the kitchen where our conversation mostly focused on flour and spices and fish filets. I chopped papaya and guava and gave her directions. All of them having to do with food. After a few minutes, she laid down her knife. And she said the words I'd been dreading hearing.

"She said: 'Dee, I'm afraid I made a mistake.'"

Rory stopped taking notes. She was hoping she could remember all this. There were so many layers to this story that she wasn't sure she'd be able to truly unravel them all until she got home and sat with the story for a little while. "A mistake? What kind of mistake?"

"Well, a decade earlier, they had reconnected on another trip—another cruise through the Bermuda Triangle on The Beatrice I. They were confident on that trip, and still confident upon leaving the ship. They believed that they were making the right decision. Both of them were giving up relationships they were in previously. Ian gave up his long-time childhood sweetheart and she gave up a relationship with a man named Rob Sutton. She chose Ian with confidence, but then spent a decade regretting the decision. Again and again. Regret paralyzed Hope's mother. It led to her depression and anxiety. It led to medicine and therapy. All over one decision she had become certain was wrong, and couldn't truly voice to anyone other than me.

"My God. How terrible. What do you think?"

"About what?

"Do you think she really made a mistake?"

Dee looked off into the distance. Rory could almost believe that honking cars and skyscrapers were melting down around her into a view of blue Bahamian water out over the porch of a seafood shack on the beach.

"I did not. I do not. None of her choices were mistakes. They were simply that—choices made at a certain time under the circumstances given. But she was distraught. She said: 'How can I love him so deeply and yet be so sure I've chosen wrong? At night I have a terrible dream. A dream that I got off that ship a decade ago and made an entirely different decision. I dream that I chose a life and a family with Rob Sutton. Why can my brain not release it? Why can't I own my decision and move forward? I'm drowning and I'm pulling Ian down with me.'

"She sat then. We had been standing cutting fish filet and fruit but I wasn't sure her legs could hold her. She had to sit."

"You were able to comfort her?" Rory felt the pain of this woman she didn't know. It was paralyzing. Rory felt pinned to her seat.

"I know loss. I know that feeling, and it pained me to experience it along with her. I have lost a mother and a husband and a child," Dee confided.

Rory looked down, saddened by the revelations that seemed both unconnected to the story between them and viscerally connected as well.

Rory tried to sort through the timeline in her own mind.

"So, the last time you saw them they had traveled on The Beatrice II?"

Dee nodded.

"And a decade earlier they had come to you on The Beatrice I?"

Another nod.

Rory shook her head in confusion. This trip that Dee was talking about? It was 9 years ago. And it followed another trip 10 years earlier. By that point, this couple had been together and childless for nearly two decades. So how could this same couple become parents to a child who was now 18 and graduating from college? A child that everyone agreed was born on 9/11, making this story so compelling?

Rory tapped her pen on her notebook in deep thought, and then suddenly realized a possibility that would allow for all the moving parts of Dee's story to make sense.

This couple could have come home from that trip in 2011 and adopted a child. Perhaps they took in a young child orphaned in the aftermath of 9/11. A child named Hope.

Rory felt sad for the child who would have to be mothered in the midst of so much doubt. Would she ever have sensed it? Did she know? Even now, did Hope know?

Rory thought about her own mother, a single mother from the beginning, but never showing an ounce of ambivalence or regret. Rory never imagined her mother felt any doubts. But that couldn't have been a fair assumption. What had her mother felt when two lines appeared not long after her lover disappeared? Had she felt something that Rory didn't know about? Did she share fears and anxieties with the troubled woman in Dee's story?

"So, what did you tell her, Dee? Did you tell her to stop fearing her decision?"

"I told her: 'I believe you have to stop thinking you missed some chance for happiness. Each time has its own set of circumstances, and its own set of events. You can try wishing them away, but it's all in vain. If things were different, my mother would be alive. My husband would be here cooking with me. My child would have survived childbirth. But if times were different, I might not have known you. I might not have had the joy of seeing you and Ian together. I might not have had the chance to see you happy and starting your life together.'"

Rory felt the sting of Dee's losses in her gut. She imagined Hope's mother might have felt them too in that

Bahamian kitchen. Rory imagined she might have taken that information and decided with Ian to forge a life together.

A life that included Hope.

Kate

THE PHONE IN her lap buzzed again and this time she took the call.

"Benton."

"I'm heading over soon. I have to get out of here. I'm surrounded by boxes."

"Ha. I'm sure you are. Your shoes alone must be taking up an entire cargo container."

"You're mocking me."

"I am not. I'm laughing with you."

"Well, I'm not really laughing as you might have noticed."

"Then I'm trying to make you laugh so I can laugh with you."

"Ah. Clever."

Kate held the phone and let Benton sit with her in silence for a few moments. Eventually, Benton broke the silence.

"I can't believe I'm really doing it."

Kate ignored the real "it" behind her words.

"Leaving your tiny Manhattan apartment? What's so surprising about that? It's time. You have a big path ahead of you. Time to get started on it."

"I'm so glad it's almost summer."

Benton and Kate laughed together then as they said the words, "Summer glow follows winter snow."

It was Benton's saying but Kate had adopted it after a heart-to-heart they once had years ago.

"God. I feel ugly in the winter."

"Oh Kate, darling. Don't worry. Everyone does."

At the time, Kate was helping Benton with a donation drive at her office. Hundreds of gently used shoes donated for a group called Soles4Souls and now they needed to be sorted and bagged. Kate had signed on to do a good deed, but now the monotony was killing her. She started bringing up random topics just to kill the time. Maybe more.

"Really? Why is that?" Kate asked.

"Countless reasons. The sunlight is gone. There's hardly any natural light on our faces when we catch our reflection. Our skin is deprived of all Vitamin D and has gone completely crepey on us. It's just a horror scene. Why do you think I hop on a cruise ship or a plane every winter? I can't bear it. But don't worry—summer glow follows winter snow like clockwork every year."

Kate laughed. "That's a good one. You do escape every winter, don't you?

"And you used to enjoy the getaways too for a while, as I recall. Until you got all love sick on me." Benton laughed and rolled her eyes. Kate felt that uncomfortable feeling she got whenever Benton brought up Ian without mentioning his name. It felt like a dare from Benton.

Go ahead. Say you still love him. I dare you.

Benton was supposed to be a friend. A good friend. And so this taunting felt unnecessary. Kate always felt like she hadn't quite satisfied Benton with her choices. There was something passive aggressive in the way Benton dangled her past with Ian over her head maniacally.

One time Kate had asked her point blank.

"Why did you two never get together, Benton? Or did you? Do you have some history with Ian that I never really knew about?"

Benton swore they didn't. And it seemed genuine.

"No. Ian and I never got together. We were always friends. Nothing more."

"Why not?"

"Well, he never asked, for one thing."

That seemed incredible. Benton and Ian had been friends for years before Kate met either one of them. How could they not be interested in each other? Both were beautiful, successful, and ambitious people. It seemed crazy that they wouldn't have at least tried to see if they were a match.

"Come on, Benton. You're always bringing up Ian. And I never bring him up anymore." Kate left out the fact that he lived in her memory like a warm blanket. "It would seem one of us is still hung up on him. And it's not me." Kate tilted her head at Benton while she held up a pair of too worn canvas sneakers.

"No," Benton replied.

"Are we talking about the sneakers or Ian?"

"Both." Benton dismissed Kate summarily, and Kate threw the canvas sneakers into the discard pile while she continued sorting.

She would have let it go then, continuing only to sort shoes, but Benton kept talking. "It's just that Ian? He's not for women like you and me, Kate."

That seemed a more incredible statement than the confession that Ian had never even asked Benton out.

"What do you mean 'not for women like you and me?'"

"He's too much. That kind of intensity—it's consuming. It sounds romantic and lovely on paper, but when you get right down to it, could you live with a man who was obsessed with your every waking move? With talking about every emotion you were feeling when you were feeling it? Who was attentive to every move you make and word you say?"

"I don't know, Benton. You're making Ian sound better and better. Don't forget I'm an old woman. Hardly anyone pays attention to me anymore." Kate tried to make the laugh that accompanied her words sound natural. But she hiccupped. Benton's words reminded her what it was to be heard and listened to and yes, even watched closely.

There was a time Ian had done all those things. Now no one did any of those things for Kate.

When she and Ian had been together, she had savored the attention and intensity. Every moment of it. But was Benton right? Would it have been too much for the long term? Ian wasn't the kind of man who would allow for anyone to take care of him in return. Would the relationship have become too much eventually? It was hard to know.

And now I'll really never know, Kate thought to herself.

"Anyway," Benton said as she tossed a pair of red stilettos on the pile, "I wouldn't worry about looking ugly. You don't. And you don't have to worry about that nonsense any more. Need I remind you that you're married?"

It felt like another dare.

Kate put a matching pair of navy pumps in the yes pile, and excused herself to the bathroom where she locked the door, turned on the water, and stared at herself in the mirror while teardrops streaked her cheeks. Then she inhaled deeply, washed her cheeks and rejoined the shoe sorting.

Turns out she *did* like a few moments now and then when no one was watching. Maybe Benton was right about everything after all.

Or maybe she was completely wrong.

Ian

"YOU'RE SURE SHE'LL be there?" Ian asked again about Dee while they sat through a third and a fourth light without moving on the West Side Highway. The traffic was almost unbearable.

"She said she would be, so she will be."

Ian didn't respond the way he wanted.

Dee told me you got married.

You told me you didn't.

I'm not sure who I should believe anymore.

"You have to have faith in your choices, Ian. And you have to have faith that the universe knows better than us sometimes."

Dee had said these words in his ear while saying goodbye to him in the Bahamas on his last trip there with Kate. It was 2011; at least he thought it was. It was the cruise meant to save Kate from seeing shadows any longer. The trip meant to save Kate from her final descent into madness as she insisted again and again that there was another life she'd abandoned by choosing Ian over Rob Sutton.

After that day with Dee in the Bahamas, and her parting words of wisdom, Ian and Kate returned to The Beatrice II and Ian tucked Kate in for the night. She was happy and peaceful in a way Ian hadn't seen in quite some time.

He stopped at the restaurant on the 9th floor of the ship for a nightcap. There was a family on the deck of the 9th floor, and they were all dressed alike. There was a theme designated for dinner that night. Kate and Ian had eaten with Dee so they hadn't bothered to take note of the ship's dinner times or dress code that evening, but this family had.

Everyone was supposed to wear black and white, and this family had taken the directive to heart.

Mom was in a white shift dress and Dad was in a white button down with black slacks. Two small daughters, close enough in age that they might have been mistaken for twins, were in white and black clothes that looked stiff and uncomfortable and like they might have been purchased just for this evening. Ian watched them. He watched the dad lift one and then the other high over his head while the mother captured the moments on her phone camera. But the dad didn't seem to notice her. He wasn't performing for the camera. He was performing for his daughters.

Deep guttural laughs exploded from each girl as each took turns being lifted to the ceiling by her father.

Ian listened to the laughs crescendo and then subside, over and over. He felt a mix of emotions that he couldn't quite sort out as he watched them, so he ordered another Manhattan and took it to go.

Ian ended the night up on the ship's bridge, where he headed to talk with his friend, the ship's captain, Mauricio. The talk with Dee had done Kate a world of good, but Ian couldn't help but think that when they returned home, the desperation might return. And he was terrified to face it again.

After all, it was still 2011. Wasn't it?

The recurring time travel pattern Kate and Ian were wondering if they were living in was starting to feel like a bad dream and not reality at all.

Ian sat and talked at Mauricio while he worked. Mauricio was checking and rechecking charts. A veteran of these seas, Mauricio had traveled in and out of the Bermuda Triangle week after week, year after year. And Kate and Ian had sailed with Captain Mauricio God knows how many times.

Come on board in 2011. Leave in 2001. Come on board again in 2011. Leave again in 2001. They never dwelled on it. They just kept traveling. Always out of the Manhattan Cruise Terminal. Always with Mauricio. They felt the effects of time travel but could not recall the memory of it.

Of course, this time felt a bit different. They were on a different ship for one thing. The Beatrice II was nearly an exact replica of its predecessor, but it *was* different. And maybe Kate and Ian were different on this trip as well. Ian thought that Mauricio might understand what Ian was struggling with between the lines of his spoken words.

"She fears there might have been another path for her. A path with that damn Rob Sutton. A path that involved marrying him and having his children. I just can't imagine her having children with someone besides me. I can't imagine her having a life with someone besides me. How can the present moment feel so real to me and yet, she has some other reality haunting her that doesn't involve me?"

Mauricio let Ian talk on and on, but he was quietly focusing.

Of course. He has to keep the ship afloat, Ian thought to himself.

Mauricio refused to look up from his monitor, instead leaning in closely to trace a green iridescent line in the middle and then turning to his charts to fill in some numbers and other information.

Ian was reassured by the fact that Mauricio was ignoring him. He could keep babbling on about Kate's fears concerning some alternative or parallel life without feeling like a crazy person.

The thing that plagued him, of course, beyond Kate's fears that she'd chosen the wrong man, was that Kate dreamed of being a mother and yet there was no child. Perhaps, Ian feared constantly, he had pushed Kate into giving up the only life she was meant to have.

How could he live with that?

How could she?

Ian leaned far back in his chair and tilted his head up

to the ceiling of the bridge while his Manhattan sloshed in his glass. He sat up suddenly when the sloshing became aggressive. A big puddle of Manhattan ended up in his lap. He nearly dropped his glass as he jumped out of his seat. But on his feet, he felt dizzy. The ship was moving quite a bit.

"What the hell? What's going—" Ian was interrupted by one of Mauricio's team.

"Captain, here are the updated numbers." He handed Mauricio a print-out that smelled of fresh ink.

Ian felt his way back into a seat, while the ship continued moving unfamiliarly. Mauricio's brow looked furrowed while he studied the newest paper he'd been handed and he nodded.

"Ok. My decision is now made." Mauricio spoke over Ian's head and when Ian turned to see who the Captain was speaking to, he noticed a small group had assembled, apparently awaiting his instructions. "We've been pushed out another 30 nautical miles by the storm. The storm is erratic and gathering intensity. We need to continue on this changed course—west instead of east. We'll dock in Bermuda in less than two days from now, only about a day later than we are expected in New York City. Call ahead to the dockmaster at The Royal Naval Dockyard in Bermuda. We'll make arrangements to fly passengers meeting emergency criteria home from there. The rest can wait out the storm with us in King's Wharf in Bermuda while we restock the ship and then head back to New York. We'll arrive back in New York City on Wednesday evening. Tropical Storm Althea will have dispelled by then, according to even the most conservative reports."

The team sprang into action. Radios and phones and keyboard tapping drowned out Ian's thoughts. He sat speechless.

Mauricio finally turned to him and acknowledged all that Ian thought he'd been ignoring for the last hour. Mauricio looked him squarely in the eye and said, "You're right, my friend. You cannot make her choose something other than what she is meant to choose, any more than I can move the course of this storm."

"A storm? Derailing the trip home? But it's not hurricane or tropical storm season is it? That season is still months away, no?" Ian heard the unfamiliar anxiety in his own voice.

Mauricio kept his attention focused on monitors and maps while he answered. "Althea is an off-season tropical storm. It's rare but still very powerful."

A thought began to take form in Ian's brain. He hadn't brought Kate on this trip for relaxation or kind words from Dee, but with the hope that they'd go back to 2001. He was hoping for a do-over of sorts. After all, they left The Beatrice I with such hope, such promise, a decade earlier. And then a decade of pain had eroded *everything*. Wasn't he secretly hoping this trip would take them back in time?

Was it all a mistake?

Now that the ship was off course, *when* would they make it back home?

Ian felt dizzy, and sat back down trying to steady his roiling stomach by holding onto the side of the tabletop on which he had just been resting his feet carelessly. It was a baffling feeling. He had never been seasick a day in his life.

Mauricio glanced over his charts at Ian, who was green and confused. "The ocean is a fickle mistress. She changes a little every time I travel her. Nothing is ever the same. Blame it on global warming. Blame it on the changing tides. Maybe I've arrived in this same spot hundreds of times before and just simply don't remember it. Or maybe this is indeed a fresh new scenario causing us to change course. No matter, now. We need to act with the information and circumstances we have at this time. Things are not, as we sometimes deceive ourselves, ever constant."

"So, we go to Bermuda, now? Until it's safe to head back

to New York? That's really what you're saying?

Mauricio nodded and shoo'd Ian out of the bridge. But not before saying, "We have to change course this time. And maybe the next. And what this means for you my friend, is that you have this time with the love of your life. The only advice I can give you is to make it count."

As Ian left Mauricio and headed back to his cabin, he wondered nervously whether this detour would ruin any hope for time travel. Would they be staying then in 2011?

As Ian walked into their cabin in the middle of Tropical Storm Althea, and saw Kate sleeping peacefully in the semi-darkness, he realized he didn't mind staying put in 2011, as long as he could stay there with Kate at his side.

In Bermuda, the sky was clear and the ocean was calm. There was no sign of the storm they were running from, which wasn't completely reassuring from Ian's point of view.

The eye of the storm is still inside the storm, Ian thought nervously as he stood at the window of their cabin.

"What should we do?" Kate joined him at the window as they docked at The Royal Dockyard. "I've never actually been to Bermuda. Have you?"

Ian shook his head. "Nope. First time. But Mauricio suggested we get a local tour guide at the dock to take us around the island for the day. He said a local can show us the best of the island. We're going to be here for a few days. We can explore today, and tomorrow we'll spend the day in the area of the island we decide we like best."

Kate nodded. "Sounds like a plan." Ian saw a rosiness in her cheeks that had been gone too long. Her eyes looked clearer than they had in years. She looked beautiful, but more than that, she looked happy.

They exited the ship together and walked through customs—a small pink building that housed a single x-ray machine and a cheerful officer.

"Good morning!" The officer greeted the couple exuberantly. "Where are you off to?"

"We thought we'd get a local tour guide to show us around."

"Great idea." The officer slapped Ian on the back with ease and familiarity.

"Got any recommendations?" Ian asked him.

"Sure. Look for Charlie. Tell him to make sure to take you to Tom Moore's Jungle. You two enjoy yourself." The officer turned his attention to a fresh batch of tourists making their way into the customs house, and Ian and Kate were left wondering how they'd ever locate this Charlie.

They needn't have worried. As they turned the bend from the area where the cruise ships were docked, they saw a cab line and right beside it, a gentleman dressed head to toe in pink and blue argyle with a large sign reading "Charlie's Tours, best on the island!"

"Charlie?" Ian smiled as they approached the man.

Charlie lowered his sign and started ushering the couple to the nearest car. "I've been waiting for you."

Ian put his hand out. "Oh, hold on. Sorry. If you have a reservation already, that's not us. We just heard about you. We literally just got off the boat and the customs officer told us if we were interested in a private tour, we should go find Charlie."

Charlie nodded. "Yes, yes. That's how I get all my customers. No reservations. This is easier. Come on."

Kate looked at Ian questioningly at first, but then nodded and shrugged.

A silent *Why not?* was shared between the two.

"What's your fee to show us around the island for the day?" Ian reached for his wallet.

"For you? A special rate. $200."

Ian nodded. "Whoa. That's steep, but I appreciate your

giving us a special rate."

After they got in the car, Ian leaned forward to Charlie and handed him the bills. "So, Charlie, what's your regular rate?

"$200."

Kate laughed. "I thought that was just your rate for special people. Like us."

Charlie looked indignant. "But I don't drive anyone who's not special."

Ian looked at Kate who was glowing in a way he hadn't seen in a while—maybe not ever. This island was clearly good for her. He was going to find a way to enjoy it as long as they could.

"Fair enough," Ian laughed. "Show us what you think we need to see today. But the customs officer said to ask you to be sure to show us Tom Moore's Jungle."

Charlie tapped the steering wheel with one hand and shifted out of park with the other. "As if I'd need reminding!"

Charlie drove them to an isolated and overgrown area outside of an island pub. When he pulled the car over, Kate and Ian assumed they'd misunderstood.

"You want us to get out here?" Ian asked incredulously.

Charlie nodded and got out of the car himself as if to set a good example. He headed toward the overgrown path and looked over his shoulder at Kate and Ian still sitting confused in the back seat of the car.

"Come on, you two!" He waved wildly.

Ian shrugged at Kate and they got out and followed behind their guide in a single file along a woodsy path waiting to see where it would lead.

They walked this way for some time. Charlie in the front, with Ian next, and Kate behind Ian. Ian tapped out the path for her with his shoes and looked back now and then to make sure she was able to stay in his footsteps. Every few feet, he'd glance over his shoulder and see Kate following along brightly. Each time his eyes would stumble on her, he'd see that she was happy. Her happiness lit Ian up from within.

"I'm relieved we have more time," Kate had responded, when Ian told her about the detour. He'd been worried that she'd become anxious. A deviation from the routine, from the plan, was not what either of them had expected. There was a chance that they had missed the window to return to 2001, a time when their reconnection was fresh and their choices felt right. The possibility lived like an unspoken brick between them. But Kate seemed genuinely relieved, and she'd nodded when Ian had explained that they would be back in New York City just a few days late.

Ian felt validated by her positive reaction, and by her happiness. *This is our reality*, he thought. *There can't possibly be another reality that doesn't involve us being together. There can't possibly be one that involves Kate being with someone else.* He wanted to ask her—didn't she agree with that, but he didn't want to ruin the moment by casting any doubt on it.

After a few turns on the overgrown path, Kate and Ian fell farther behind Charlie. They had some trouble keeping up partly because the recent storm rains made the muddy path slick and ill-defined. But also, because Kate and Ian couldn't stop staring. Overhead the trees made perfect, welcoming arches inviting them deeper into the jungle with their symmetry and beauty. Ian couldn't speak for Kate, of course, but he was struck by the beauty and by his own lack of fear. They continued following a stranger fearlessly into a remote jungle, past signs boasting private property flanking the path they were on. The path itself was marked only by twisted gnarls of branches that at each turn looked exactly like the ones that came before and the ones that came after.

The smell of the foliage was wet and thick and mossy. It was vibrant. The entire jungle was alive and buzzing with life, and Ian was caught up in it. As they walked, he pointed out pink flowers and small ponds with fish teeming just under the surface. He pointed out to Kate all that he saw, soundlessly, just a few seconds before she saw it as well. They fell further and further behind Charlie and soon Ian felt he was Kate's private guide on this trip. He reveled in the role.

As they turned the corner, a cave came into view, with a pool of blue water escaping from it. They found Charlie standing at the mouth of the cave, pointing and smiling, as if he'd been there all along. "Here is the cave. Feel free to swim in it. Its waters are refreshing after this long walk." The path opened up and Kate was able to walk alongside Ian for the first time since they'd set out on the walk. Ian pulled her into his arms. The canopy of trees had opened up as well, and the sky was more visible here through breaks in the jungle trees.

"Oh Ian. It's breathtaking," Kate put her hand up to her mouth as if to physically catch her breath before it left her. Instinctively Ian leaned in to kiss her as if resuscitating her. It was a familiar impulse to want to save Kate, and Ian gave into it. With the stalactites in view in the cave just ahead of them and the blue water beckoning them, Ian turned to thank their guide. But Charlie was gone. Ian turned quickly in a few different directions; it didn't seem possible that he'd have been able to make his way back down the path they'd just come from so quickly. And there didn't appear any other way forward unless one traveled through the water and through the cave. Ian thought for a moment that he'd imagined Charlie standing there at the cave mouth beckoning them.

Maybe he'd left a long time ago, and they really had been all alone in the jungle.

Ian saw Kate craning her neck looking for Charlie too.

His absence was odd, but not unwelcome.

Ian leaned in and kissed Kate long and deeply.

When Kate pulled away, she asked Ian, "Where do you think Charlie went?"

Ian shook off the startled feeling. "I don't know. He was simply done with us, I guess. Right?"

Kate closed her eyes, shaking off her own uncomfortable feelings, or so Ian assumed. Ian waited for her, and she came back to him in a little bit. "Well, should we try to find our way back, then? Just you and I? Do you think we can sort of retrace our steps?"

Ian pulled her to him. "I don't want to talk about leaving just yet. I don't want to go back. I want to be here. *Right here.*"

Kate kept looking around like Charlie was going to materialize. Ian reassured her. "Kate, we're not in a hurry. We'll find our way back eventually. Don't worry. We'll turn back and follow the path. It was overgrown, but it was worn, and I can find my way when it's time. The path leads out to a pub, and we can easily get another cab back there. But let's not hurry."

"But where did he go?" Kate wondered aloud again. Ian shook his head. It was enough for him that Charlie was gone. He didn't need to know where.

"And with your money? That was an expensive trip, Ian."

"Or maybe it was simply worth it," Ian winked at her. "Come on, let's swim."

Kate nodded and lifted her sundress over her head and Ian admired her swimsuit-clad body. He studied her long legs and muscular arms. She had grown thin—too thin—over the last years, but she was working on becoming stronger, and the work was reflected in her body.

Kate's swimsuit was really a dress and it was the color of the pools of water. Turquoise with flecks of bright green. For a moment Ian worried he'd lose her—she was perfectly matched to her surroundings. But she grabbed his hand

and pulled him to the rocks with a grip so firm, he stopped fearing he'd lose her. His fears started to take another shape altogether. Something he couldn't quite put words to. He stood speechless while she pulled on his hand.

"Come on," she insisted.

Ian stood still. He was stuck.

"Come *on*," she said again impatiently.

Ian complied and walked right up to the edge of the water with her—still clad in his oldest intact sneakers and favorite NYU tee shirt over floral swim trunks. If she blended into the jungle, then he was their milepost of distinction. He pulled his hand out of hers and lifted his shirt up and over his shoulders. He peeled each sneaker off with its opposite foot. He lifted his hands high in the air like he was about to jump—cannonball even—off the closest rock, when Kate reached up and grabbed Ian's hand again abruptly.

"Wait!" Kate yelled out and the fear in her voice stopped Ian rather than the word itself. "We don't even know how deep it is in here." Ian looked down past his bare feet. The water was clear and looked deep, but he realized she was right. The unbroken surface of the blue pool provided an optical illusion and Ian couldn't really know the depth standing there above it. Ian sat down on the rock ledge and slid slowly off its mossy surface into the water. He treaded for a moment and then raised his hands over his head and lowered himself down. He was surprised by how long it took. It was deeper even than he had hoped. He felt the soft ground finally and pushed himself up quickly, breaking through the surface with a loud and labored gasp. He waved at her.

"Come on in. It's deep enough here for you to jump. And it's cold enough that you're going to need to!" Ian reached his arms out to her like he was trying to catch her.

Kate stared at his open arms, smirking as she kept him waiting and the goosebumps popped out across his chest and arms. He thought she was going to change her mind about coming in—after she'd been the one so insistent from the beginning, but suddenly, as he shivered, she disappeared from the banks—transformed into a water nymph—a splash of cool spray not far from where he treaded water. She bobbed up again next to him, treading water and flapping the water with her hands.

"This feels wonderful," her voice was shivering.

He wanted to hold her but the water was too deep. He turned to see where the cave led behind them, and noticed a rock formation around the corner, with light streaming behind it betraying an opening. Ian waved at her to follow him and she obeyed soundlessly. They swam in the cold spring through the hushed cave while water splashed behind them occasionally. Ian led the way and headed for a rock near the opening of the cave, and when he reached it, he took Kate's hand and pulled her up next to him. Beyond them was a clearing, with light speckling on water and grey rocks just beyond them. The water clapped loudly as their bodies came together.

Ian held Kate for a long time on the rock, warmed by her, while their breath mingled and echoed against the cave wall, until their body heat gave out and the shivering began anew. Then, Ian swam off the rock and pulled Kate back into the cool spring with him. They moved together into the clearing, where the water turned warmer. When they reached the nearest bank, they pulled themselves up and out of the water under the jungle-fed sky.

Kate was still shivering, so Ian released her. "Take your suit off, we'll hang it to dry a bit before we head back." They took off their suits and lay on a bed of leaves by the water, twisted up like the branches surrounding them.

Ian thought briefly about Charlie the tour guide who had disappeared suddenly on the walk, and he wondered if there were any other lone souls who might stumble upon them here, naked and warming up very slowly under the

Bermuda sun that was making its way through the tree limbs like a maze.

Kate told Ian once, "You have a way of kissing me in the place where the muscles hold me upright." It was sexier than "You make my knees buckle" and he'd told her so. She had said it again and again that one time, but never since. Still, Ian remembered it. As they lay there on the bank, he tried kissing her there again, and imagined that if she was standing, she wouldn't be able to remain doing so. They lay together like that for what seemed like an eternity—in the clearing in the jungle as Kate held onto Ian for dear life.

A few days after the Tom Moore's Jungle outing, while the rare but real Tropical Storm Althea still swirled and churned in the ocean behind them, Ian and Kate found themselves in a familiar place aboard Mauricio's ship. Ian found the notes again that he thought he had shredded in late 2001. He had a vague sense of déjà vu as he said to Kate, "I think we went back in time again. I know this sounds crazy, but I believe it. I really do."

Even with a new ship, and even with the ship veering off its course, Ian believed they had landed in a place they'd been before.

"Ian where do you think we are?"

Kate's eyes darted back and forth on that last day of the last cruise they took together.

"There have been clues all along of course. But I think I ignored them. Deliberately. And then this morning, I found notes in my bag. The notes I made in preparation for a trip to India in 2001. I hadn't seen or thought about those notes since that trip. I shredded those notes in late 2001 after I wrote the article."

Ian watched as Kate put the pieces of the puzzle together.

Her hands went to her throat and she backed away from him. Ian thought for the first time about how going back in time might be frightening to Kate. While he was envisioning a fresh start and renewed confidence about their life together, she might be envisioning going through all the same pain again that she'd just been through that last decade.

It hadn't occurred to him that Kate might very well want to stay in 2011 while he had tried desperately to drag them back to 2001 again. There was an uncomfortable familiarity to the moment that engulfed him—in which he wanted something desperately that Kate did not seem to want in return.

Kate kept backing away from Ian toward the pool. Ian lunged toward her but it was too late. She was in the water, sinking fast.

Ian dragged Kate out of the pool, and as he crouched over her, exhaling loudly and painfully, the familiarity of the moment was over. If his brain was telling him they had been there before, then his heart was telling him it was *never like this*.

"I saw it," he said to her with a ghostly voice. "You were right."

"What did you see, Ian? Because I saw something too. *Someone*, rather."

"What do you remember? Before you came on board? Do you remember your conflicted feelings about Rob Sutton?"

Kate propped up on her elbows and shook her head vigorously. "There's nothing for me in that relationship anymore. No future there, whatsoever. I don't want to talk about him anymore. You were right. We are meant to be together, Ian. You and I. No one else."

The ship doctor arrived then and knelt and shone a light in Kate's eyes. Ian stood up and let the doctor take over. He shivered and tried collecting his thoughts. Ian had breathed for Kate. In and out. He hadn't meant to steal her breath. He'd meant to replace it for her. But in breathing for her, he'd also seen something she clearly didn't remember anymore. He'd seen Kate's children. More specifically, he'd seen the boys that had been haunting her dreams for all those years.

He saw them.

But now she apparently didn't remember. She didn't want to go back to Rob.

There's nothing for me in that relationship anymore. No future there whatsoever.

It was as if in breathing for Kate in those moments, Ian had taken away a memory. He hadn't meant to, but there it was. She no longer remembered the sons she might never have.

As Ian watched the ship doctor shine a light in Kate's eyes and ask her what year she thought it was. She answered confidently.

2001. It's 2001.

He started to step in. To interrupt. To help her. But the ship doctor nodded, confirming. "Yes, it's 2001. Good. Now, how are you feeling?"

"Fine, I feel fine."

"Ok, let's help get you to a chair and off this hard concrete."

"It's ok," she said. "I just feel a little dizzy. But that's to be expected. I think I might be pregnant, you see."

Ian gasped. "Kate?"

She nodded exuberantly. There was no trace of grief or confusion in her face.

"Ian, it's true. I saw her. I saw *Hope.*"

chapter seven

Rory

RORY'S PHONE BUZZED on the bench where she and Dee were sitting, and she jumped at the noise. Then she glanced down at the screen and apologized to Dee. "Oh, I'm sorry. I have to take this. It's my mom calling from out of the country."

Rory saw Dee's eyes glisten as she stood up and stepped away from Dee to take the call.

Rory could feel Dee's sadness, presumably over another mother who might not be able to make it to see her daughter on this special day. Rory turned as she walked away with her still buzzing phone and hit "Accept."

"Mom."

"Hello, sweetheart. It's beautiful here. We'll have to come back together sometime. I mean, you'll bring Marcos too if you want. I'm not suggesting we'd leave him out. It's just that I don't know what his paperwork situation is. Oh for heaven's sake, that sounded bad. I didn't mean it that way. Dear Lord, can I just start over?"

"Mom, relax. Isn't that what you're supposed to be doing? Relaxing? How's the retreat?"

"Glorious. Utterly glorious. I am completely relaxed. I even met a friend."

"Really? What kind of friend? A *boy*friend?"

Rory drew the last word out nonsensically.

"Oh you!" Rory knew just what face her mother was

making at that point. Sarcastic and endearing and acqui-escing all at the same time. "Just a friend."

"When are you coming back?"

"I don't know, dear. I'm thinking about staying another couple of weeks. I'm doing so well, they've asked me to be one of the retreat leaders for the next session."

"Really?"

"Well, don't sound so surprised, Sweetheart. I'm not so bad at downward facing dog, as it turns out." The laughter coming over the line was sweet and refreshing. Things had been so tense between them lately; Rory had forgotten the old ease of their relationship.

Something about the carefree tone of her mother's voice and the phone and space between the two women made Rory bold.

"Mom, can I ask you a question about my dad?"

A pause and then, "Sure, honey. What is it?"

"Did you ever try to, you know, find him? Tell him about me?"

"Sweetheart. Your father was a wonderful and hand-some and kind man. But he was a gypsy. He didn't want children. He wanted his freedom. He was adamant about that fact and I didn't ever want him to feel trapped by a child. And I certainly never wanted you to feel rejected. We've been through this. He left the country before I even knew I was pregnant with you, and I never even really knew how to start the process of finding him, and maybe that sounds like a cop out, and if so, I'm sorry."

"No, I know. And I'm not saying you should have pushed him to accept me. I'm just wondering if we could have looked a little harder for him."

"We?"

"Well, you know what I mean."

"Yes, I do."

Soft exhales from both women connected over the dis-tance.

"Anyway, Mom. I get it. You said he was really certain back then that he didn't want kids. You can't force someone into something that important."

Her mother had never even told Rory his name. And Rory never pressed. She knew her mother was trying to protect her. But she didn't want to hide under her mother's cloak of protection any more. Her mother seemed to hear her thoughts.

"Well, Rory, I guess the thing is you're not a kid anymore."

"No, I'm not."

"Frankly, I've been giving this a lot of thought myself lately. So, when I get home, if you want, I can help you figure out where to start."

"Thanks, Mom. I appreciate that. I'm not saying that's what I want to do. I'm just saying I'd like to think about it."

"Well, Sweetheart, I better go. I have class in 15 minutes. I was just calling you between sessions. We're making homemade granola next."

"You're something else, Mom. Have fun."

"You too, Sweetie. Goodbye!"

The call jolted her back to reality and reminded her why her problems with Marcos were so much more complicated than she was letting on. Rory turned back to Dee, half expecting her to have disappeared. But she hadn't. She was sitting right where Rory had left her.

Waiting.

Rory looked over her shoulder at the city street and the traffic at a standstill outside Carnegie Hall. Horns were blaring and the police were setting up new roadblocks.

They must not have expected these crowds. They kept this whole thing under wraps but it appears news is getting out after all.

With her phone still in her hand, Rory texted her editor quickly.

Change of plans today. Covering the 9/11 survivors' graduation at Carnegie Hall instead. Getting some inside scoop. More soon.

Over her phone, Rory saw a biker weaving through the traffic with a delivery hovering over his handlebars. When she watched the city moving at this speed, she often willed it to slow down. At the same time, she found herself wondering where everyone was moving at this breakneck speed?

Rory rejoined Dee.

"Do they live far from here? Is that why Hope's parents still aren't here?"

"Sort of. It's a long story. So you've heard."

Rory chuckled and looked at her watch. It was 11:15. She'd been sitting with this stranger over an hour.

A long story indeed.

If Ian and Kate were happiest in the Bahamas, did they just stay there in the Bahamas? Did they outsource Hope's learning and raising to this makeshift boarding school of 9/11 survivors? And were they still there? Drinking beer and eating homemade conch fritters on the wooden porch of Dee's restaurant?

Was this why they weren't back in time for Hope's commencement speech?

And if so, Rory wondered how Hope felt about this. It was wonderful to have happy and fulfilled parents, she supposed. But it also seemed a little self-centered. Suddenly Rory had a vision of these two lovers hanging out by the blue Bahamian sea while Dee was standing in for them at their daughter's commencement speech.

My mother would never do that. My mother will drive me crazy until I drop dead, but she would never disappear on me, Rory thought, as she remembered her mother actually *had* disappeared recently.

She'll come home from that retreat sooner rather than later. And when she does, we'll sit down and have our own long talk.

Kate

KATE ROLLED HER window down for air and caught a scent of the city and the river and something vaguely citrusy and salty wafting on the air.

The scent was familiar and reminded her of an old friend.

Dee.

She and Dee had kept in touch only erratically over the years.

She assumed that Dee kept in touch with Ian but she never felt that Dee's calls were fishing expeditions for Ian. Dee seemed genuinely interested in how Kate was doing. And Kate was always happy to hear from her.

Each time they spoke, Kate did most of the talking. She would fill her in. She'd tell her what was new. And what wasn't.

The most recent call had been just a few weeks ago.

She told Dee about the planned trip to Mexico, and Dee seemed genuinely happy on the other end of the phone. That was the thing about Dee. She took on everyone's joys and sadnesses as her own.

"What wonderful news!"

"Yes, yes it is."

"And how are you holding up, Kate?"

"It's been a long road."

"Indeed."

"I've often gotten discouraged along the way, believing I know how this ends."

"And do you?"

Kate had laughed then at the implication in Dee's voice.

"No. Of course I don't. No one ever does."

"Good girl, Kate."

Of course, Dee wasn't completely caught up. A lot had changed over the last few days. The trip to Mexico had not gone as expected.

Kate couldn't help but wonder what Dee would say about the newest developments in Kate's life. Would she embrace them? Would she judge them? Kate told herself it didn't matter what Dee thought. It only mattered what Kate thought.

She also tried to tell herself it didn't matter what Ian thought. That was a harder sell.

Ian

TROPICAL STORM ALTHEA stayed mostly at sea, and eventually it was safe to travel back to New York City. Hours after The Beatrice II docked in New York, Ian was the one who went directly to the pharmacy.

He stood in the pickup prescription line for a half hour. It was longer than usual, but he was used to waiting for Kate's prescriptions. During the previous decade, Kate and her doctor tried cocktails of all kinds, trying to get her well. Ian felt hopeful as each attempt worked for a short time and then ultimately failed.

As Ian moved forward in the pharmacy line, he was troubled.

What if all along Kate was right? What if she was experiencing loss and grief for sons and a life that she was meant to have with Rob Sutton?

What if all along the shadows represented another life? What if all along she was grieving the loss of sons she may never have now?

Ian stood quietly in line as it moved steadily forward, putting him closer and closer to the truth with each passing moment.

Kate had been weaning off the particular drug combination she was on just before the last cruise. She'd have to return to the psychiatrist for a new regimen, and so she wasn't likely to have any prescriptions awaiting their return. But still Ian stood in that line for half an hour.

When he finally got to the counter, the pharmacist, a familiar person in their lives, who knew Kate and Ian well, and knew about Kate's mental health struggles, looked at Ian blankly.

Ian paused for a moment. The pharmacist knew Kate's medical history better than anyone except her psychiatrist. No doubt he'd be worried with the news that Kate was likely pregnant. Ian watched the pharmacist standing in front of the clear acrylic bins for several long moments before the pharmacist interrupted his staring gently.

"Sir. Can I help you?"

Sir?

Ian was jarred back to reality with just the word. It wasn't 2011 any longer. He wasn't there to pick up a prescription. He wasn't standing in front of a familiar face. He was standing in front of a stranger in 2001. One who would become familiar, gradually, over the next years, as they battled Kate's struggling health together. As they battled Kate's demons.

Unless.

Unless this time was different.

"Um. I'm sorry. I'm not here to pick up a prescription." Ian looked over his shoulder for any known faces in line behind him but didn't see any. He said the words he'd been saying only in his head for the half hour he'd been standing in line. "I need a pregnancy test."

"Oh, you don't need a prescription for those, Sir. They're over there in aisle eight."

The pharmacist pointed behind Ian and Ian followed his point without another word.

"Not pregnant."

Less than an hour later, Kate held the stick up to the box to interpret the results and read them aloud to Ian, the sadness clearly evident in her voice.

He wasn't sure what to feel with the news.

"How can this be?" Kate was sure she was pregnant, and Ian reminded her that she very well may be, but it was too soon to tell with the pharmacy-issued test.

"You need to give it some time. Wait. Be patient," he told her.

The light in her eyes that had settled there on the ship

remained. Ian watched her over the next few weeks with tentative happiness. He ignored the lingering doubts and fears and the vision he'd had while resuscitating Kate in the middle of an off-season tropical storm—a vision of two boys who weren't his.

Two days after a missed period, Kate looked at Ian with fear and excitement in her eyes and asked him to go get another pregnancy test. This time he bypassed the pharmacist and went right to aisle eight and purchased three tests. Kate took all three tests in rapid succession. Sitting in the bathroom in her small Manhattan apartment that she had either lived in alone or shared with Ian for the last decade, depending upon whether it was 2001 or 2011, the couple stared together at the two pink lines for an inordinate amount of time.

And then Kate looked up with the most radiant smile. "Ian, we've gotten a restart after all. A do-over. I don't know what happened on that ship. And I don't care. I don't know why I vaguely remember a decade of confusion and unwellness. Maybe it happened; maybe it didn't. But this—"

Kate held up the stick covered in urine and pink dye triumphantly. "This is our brand-new start."

Ian felt emotions he didn't even know were possible. Amazing, incredible joy. Excitement. Anticipation. Nervous fear. But beyond that, behind that, he felt something else. Something he didn't want to name or acknowledge.

It was the feeling that by having a baby with Kate, he was now forcing her to give up something else. *Someone* else.

That feeling was *knowing*. And he could not make it go away.

It was *that* feeling that drove him away eventually.

Kate's therapist, Dr. Nancy Gothie, called Ian and Kate both in for a session soon after the pregnancy test confirmed what they'd suspected from the minute they left The Beatrice II.

Kate had told Dr. Gothie that there was a fuzzy memory of a lost decade. The therapist knew nothing about that lost decade, of course. As far as she knew, she took Kate on as a new patient fairly recently due to a reported feeling of "stuckness" she was feeling in her relationship with a man named Rob Sutton. Now Kate was back from a trip through the Bermuda Triangle with a new joyfulness, a new pregnancy, and a new boyfriend. And everything felt very sudden to this no-longer-old therapist.

So Dr. Gothie had asked Kate to bring Ian to her next session to help her help Kate. Kate was trying to end the therapy. She was honoring the appointments she already had booked with Dr. Gothie, to try to talk through this fuzzy memory of shadows and regrets. But she was determined that she wouldn't be needing this therapist for the long term. Nevertheless, she asked Ian to come with her as per Dr. Gothie's request.

As Ian and Kate sat alone in the waiting room, before their joint session together, Kate said, "I wish I would have just canceled all my remaining appointments. She seems to be making everything cloudier rather than clearer."

Ian nodded with trepidation before they were summoned out of the waiting room by the therapist. The therapist read from Kate's last session notes, with Kate's permission, taken in an appointment just days after Kate and Ian returned from the cruise ship detoured by Tropical Storm Althea and discovered it was 2001.

Kate had used her prescheduled therapy sessions to work through the confusion she was feeling returning to 2001 yet again. It was a familiar loop. Still, it wasn't easy. Ian understood that. He didn't mind hearing about Kate's confusion over landing yet again in 2001. This time, unlike the other times, there was something sweet about it and not ominous.

Kate told Ian before the joint session that she was careful not to use words like "time travel" with Dr. Gothie, for fear of being disbelieved, or worse, committed. Ian agreed to be similarly careful.

At the session, Dr. Gothie read Kate's words aloud. "I feel like I've woken from a long slumber and I can't shake the sleep off my brain to remember clearly the nightmare I've just had. I know I've had one, but I can't remember the details. I like it this way, though."

Kate nodded along with the therapist's reading.

The therapist continued.

"I know I've been through some shit, to put it bluntly. I know I have struggled to find a rhythm and I've struggled with guilt and depression ever since Ian and I reconnected. I know all these things and yet I know too that these things are like a fog rolling off my brain that I feel like I'm finally emerging from."

More nodding, and then Dr. Gothie stopped reading.

"Kate, do you want to talk more with Ian about these feelings of guilt and depression that you've been having since you and he reconnected on the trip?"

Kate shook her head. "No, you're getting it all wrong. And I don't blame you—because it's confusing, but I was talking about the guilt and depression I felt since the first reconnection—a decade back or so."

"But I thought you and Ian met around the same time you met Rob? 1997? That's only about 4 years ago."

Kate shook her head and nodded too.

"I know, I know. I sound crazy. You're right. We did meet in 1997, but there have been reconnections with Ian all along. It's confusing. But we don't need to get bogged down in the timeline right now. The fact is, I'm over the guilt now. I'm over all the sadness. And it's all because of a baby. This baby changes everything."

The therapist shook her head. Ian realized she did not agree with Kate.

Or at least she wasn't sure.

The therapist wanted to talk about Rob, which made Ian uncomfortable for so many reasons.

"What about Rob?" the therapist prodded.

"Rob Sutton? That's over. We broke up as soon as I got off the ship. He's sad, naturally. But I can't get bogged down in his emotions. I have to do what's right for me."

"You're moving on?"

"Indeed I am."

Ian looked back and forth at Kate and the therapist searchingly. Neither seemed to remember that the therapist advocated for Kate to move on at every session over the last decade. A decade which didn't exist anymore.

"Well, you mentioned something about a shadow in our last session? A shadow that—before the cruise ship—you felt was following you?" the therapist continued on.

"Yes, a shadow. That used to follow me. But it's gone now. I mean it's there when it's sunny out, but I'm not really sure why I even mentioned it. It's not really a thing right now."

Kate stood up to finish the session. Ian remained sitting.

He considered saying some things out loud that might help the therapist fill in the missing pieces.

Kate was lost because she chose me over the father of her sons.

She remembered them but we all kept telling her they weren't real.

We did that for a decade. A long tumultuous decade. Maybe longer. Who can know now?

But the world has shifted and now Kate and I are having a baby together.

We've gone back in time from 2011 to the year 2001. Again.

And miraculously, Kate doesn't remember those sons anymore.

And she doesn't want to be with their father.

So they will not exist.

There will only be this new baby.

You think Kate is a new patient, but you've actually given her a decade of advice.

A decade that neither of you really remembers now.

But I do.

I remember everything. I resuscitated Kate in the middle of a tropical storm that we had no business traveling through.

While I gave her breath, she traded me with memories.

I'm the only one who remembers Kate's sons.

Which means I'm the only one now who knows what Kate has given up.

Ian wanted to say these things but he stayed silent. He took all his cues from Kate. It was so unlike the last decade as he remembered it, when Kate needed to be cared for. A decade when she was broken. This Kate—the one who was cutting the therapist appointment short and talking about moving on—was healed. Or at least was on her way to being healed.

Ian was so happy to see this Kate, he ignored the nagging feeling that lingered in his brain, reminding him that Kate was meant to have more babies than this baby she was carrying of *his*.

As she stood, she replied, "Dr. Gothie, I'm ok. I'm just tired. And now I have baby brain on top of everything else. Remember: I'm having Ian's baby."

The therapist looked like there was more to say, but Kate walked out and Ian followed her. He stopped short behind her as Kate paused at the receptionist desk. "I'd like my records to be sent to my home address. I'll be discontinuing therapy. Thank you."

The receptionist shrugged and nodded, and they left the office without even a goodbye.

At first Ian wanted Kate to get a new therapist, but Kate

refused. She also wanted to stay off all meds because of the pregnancy. Ian was reluctant but understood. Kate agreed that medication had been the right answer for her before, but now, things felt differently. Her entire internal chemistry felt new. Kate said she didn't want to get a new therapist or a new psychiatrist and start at the beginning.

In the meantime, Dr. Gothie called a few times. She kept telling Kate that she hadn't given her therapy enough time, but Kate insisted that she'd given it plenty of time. A few months later, with a baby on the way, and a new lease on life, Ian noticed Kate was doing well, but he wasn't. He called up an old friend and asked if she had time to talk. She said she had a better idea.

"I'll come stay with you, Ian. I'll help you and Kate get ready for the baby."

"Thank you, Dee. That would be wonderful."

Dee came there from the Bahamas in Kate's seventh month. When she arrived on the doorstep, she held Ian and they cried together.

"Dee, isn't life amazing?"

"Yes, it is. It certainly is."

Dee went immediately into the kitchen and started cleaning and cooking, and Ian followed her there. He saw how she took charge of everything and he felt some relief in her control.

Tomorrow Kate and I will take an overdue walk through the Central Park Zoo, Ian thought.

Then he watched as Dee noticed the calendar on the kitchen wall. She flipped it over to a new page and secured the tack above it.

September 2001.

chapter eight

Rory

"SO, ARE THEY still in the Bahamas? Hope's parents?" Rory took a wild guess.

"Oh no, the time I told you about? That was their last time."

"So, you haven't seen Hope's parents since that trip to the Bahamas in 2011?"

"Not exactly. I guess it wouldn't make much sense to you if I told you that *after* I saw them in 2011, I saw them again in 2001, actually."

"No, it definitely would not. But I guess that's just more of the time travel stuff that I really don't understand."

Dee nodded and smiled. "Let me just say this, then. I was there when Hope was born, and it was one of the greatest joys of my life to see her into this world. I'm proud to have been there at the beginning of her journey. I can't say that about too many people." Dee looked longingly over her shoulder at the crowd assembling around the doors of Carnegie Hall.

"We should go reclaim our seats. I'm not sure that Hope is destined to make this journey again and again. We should be there for this one time."

"We only have one life, right? Make it count," Rory said as she started to stand up.

"Well, that hasn't exactly been my experience," Dee said. "Which makes Hope all the more special." While Rory stood, Dee remained in her seat.

"I thought we were going back in to reclaim our seats?" Rory asked.

Dee said, "Actually, sit back down. I want to tell you what happened to her parents after Hope was born."

Kate

"I'M SORRY. What did you say?"

The driver had been on a phone call, but now Kate realized he'd hung up and was speaking directly to her. She was pulled out of her thoughts.

"I said, a driver friend of mine just called to say the city is all but shut down in that direction. Said he hasn't seen anything like it in quite some time."

"Oh no. What do you suggest?"

"We have to be patient and take some detours. You in a hurry?"

"Well, I was. But I'm not sure we're going to make it. I might have to just accept that."

Kate rubbed her temples and as she did so, she looked at the tattoo on her forearm dancing as their driver navigated over some potholes, and changed direction.

She texted Benton.

I forgot to tell you. I got a tattoo.

Of what??

Kate typed out "warrior," and then deleted it.

A crazy monkey.

There were few things that surprised Kate anymore. Benton was one of them.

Benton had called Kate nine months earlier to ask questions that made little sense at first and seemed very unusual questions coming from Benton in particular.

"When did you first know you wanted to be a mother?"

"Was it something you always knew you wanted to do or was it something that came to you gradually?"

"How did you know you would be any good at it?"

"Benton, where is this coming from? Are you pregnant?

Are you thinking about getting pregnant?" Benton and Kate were the same age and the thought of having a baby while staring down 50 seemed incomprehensible to Kate.

"No," Benton laughed. "I do believe that ship has sailed. But I'm thinking about fostering the most amazing kid."

"Really?" Kate tried to hide the overt shock in her voice. Over the years, Benton had been a fierce volunteer, organizing shoe and clothing drives and working at food banks and animal shelters, but Kate never imagined Benton would sink her teeth into something as special as fostering.

"There's this girl I've been mentoring at the soup kitchen. She's bounced around from foster family to foster family since she was 5. She's now 14. She's going to age out of the system in a few years, and then what? I've been giving her advice about high school classes and even possible internships next year. She's interested in animals, so I took her to the Central Park Zoo to fill out an application for a volunteer position, but her current foster family can't commit to helping her get there. She comes to the soup kitchen every weekend to help give back. She's grateful for everything she has, which is so little. She's really extraordinary."

"Oh Benton, that's amazing. Do you think her current foster family would agree to you taking over the role of her foster parent?"

"Well, it's my understanding that they'd have to."

"Have to? What do you mean?"

"Well, I'd be fostering with a plan to adopt. They are not currently on that track."

"Wow. Benton, that's huge. Are you sure?"

"No. That's why I'm asking you all these questions."

"Well, Benton, what I can tell you for sure is that it's sort of impossible to prepare adequately for motherhood. But if you wait until you're 100% ready and you know all the answers, you'll wait forever."

"I was hoping you'd say that. I'm pretty sure I'm going through with this, and it would mean everything to have your support along the way."

"Of course, you have my support, Benton. I'm honored that you trusted me with your plans. So, tell me more about this girl."

Ian

IAN AND KATE'S daughter made it into the world in three pushes.

"Just three pushes!" The resident on call yelled triumphantly, and Ian wanted to punch him in his fat, smug mouth the moment he said it.

There were four hours of excruciating back labor before those "just three pushes!" Two traumatized parents-to-be navigated a maze of collapse and death as they tried to make it to the hospital for the one joyous reason anyone would be seeking medical care that day, before those "just three pushes!" They walked uncomfortably much of the way, because the roads were not navigable by anyone, let alone speeding cars carrying women in labor, before those "just three pushes!"

On the morning of September 11th Kate had gone into labor at school, moments after classes had been suspended at the university due to a confirmed terrorist attack downtown. She had managed to get a call into Ian just before cell service was jammed up for the rest of the day, and he'd come to get her and they had walked to the hospital a few blocks from the university because they couldn't get a cab and they didn't know how to deliver a baby themselves.

The resident who Ian wanted to punch in his mouth put the newborn baby girl in Ian's arms himself, erasing his ridiculous "just three pushes!" remark from Ian's brain. Bloody and oozy and still connected to Kate, Hope cried into Ian's chest, and Ian whispered to his daughter, "You're here. I remember now. You're supposed to be here too."

It should have been enough.

And it was. For that one day—Hope's birthday—it was all enough.

There was a lot of commotion then. They asked Ian if he wanted to cut the cord, which he decidedly did *not* want to do. He looked at the connection between Kate and Hope and he thought he'd be a fool to welcome cutting through that. He gave the task to strangers instead. Hope was whisked away to the scale and cleaned up and Ian stared at Kate as she lay in the bed sore and bloody and sweaty and never more beautiful. The nurse in charge said they had clearly miscalculated Kate's due date, as the baby weighed in at 6 full pounds, required little intervention, and didn't appear to be a preemie. "Either you miscalculated or this baby is a miracle." The nurse smiled over the scale at Ian. And he nodded, because of course she was a miracle. The "just three pushes" resident poked his head up from between Kate's legs and announced excitedly "Ok! Hold still! Time for a few stitches!" And Ian remembered something that he had forgotten when the resident placed his daughter in his arms a moment earlier. Ian remembered that he hated him.

Soon enough, Kate was stitched and cleaned up and propped back up in a sitting position, and a swaddled baby was placed in her arms. Ian leaned over the bed, and sniffed their newborn, who had a scent coming from her head that made Ian forget his own name. One of the nurses covered her hair—while Ian was still nosing it—with a knitted cap and as Ian drowsily tried to take it off, the nurse chided him, "She needs to stay warm, now. She's little and she came a bit too early, but she's a fighter. Still, she needs to stay warm. Leave the cap alone."

Ian moved his fingers and let the nurse pull the cap back on. Tufts of black hair sprouted from the bottom of it. The baby was sucking on Kate just under her neck and the skin puckered tightly under her mouth. Ian watched as Kate shifted the baby to her breast and she latched on easily. Ian crawled into the bed next to Kate and held his two girls.

As they lay there content finally, Hope swaddled tightly in a hospital issue blanket with Ian counting her fingers and making a mental note to check toes later, Ian caressed Kate's face and felt tears as she leaned her wet cheek into his hand.

"You ok?" he whispered tentatively.

"Perfection." She sighed.

"Look at her. I can't believe you did this. In the midst of hell, you brought a piece of heaven into this world. Kate, I will never ever stop being grateful for this moment. I'm so sorry about everything you had to endure to get here."

"Stop. No more regrets. No more what ifs. We live this life from here on out. You hear me?" Ian was surprised by her confidence. It had been evolving within her throughout the pregnancy. But now the transformation was complete.

Ian rolled over and climbed off the bed. He propped another pillow behind Kate's head, and helped her adjust the baby as she switched to the other breast.

Ian started to pull a chair away from the wall close to the bed. There was a sink and mirror next to the chair and he caught a glimpse of himself. Unlike Kate who had grown more radiant throughout the day, Ian looked like he'd absorbed the hell. His eyes were sunken and his skin was not a familiar color at all. His clothes had speckled dust and dirt on them. He looked like he'd just come in off a construction site.

Ian suddenly noticed the television was on in the room with the volume muted.

"I have never witnessed anything so terrible in my life." Ian waved at the television images and shuddered. "Those pictures don't even compare to what it really looks like out there."

"I know, Ian. I was out there too. Remember?" Ian nodded gently at Kate. She was serene and content, but he was still wearing the day on him. While the entire city was walking uptown—away from the scene on the television—they had been walking downtown—toward it—in hope of finding an empty hospital that could welcome them.

As it turned out, the hospital had plenty of room for them.

"I expected the hospital to be a madhouse," Kate said questioningly as Hope nursed loudly. "But it's so quiet out there. Where are all the injured people?"

When they arrived, the nurse at triage told them they were expecting to be overwhelmed with overflow from the Trade Center buildings. She rushed them through. She was a pudgy woman with perfect skin and hospital scrubs with pugs of different sizes and colors. Ian had found himself staring at her scrubs, counting the black pugs, wondering why there weren't more black pugs in the world. While she was trying to glean pertinent health and insurance information, he was still wondering why pugs were relinquished to a spot on this buxom woman's madcap scrubs and not allowed time to materialize. He was in a state of shock brought on by Kate's labor and the tragedy that had befallen the city and ultimately, as he was coming to understand now from the television screen—the world.

Now that he had a moment to reflect, away from the nurse's pug-covered scrubs, he realized the truth.

"Kate. There are no injured."

"But what do you mean? It wasn't as bad as they thought? But those images? And all that we saw?"

Ian continued shaking his head sadly. "There are no injured. There are only those who got out. And those who didn't."

"But—

"Kate, they are listing the death count at over 2,000. And climbing. And there are planes still missing—"

Even though he was saying them, Ian had trouble wrapping his head around the numbers. He had trouble wrapping his brain around what he was saying out loud. He suddenly felt the recklessness of bringing a child into the world—into *this* world—acutely. He wondered anew:

What have we done?

But this time, he was not dwelling on forgotten sons from the past who may or may not be real—the same ones who haunted his memories so wildly throughout the pregnancy. This time he was facing down a fear about the very real future.

Ian stopped talking about death and destruction and said, "Let's turn this off for a moment. We can't ignore what's happening forever, but we can—for just this one moment in time—choose now." He walked over and reached up to the wall-mounted screen and turned it off. Then he pulled a chair next to the bed and lay his head gently on the bed next to Kate and the baby.

"Dee?" Kate spoke one word as a question and a fear and a sentence all in one.

"She's safe. She'll meet the baby when we get you out of here tomorrow. She says she can stay for as long as you want."

"I'm not sure yet how long I'll still need her."

"She knows that."

Ian hadn't realized until then that the television had been the main illumination in the room as the sun had set sometime after Kate had given birth. Time had passed without acknowledgement as they fought to bring new life into the world. Now that the television was off, they sat in the darkness of the room, with only a small cone of light making its way in from the outside corridor. They rested in comfortable silence, the three of them, listening to the sounds of their own breath. The rise and fall of the baby's sleepy breath on Kate's chest and the far-away sounds of beeping and hospital voices made their way up and down the hallways and lulled them all. They were suspended in time.

"Hope," Ian whispered.

"Hmmm?" Kate was close to sleep.

Ian saw her sleepiness, and picked up the baby—keeping her swaddled—and leaned back in the chair with her. She squirmed in the new position until sleep found her again and her breath pattern resumed. Ian waited until she was settled and then said, "We have always been calling her Hope. Is that name still ok with you?"

"Of course, darling. I'm not sure any other name would fit." Kate lay back into her pillows and Ian watched her drift off to sleep. He closed his own eyes and saw the three of them ankle deep in clear blue water, holding hands, with Hope in the middle. Ian could feel cottony sand buckling under and pouring over his feet and toes. He felt relief and fear and contentment.

They had brought this girl, who was meant to be, into the world. He understood now that time had a sequence—an order. They hadn't given up anything.

They'd merely added it.

Kate and Ian had their daughter.

Now Kate would have her sons.

And for that to happen, Ian would need to leave.

chapter nine

Rory

RORY WAS BREATHLESS.

Dee had told her a story of miracles and childbirth amidst chaos and then dropped the bombshell.

"Ian left her? With a new baby, a world in chaos, and a history of mental struggles?"

Dee nodded matter-of-factly, over her nearly empty coffee cup.

"That doesn't seem quite right."

"He believed that there was another path for her too. He believed that in addition to being Hope's mother, she was meant to be a mother to others."

"Like in some parallel universe?" Rory couldn't believe the words she was uttering. These strangers were getting to her. And it was definitely Dee's fault. The story she was weaving may have been far-fetched and nonsensical, but it was also beautiful and hopeful.

Dee continued on.

"He didn't know. He just feared that the dreams they both had experienced meant that she wasn't living her best life. And he didn't want to stand in her way. So, he left and he gave her his blessing to love again, and to have more children, and to live her life joyfully."

Mom would love this story, Rory thought. She pictured her mother striking fierce yoga poses in her matching leggings and sports bras. Her mother had always been the right combination of realistic and dreamer. Her mother would have embraced the magic of it, discarded the truly tall parts of it and accepted the rest at face value. She was complicated, her mother, but she was also a dreamer and a believer of love. That was why it made her reluctance to accept Rory's relationship with Marcos so difficult.

"So, he left her? Right away? Right after Hope was born?" Rory repeated angrily.

Dee nodded solemnly. "Yes, it didn't take long. Not months or even weeks. In the immediate hours after 9/11, Ian decided—no, he committed in a way he'd never done about anything before—to fight for his country. He'd been greatly affected by the destruction of the day as he fought to bring his baby girl into the world. He'd been impacted by it in a way none of us could have predicted. He thought this was his destiny. And in turn, he believed that Hope's mother had another destiny away from him as well."

Something tempered Rory's initial anger at Ian's decision to leave Hope's mother. A memory.

Rory remembered being a sophomore in high school and doing school shooter drills. At first, she'd felt like a sitting duck. In drills, she behaved like a wounded animal, staking out hiding spots in closets and under lab tables. But then she had a teacher who taught them how to barricade themselves into whatever room they were in. "When they deconstructed the Virginia Tech shooting," the teacher told them, "they learned that the victims in the rooms that barricaded fared the best. You must barricade. With everything you can find. Make it difficult for the shooter to get in. Make it impossible."

Make it impossible.

Rory had been such a timid student, but in those drills, she found herself suddenly empowered, emboldened. She wasn't afraid. She survived the rest of her high school years imagining herself a hero, a warrior who would be able to defend herself in battle. She'd be able to defend not only herself, but also her fellow students. She'd help the weaker students, the ones who cried during every drill, the ones who refused to participate. She'd save everyone, and not by sitting still, either, but by jumping into action when the time came.

Rory could imagine that living through 9/11 and being old enough to really experience it—something she had not been—could embolden and empower a person to take action rather than sitting around waiting for the next attack.

Ian must have felt like that after 9/11. Especially with a new daughter just coming into the world. Rory had been three on 9/11. Her memories of the day were non-existent. Her first memory was when she was four, throwing a temper tantrum in the middle of a store because her mother wouldn't buy her the jumbo lollipop she wanted at the checkout area. Her mother had been calm and collected and ignored the temper tantrum. She'd put her cool hand on Rory's warm forehead. "I'm sorry you're upset, Sweetie, but that's a firm no. You're not getting it. Might as well get over it." Rory didn't get the jumbo lollipop and to this day, lollipops triggered feelings of embarrassment.

Her first memory was a lollipop. And it was post 9/11. She too was technically a survivor of the day. Just like Hope Campton, and Hope's parents, and everyone else inside Carnegie Hall and those waiting to get in.

"Ian decided to enlist in battle. He was eventually assigned to a battalion in Afghanistan," Dee continued.

"Ah, it sort of reminds me of the Pat Tillman story."

"Well yes." Dee cocked her head, anticipating the next question with a gesture. Or perhaps warning her not to ask it. Rory asked anyway.

"I don't remember ever hearing about an Ian Campton. I've read plenty about the Pat Tillman story."

Dee nodded. "Of course. There was decidedly less media coverage about a former reporter turned soldier at a time in which over 4,000 men and women were becoming new soldiers as well. But he did enlist. And he did fight. You can trust me. And, there was sadness."

"What happened to him?" Rory's breath caught and she felt the words escape her before she had a chance to filter them. Dee's eyes were watering all the way to their edges and Rory didn't want to be the one to help them overflow.

Rory thought back to the beginning of this meeting when Dee had first flagged her down. Rory had taken the seat next to Dee. Was Dee saving only one seat? Was she saving it for Hope's mother only? Surely Ian wasn't—*gone?* Rory tried going over Dee's story from the beginning. Had Dee said Ian was on his way? Or had Rory only assumed he was?

Rory watched Dee inhale sharply in the silence between them. And then Dee stood and turned toward the doors to Carnegie Hall.

"We should go. Hope will be making her way to the stage any minute now. I don't want Hope to look out and see an empty row. I want her to see me at least."

They found their seats easily again. No one had taken them despite the fact that the auditorium had filled up around them. In fact, there were not just two empty seats. There were four empty seats still waiting for them as though they had reserved stickers on them, but of course they did not.

The seats brought Rory comfort as they made their way toward them. Surely, Hope's parents—*both of them*—were on their way now, 9/11 and Afghanistan and war, notwithstanding.

There was a family sitting in front of them who hadn't been there before. A little girl sat in front of Rory and Dee in a yellow sundress. Rory noticed Dee looking at her with that indulgent amusement most adults looked at children with. Rory couldn't conjure up the same expression; nor did she want to. She'd never subscribed to the theory that every little child was adorable beyond belief.

"Did you know?"

The girl in the yellow sundress was pulling on Rory. Rory rubbed her own arm and saw Dee looking at her questioningly as she ignored the little girl trying so desperately to get her attention.

Rory looked around. The little girl's mother appeared to be the well-coiffed woman who'd moved to the end of the row, ostensibly to save seats. She had left her precocious daughter to be a bookend and to talk to strangers. Rory tried to get the mother's attention by staring at her. Either the mother noticed or she didn't. But she didn't bother looking back. She seemed to believe her precious daughter was being taken care of by this stranger. Rory grew increasingly annoyed.

"Did you know?" The little girl asked again.

Rory noticed Dee watching as she interacted with the little girl.

The little girl was relentless. Rory gave in begrudgingly, more because of Dee's expression than the little girl's.

"Know what?"

"That light we see. From the stars." She pointed up at the golden stars decorating the ceiling for the event and Rory felt suddenly embarrassed for the little girl, as she worried she might believe the decorations hanging from the ceiling were actual stars. Clearly, she'd been indulged way beyond the norm, even for girls of her age.

"What about it?"

"That light we see from stars? It's not really there."

"Ah. What is it then?"

Rory looked over at the little girl's mother. This time the mother looked back at Rory, and she shrugged. It was an ugly expression and gesture. The mother spoke for the first time. "She's really into this astronomy nonsense right now. Sorry. It's her father's fault."

"Fault?"

Her interests were someone's fault?

What about her uncanny willingness to engage strangers without knowing if they are safe or not? What about the fact that she is obviously so starved for attention she doesn't care about her safety? Whose fault is that?

Rory wanted to ask the mother all these questions, but she didn't.

Rory suddenly became more interested in what the little girl was saying. She nodded at the little girl, encouraging her to keep going.

"It's just left over from a star from billions of years ago. The star dies but the light lives on, and it travels through billions of years just to find us. But the light's not really there now. It was there a billion years ago."

Rory caught the mother shrugging again out of the corner of her eye. Rory glared at her. The woman said, "I told you. Nonsense."

Rory said, "Well, it sounds kind of romantic to me." Dee nodded approval in Rory's peripheral vision and she felt proud.

The mother laughed then, but not a happy laugh. "Oh Lord. You sound just like her father now. So sorry for you." The mother went back to scrolling through her phone, and the girl in the yellow sundress went back to looking up at the stars.

Rory let an unbelievable sadness wash over her. She felt the entire timeline of her relationship with Marcos looming ahead of her including its end. And it was the part *after* the end that made her panic. She wasn't sure there'd be any light that would outlast it. But maybe if she could convince herself the little girl's "nonsense" was true—she'd accept whatever was coming next, a little more easily.

Kate

KATE LOOKED DOWN at the dress she'd chosen for the day and smoothed down its golden fabric as it stretched onto the black leather seats of the taxi cab.

"An unusual color," the woman at the boutique had said obviously.

Lemongrass. Kate had explained.

It reminded her of a long-ago magical dress. One that she'd worn on a very different trip. She'd worn it with Ian on a cruise on The Beatrice and they danced the night away and reconnected and fell back in love and then, miraculously, but tragically too, found themselves traveling back in time.

The one-of-a-kind lemongrass dress with the red velvet lining hadn't made it home after the trip, but she'd found this one—a different, more practical version at a boutique near the home she shared with Rob Sutton for many years. When she bought it, she imagined wearing the dress with Rob and having its hopeful color transform their lives.

It was a silly thought, she could now admit. But at the time, maybe she'd been desperate. After letting go of Ian, her life had taken a different route altogether.

And she'd been willing to believe in a dress again. And in magic.

It hadn't worked, unfortunately. The first time she'd tried this particularly exquisite dress on for Rob, the result had been less than stellar. She'd zipped up the side and walked out of the closet.

"Rob, what do you think of this dress?"

Rob had looked at her distractedly. "Pretty. You don't look a day over 35."

"Ha! I'll take it."

He looked back down at his laptop. Kate walked over to the desk in the corner of their bedroom where he was working and pulled up a chair next to him. "What are you working on?"

"A brief. Trying to fix some second year's work and make it a compelling summary judgment motion."

"What does that mean?"

"Oh, it would bore the hell out of you. Just let me finish and then we'll go out to dinner. You can wear that new dress of yours."

Rob leaned over and gave her a peck on the cheek. Kate took the hint and left Rob to his work. Back then, she was still trying. So many years of marriage had taught her to never take her eye off the ball. But she was growing weary by then too. Rob's distracted dismissal of the dress had seemed a small thing in the moment, but when she thought back on it from the cab ride, she realized it had been a very big thing indeed.

After Rob's dismissal that day, Kate headed into the walk-in closet and took off the dress, hanging it gently back on a velvet hanger for another occasion. She had rubbed her hands along the smooth material of the dress and admired the golden color. She'd wear it another time. It deserved an "occasion." She didn't want to waste it on a dinner with her husband who was mostly distracted by a brief he thought she was too simple or too uninteresting to truly grasp.

Grabbing at straws of intimacy with Rob was always a little harder than it should have been. But there had been reasons for staying. Even as she put the dress away for another occasion—one that wouldn't come until a year or so later as it turned out—Kate couldn't really dwell on the overwhelming sadness of being dismissed by Rob because there had been a loud crash in the basement not two minutes later, followed by a yell.

"Mom! Where are you?"

"Mom! Michael's been playing Fortnite for four hours! Tell him to get off the console right now."

The boys' screams and yells carried up two floors and mingled together.

Kate leaned her head out of the closet to see if she was the only one who heard the boys. Rob was tapping busily on his laptop. If he heard them, he had a damn good poker face.

"Mom!"

"Mom!"

She had taken one last look at the golden dress and bid it adieu as she headed downstairs to mediate a fight over video games.

Yes. There had been trade-offs. Letting go of Ian had given her the chance to find the other great loves of her life.

And she had.

She'd birthed them.

In the end, neither Kate nor Rob could really pinpoint when things had gone wrong. Kate suspected they'd never really been on the right track ever. They'd found each other at a time in their lives when they thought getting married was the next right step. But maybe it wasn't.

Or maybe getting married to *each other* wasn't the next right step anyway.

On the last day of their marriage, Rob stood at the door, ready to leave, the fighting and the volatility over, due to sheer exhaustion, and Kate looked at him levelly and said, "What if there's a totally different narrative here, Rob? What if you strip away the worst things I've done? And you strip away the worst things you've done? And there's something just lying here underneath it all?"

"What's that?"

"A man who wanted to be married to a woman who loved only him? And what if on the other side of that equation, was a woman who wanted to be married to a man who loved only her?"

Rob's eyes softened like they were getting somewhere finally.

"And what if it was perfectly ok for that man to want what that man wanted? And for that woman to want what she wanted?"

Rob nodded. It was the first time he had appeared to agree with her in some time.

Kate continued, "But what if it was not ok for that man to want it from that woman? Or vice versa?"

"Or vice versa," Rob conceded, painfully.

"I don't think you're a bad person," Rob said.

"I don't think I am either."

He chuckled a little and a clump of hair fell over one eye. Kate reached over to move it out of the way the same way she'd done for her sons a thousand times. The move felt stiff and awkward. Her husband had become a stranger to her, a benign stranger, but a stranger nonetheless. Which made it both easy and heartbreaking to say the words that came next.

"I think it's time for us to stop trying to make each other fit some sort of mold we have no business insisting on."

Rob nodded in agreement. And for once, Kate hated to be right. And yet, she knew she was.

Ian

HE LEFT ON a Wednesday.

Of all the important details, that one stuck out the most, and forever after that day, Wednesdays were terrible for him. It seemed like such a mean thing to do. To ruin Wednesday. After all, it fell in the middle of the week and so the days leading up to and leading away from it felt like they were ruined too.

He had convinced himself that he had actually ruined *every* day by leaving on a Wednesday.

Kate cried and begged him not to go. Dee stood back stoically surveying the scene, seemingly understanding the best aid she could provide was silence in the moment, and to catch Kate in her arms afterward.

"Don't leave now. You have time," Kate kept saying. Ian shook his head. Time felt like the one thing they didn't have. They had a new baby food puree machine, a diaper wipes warmer, all the green and yellow gender-neutral clothing anyone could ever ask for, and diapers in huge quantities in graduating sizes starting with newborn and moving up to toddler-sized pullups.

They had everything.

Except time.

"I can't stay, Kate. I can't in good conscience do nothing, when so many are dying and putting themselves in harm's way. I can't stay. I'm sorry."

"This is an excuse. This is your way of getting your precious freedom back, isn't it?" Kate spewed hateful words at him. "You never wanted this life, did you? Parenthood and all its trappings? You never wanted this life, and now you want out. You're leaving us to travel the world and all that comes with it."

Ian was afraid Kate would say more things. Things she could live to regret.

He knew he needed to leave quickly. And he even knew she had to hate him a little so she could move on.

He made a suggestion that was like salt in her wounds. Kate and Ian had never married. They had never thought it necessary. But now he had concerns. And it seemed like a good way to get Kate and Rob back together.

"We'll need some legal papers drawn up. I want to make sure Hope has my name and is my beneficiary in all legal ways. If it's all right with you, maybe Rob Sutton would do some legal work for you. For us. I mean, he's a lawyer, and at least you know you can trust him, right?"

Kate had thrown a pillow across the room at him and told him to get out.

He'd been planning on leaving that weekend. But he moved his departure up a few days. Ian left on a Wednesday, leaving behind some bank account numbers and passwords, a copy of his life insurance policy and a note.

Kate,

I don't want you to wait for me. This isn't me being kind and generous. This is just the opposite. I don't want to be alone on the other side of the world, and so I can't ask that of you either. War is an ugly world, but I'll be in this world now and I have no business in your world. I will always love you and our daughter but I'm not sure I'll be able to come back, and if I do, I'm certain I won't be the man you're expecting.

Goodbye, Kate.

chapter ten

Rory

"OUCH." Rory listened to Dee recount the words of Ian's goodbye letter with a hole in her heart.

She couldn't help but make the story personal.

Is that the sort of goodbye awaiting me in the future?

Dee nodded. "Yes. Very painful. Very painful indeed."

"And that was it?"

"Well, I don't know if that was *it*. But it was certainly what happened next."

"How did she take it? Did she relapse into her mental struggles?"

Rory pictured suddenly a woman who would be seeking leave from a mental hospital to see her daughter receive her high school diploma. Was *that* why they still weren't here yet?

"Well, she was understandably distraught. She kept asking over and over, 'How could he do this? Not to me? But to Hope?'

"I told her, 'He wants you to love. He doesn't want you to be burdened by this decision he feels he has to make.'"

Rory shook her head. "But she *was* burdened, or course. She was left there, alone with Hope. She had to be father and mother to that little girl, no?" Rory knew she was taking this all a bit personally, what with her own father leaving her pregnant mother for his own selfish reasons. It occurred to her that maybe this was the reason she was so adamant about never moving from New York City.

Maybe she'd never really forgiven her stranger of a father for leaving?

Or maybe she'd been waiting for him to return to find her for all these years?

Rory shook off the thoughts. "I just can't believe he'd leave and tell her he wasn't coming back."

"I think what he really wanted was for her to love again. To have a full life. A life he was afraid he couldn't provide for her. But she was uncertain, as you might expect.

"She said, 'How could I love someone again after loving so completely? I gave everything to Ian. I have nothing left.'

"I told her that was certainly *not* true, and when she asked me how I could know, I nodded down at the baby in her arms, swaddled and nuzzled under her chin. Without realizing it, after reading Ian's letter, she had instinctively straightened Hope's small cap back onto her head and tucked Hope back onto her breast, where she'd nursed hungrily, her small hands wrapped around her mother's in a locked position.

"She waved off my conclusion, saying, 'This is different, a mother's love is different.'"

Rory thought of her own mother dedicating her life to Rory. She had to wait until Rory moved out and then she had to go to another country to find a new "friend" as she put it.

"It *is* different," Rory agreed aloud. "A mother's love can be, well, consuming. It leaves little room for other new love to come in. I can understand her reservations about—"

Dee interrupted her. "Where love blooms—there is fertile soil. More love can grow. You can love again. This is what I told Hope's mother."

"How did she respond?"

"Well, she said she didn't know if she could let go of Ian. And I told her, 'My God. Of course, you can't. You shouldn't. Why would you ever want to?'

"What she needed to do, what Ian *wanted* her to do, was to embrace life. To have a rich and full future."

"Wow. And is that what she did?"

"Well, I remember that after she read the letter, and after she finished nursing Hope, while Hope was fidgeting off her breast, I reached over to take the baby while she buttoned up her nursing bra and she walked over to the dining room table where I had placed a bowl of soup and a sandwich for her lunch. I told her to eat."

"And then what?" Rory asked.

"I told her to eat and then she'd have the strength to do whatever came next."

Kate

"YOU MARRIED?"

The taxi driver's boredom with the difficult trip was making him nosy. He threw the private question out into the public space.

Kate just shook her head. She pulled out her phone to scroll through it in the hopes that he'd get back to driving quietly. She couldn't see a thing, so she tried rummaging through her bag for her reading glasses. The only ones she could find were scratched ones with bright purple frames that clashed with her new hair color.

No matter.

Kate grimaced as the faintest of twinges were starting to make their way around her back. She reached down and massaged her lower back with her hand. She hadn't had any back pain in quite some time. This would be an inconvenient time for it to resurface.

The driver must have noticed her expression in the rearview.

"You ok?"

Kate shrugged. She didn't want to answer that question any more than she wanted to answer the one about being married or not.

Kate woke one Monday morning far too early, drenched and freezing and reached for her reading glasses first.

She reached for her phone next and gave it a quick scroll with held breath to see what the night had brought. It usually brought nothing. This night it had also brought nothing.

Kate replaced the phone and the reading glasses clumsily back on the narrow nightstand. They toppled off the edge, and she lay back and rubbed her temples, frustrated.

After a moment, Kate rolled over and stretched her hand toward the floor for the fallen glasses and phone, and that's when she felt the sharp pain in her back. She yelled out in pain.

She caught herself just before the yelp formed into a word, a word she still called out instinctually for comfort, a word she was surprised was on her lips, but there it was.

In pain, she had nearly called out for *Rob*.

Rob wasn't there to hear her call for help, of course, so Kate rocked herself over like an upside-down turtle until she was on all fours upon the bed. She crept and reached until she found the phone on the floor. By the time she retrieved it, she was sweating anew, her back spasming and twisting in such pain, she felt the stinging tears pour down her face uncontrollably.

With deep measured breaths, Kate scrolled through the phone until she got to the only doctor's number she had stored there, her gynecologist, and she hit send.

The receptionist was warm but firm. "Mrs. Sutton, you need to call an orthopedist."

"But I can't even move."

"Mrs. Sutton, you need to call an ambulance if you're not mobile and in that much distress. Do you want me to call an ambulance for you?"

"No," Kate yelled out. She wanted to correct her and tell her to stop calling her Mrs. Sutton, but she couldn't get the words out. And they wouldn't be true anyway. She was still technically Mrs. Sutton then. Soon she would be Kate Monroe again but for now she was stuck being Mrs. Sutton for a bit longer.

Only there was no Mr. Sutton. Rob was gone.

Kate found a browser button on the phone and pulled up local orthopedists. She called the first one on the list, and started a new patient intake over the phone.

Last name?

Sutton.

First name?

Kate.

Address.

Phone number.

Social Security Number.

Emergency Contact?

Kate paused. She didn't have one anymore. Rob was no longer her person. She'd now remove him from emergency forms and beneficiary forms, and he'd do the same. She felt sucker punched. How did half of America get divorced so easily? It turns out it was hard to unravel a marriage; it was like unraveling a life. In all the discussions of "you only have one life to live, get on with it all ready," no one ever mentioned that you'd need a new emergency contact person in the event of a divorce.

Kate gave her mother's name and number.

Marital status?

Kate paused a second, and then gave the easy answer. It was still legally true. Still technically true. The divorce decree had not yet been signed. Although it was sitting on a judge's desk waiting to be signed any day now. Waiting to change everything.

"Married."

"Do you want to also add your husband as an emergency contact?"

"I do not."

The receptionist paused for a moment, like she was waiting for Kate to say, just *kidding*.

After the pause, came, "Well, all right then."

Kate pressed the end call button hard. She wasn't sure she wanted to be seen by anyone at this office. She wasn't sure she wanted to be seen at any office.

Kate lay in the bed and held herself completely still until she passed out from the pain or the back spasms stopped.

She wasn't sure which came first. She just knew that when she woke up, her back was feeling normal again, but she wasn't.

Ian

IAN LOOKED OUT the cab window at the Hudson River in Manhattan as the piers got smaller but only for a short time as they were stopped in traffic again in no time.

Kate's face was backlit by the natural sunlight coming in through the cab window, and Ian noticed—not for the first time—how kind time had been to her.

He'd left right after Hope was born and pushed her away into the arms of another man, hoping that her destiny would find her. But nothing had worked out the way he'd planned, and now she'd come to find him and bring him home. She should be angry at him. He'd understand anger. But she seemed to come to Mexico with something other than anger. There was a calm resolute understanding in her tone.

Even so, he knew she didn't truly understand. How could she?

After his last tour of duty, he had landed back in Mexico. He was off the grid, intentionally, after having his spirit broken by war and service and absence from the only people he gave a damn about, but he made sure Hope and Kate could find him. And Dee. Not that they'd want to. But still, he made sure he could be found.

His days in Mexico took on a routine. He would have hoped the routine would bring comfort, but it didn't quite work out that way.

Every morning, as he worked at a private beach resort in Mexico called *Playa del Espejo (Mirror Beach)*, Ian squinted at the rising sun, calculating how soon until he would be away from the beach. He wanted to be away from all the people, back in his cottage near the ocean where the four walls felt like a cocoon, holding him until each next day.

Of course, at night, in the cottage he shared with no one, the demons were waiting for him. But the demons were everywhere. The cottage was the safest place to encounter them. He truly believed that.

Every evening, after a long day of work, he'd knock on the door to his landlord's house and ask to walk the dog for her. His landlord was also his neighbor, and he'd ask because it was as much a pleasure for Ian as it was a help for her, her legs dark and swollen with poor circulation. He'd walk along the waterline with Rolo, the dog, just before dusk, throwing sticks and letting the small matted dog run and circle back to him for miles roundtrip. They'd arrive back home just after dark. Ian would deliver Rolo tired out for the evening and he'd let himself into the humble living room of the sparsely decorated cottage next door.

Each night, when he returned from the beach walk with Rolo, Ian would mix whatever meat was in the refrigerator into a pot with rice and beans and he'd eat it on the couch, straight out of the pot, eyes fixed longingly on the small table across the room pressed into the wall to save space. The table had three chairs situated around it.

It would be nice to sit and eat at that table.

It would be nice to have people to join me to sit and eat at that table.

He'd try to keep the thoughts from entering his head, but they crept in nightly anyway, along with a thousand other haunting thoughts that he'd have to drown with tequila, some nights more than others.

On one of those mornings recently after a more-than-others kind of evening, Ian's head was pounding and his boss was calling him even more loudly.

"Ian! Vamos! Let's go."

The reason it was all too much that particular day was because of Hope.

She'd written him a letter, reminding him, as if he needed reminding, that she had turned 18. That she was now an adult. That she'd be graduating at the end of the school year. And that she expected him at the graduation ceremony or she'd come get him herself.

He honestly believed that she was bluffing. But still, she *might* come and find him. She might come and try to seek out answers, and what answers would he have for her?

He'd asked her when they spoke sporadically over the years.

"Is your mother ok? Is your mother happy?"

"My mother is fine. My mother is still carrying a torch for you. We both are."

He wanted to write back and tell her he would not come. That seemed cruel, but it seemed necessary.

If Dee was to be believed, and back then, he had no reason to believe she wasn't, then Kate had moved on with her life. She had married Rob, and she had her sons alongside raising Hope. Ian didn't want to come back and disrupt all that. He wanted Kate to be happy. He didn't want to distract her from her happiness.

He didn't want to come back and ruin everything.

Leaving had been so painful, that he wanted it to be *for something.*

"*Ian! Vamos!*" The manager always yelled at him to hurry, but Ian couldn't comply. His legs felt like lead bricks in the hot sand as he moved. And as time went on, he became more and more stuck in that sand.

chapter eleven

Rory

INSIDE CARNEGIE HALL, Rory and Dee sat in silence for a little while before Dee changed the subject back to Marcos.

"This art, you are describing, that Marcos creates. It just sounds truly extraordinary."

"It is," Rory agreed.

"Art that makes life more accessible. Fascinating."

"That's a beautiful way to describe it. Perhaps you should do his publicity."

Dee laughed. "I'm not sure I'm qualified for such a thing."

"Well, as it turns out, neither was the actual Museum Director in Miami."

"What do you mean?"

A few days after Marcos broke the Miami news to her, Rory walked in and saw Marcos sitting on the floor. The room looked bigger than it had in a while. But not in a comfortable way.

She knew there was bad news.

She simply asked, "Marcos?" And then waited for the response in silence.

"The Director was fired."

There was a fight. More than a fight, really. Inside politics, corruption, in-fighting, and an implosion within the administration of the museum. "They're mad because she hired her daughter or spent too much of the budget on my exhibit, or lost a grant, or a host of other issues—I don't know. Regardless, they've fired her."

Rory tried to conceal her relief.

This project would go away. It was all a big false alarm. If only he had waited a few more days to tell her, there'd be nothing to tell. There would be no exhibit, and no Miami.

"I'm so sorry, Marcos. I really am. But there will be other exhibits. Think of the good news of having your art accepted in this way."

"You're so right, *Bella*."

In hindsight, she should have left well enough alone, but she kept going. Later, she shuddered to think about how she'd kept going.

"I know it's hard to let go of this idea after you started to believe the universe was talking to you from Miami, but you will."

Marcos reached out for her hands.

"Oh, you are so very right. I cannot let go of this. I've signed the contract. They've even made the first payment. I can't abandon this now. I'll go. Thank you, *Bella*."

Rory's head spun with the realization that she'd talked him back into something that had been over a few moments earlier.

"Go? But Marcos, you can't, right? I mean who will promote or manage your art exhibit if there is no director?"

"I will. I will promote my own art. I will have it transported and installed. Who can be a better ambassador for my art than me? I'll fight for my art. You are right. Always right. I love you, *Bella*."

He'd kissed her then, but she'd pulled away too soon. Because that was not what she had intended at all.

That night Rory dreamt about taking photos of Marcos's art and posting them on Instagram. She dreamt she diluted their beauty and value with precious comments and hashtags. In the morning she woke in a cold sweat and had to grab her phone for a data hit to make sure she hadn't done the thing she feared doing deep in the night.

Rory looked at her watch. It was now past noon.

She saw Tanya Corbin walking toward her and she flagged her down.

"I'm sorry. Wasn't the commencement due to begin at noon?"

"Yes, indeed. But things have not gone according to plan."

"Welcome to my world," Rory said wryly.

"Anyway, things have been delayed for about an hour or so. Security is having trouble with the roadblocks. Some of the teachers and dignitaries have had trouble making their way here. You're lucky you got here early. You got a seat and you missed the hassle."

"The day is turning into a bigger news story than you expected, I guess?"

"Yes and no. We are also in competition with the days' events at City Hall. To be honest with you, we didn't really advertise today's ceremony. We've kept the students in a cocoon, and I think we expected to sort of keep that going even through today. But we weren't realistic. The kids are 18 now. They've all got social media accounts and they are adults. We can't regulate their behavior nor would we want to. That's been the whole point of this study."

"So, Operation Steel Survivors is a study?"

"Yes, these kids are part of a longitudinal study. We've studied them for emotional and physical effects of surviving, quite literally, the events of 9/11."

"And what have you concluded?" Rory held up her press lanyard to Tanya, as if reminding her that she was "on the record" if she wished to be.

Tanya chuckled. "Ah yes, another curious journalist. Well, tomorrow we're releasing the complete and official report, but I'll give you some headlines."

"Please." Rory moved forward on her chair, and took out her notepad and pen. She flipped to a new page that didn't have notes about Ian and Hope and time travel.

"It turns out these kids are a perfect microcosm of the current generation."

"How so?"

"They have the exact same rates of anxiety, depression, college acceptance and even green eyes, as the reported statistics of this current class—the class of 2020—nationwide."

"Hunh?"

Tanya just nodded in response.

"In other words, they are completely normal?"

"As normal as the rest of the American youth of this generation."

"Touché. So how many of them did you say there are?"

"Thirty-seven," Tanya said proudly.

"Hardly a reliable sample size, wouldn't you say?"

"Well, sure. That's the counter argument. But isn't it spectacular that even with this sample size, the kids measure up exactly against the rest of their peers nationwide?"

"I suppose. So, you're saying these kids really weren't affected by 9/11, the way the rest of us were?"

"Oh, no. Quite the opposite. They still have startling rates of anxiety and insecurity and paralysis. Just like the current generation. Along with equally startling rates of reliance, resiliency, and overcompensation. My take is that this entire generation has risen above the rather tangible effects of 9/11, and these 37 kids are no exception."

"Interesting. But I'm not really sure there's a story there."

Tanya nodded at Rory. "Yes, I can understand why you might think that. Agree to disagree, I guess."

Rory nodded and watched as Tanya walked quickly away.

Rory turned back to Dee who had been within earshot of the entire conversation with Tanya and shrugged. "Guess we have more time?"

Dee nodded thoughtfully.

"So, tell me more about what happened to everyone after Ian left."

Kate

BENTON TEXTED AGAIN.

Sorry if you've been trying to reach me. I have no service inside. Are you making any progress?

Not really. We might not make it.

A row of sad emojis. They seemed a little juvenile coming from the ever-graceful Benton.

Kate sent back laughing face emojis in response.

And then Benton texted a reply.

Good news! They've delayed everything. There's a huge bottleneck outside and New York City is at a standstill. Even worse than usual. You have more time!

Benton followed up with a row of dancing women emojis.

It was Kate who had taught Benton how to use emojis. Not long after the separation, Benton had reached out. She texted her to invite her to coffee, and Kate had responded immediately.

I'd love to!

Benton even agreed to come out to New Jersey to meet Kate. There was a new coffee shop in town, and Kate suggested they meet there.

You'll never even know you're out of Manhattan! Kate had texted.

Benton responded more formally. *Looking forward to it. See you then.*

At the chic café, sitting with over-sized latte mugs topped with frothy heart-shaped foam rings, Benton had reached over and taken Kate's hands in her own.

"I've been thinking so much about you."

The words alone were incapacitating.

Someone had been thinking of her. It seemed incongruous with her feelings of disconnect. The separation from Rob had debilitated her. She spent all day feeling like she was connected to no one on the planet, and yet, while she was feeling that way, as it turned out—someone was thinking of her. It felt redemptive. Challenging. Like karma was daring her to feel sad. And she suddenly couldn't meet the dare head on.

"That's so nice. I'm happy you reached out. It's lovely to see you."

More pleasantries. A string of them meant to help jumpstart the meeting between the two women who hadn't seen much of each other over the last few months and years.

"How are *you* doing, Benton?"

Benton shared things. About work and a colleague whom she thought she'd fallen in love with, but then she reconsidered. About her new foster daughter, Chloe. How things were proceeding nicely. She was readying her apartment for a home study, and Chloe and she were learning how to be together and live together. There were challenges and successes. Benton readily shared them both.

Kate shared things as well. She told Benton she was adjusting to the reality that Rob had left. That their marriage had shriveled and died on the vine, and that they were trying to find their way back to being friends and co-parents to the children they loved. The children were the only things they could agree upon.

Benton nodded sadly. "I always rooted for you and Rob."

"Me too." Kate said wryly.

Kate twisted the coffee mug in her hands, not wanting the coffee date to end. She'd been feeling alone and lost in the world, and all along someone had been missing her. Had been thinking of her.

She had been tethered to Benton without realizing it, by sheer mental connection. Kate felt empowered and lightened.

There was no telling the things she'd be able to get done now. Even though she was reluctant for the coffee date to end, she was suddenly anxious to jump into her day, something she'd been dreading just a short time earlier.

Kate waved for the check. She'd pick up the check, and she'd tip the waitress generously. And then Benton would want to do this again and again. She'd want to meet again for lunch to pay Kate back. They'd lose track of who owed whom lunch or coffee and they'd make more and more dates for lunch and for coffee and maybe even dinner.

There would be countless more opportunities for connection. Kate's warmth skipped ahead to exhilaration.

The waitress put the check down in front of them, and Kate swooped it up heroically and plucked her card from her wallet with the other free hand.

"Oh, and one more thing, Kate."

Kate looked up at Benton, still smiling, until Benton told her the one more thing.

"I was wondering if maybe you knew of any open teaching positions?"

"Teaching positions?" Kate was confused. What were they talking about? They'd been talking about themselves just a moment ago. Not teaching positions.

"At your university? I have a niece who's graduating with her Master's Degree, and I know how hard these teaching gigs are to find when you can't get your foot in the door. Don't you agree? I mean, I know you got yours through sheer perseverance, but we can agree that's the exception, no?

"Anyway, I told her about you. And I told her next time I saw you, I'd ask you. Maybe even ask you to put a good word in for her. She's a good kid. Trust me, you can vouch for her."

Kate's head spun like she was dizzy, and she reached for the seat cushion underneath her like she might fall off it.

"But I don't work there anymore, Benton. I left. To raise the boys. A few years ago. Didn't you know?"

"Oh no. I didn't. Too bad. Ok, then. Well, thanks for the coffee."

Like a snap of the fingers, Kate felt unheard and unseen. And totally disconnected again.

Benton hadn't been thinking of her. She'd been networking. And Kate hadn't been tethered to anyone. Just as she thought, she'd been cut loose, flying in the wind, without a soul in the world to anchor her. Ian was God knows where. And so was Rob. The kids didn't need her in their lives. Maybe they would again one day, but they didn't now. She wasn't connected to anyone.

No one missed her.

No one was thinking of her.

She looked up and saw her sons' Spanish teacher, Trey Dunn, walking into the coffee shop, and she reached up to wipe her eyes clean of their tears, not wanting anyone she knew to see her like this, particularly not Trey Dunn, who had been terribly kind to her since the separation, checking in to make sure she and the kids were doing well in light of the transition.

Kate had found Dunn's interest very genuine and had even started to daydream about the possibility of dating again in the future. Not necessarily Dunn himself. But someone *like him*. She didn't want to ruin those daydreams by having him see her tear-streaked and blotched.

Benton noticed her tears and responded. "Oh, Kate. I'm sorry. I'm being insensitive. You're struggling, and I'm job networking for my niece. Chloe says sometimes I need to stop barreling through life like it's one big business deal."

Kate smiled. "Chloe sounds wise. I'm looking forward to meeting her soon."

Benton said, "I'd like that."

There was a pause and then Benton said, "I don't even know how to use emojis."

"Emojis? What does that have to do with anything?"

"I never use emojis when we text, and Chloe says it changes the entire tone of a conversation when you're able to sprinkle emojis in. It seems kind of crazy to me, but she insists."

Kate laughed. "She's right, though. Pull out your phone."

Benton complied and Kate said, "Text me your request to put in a good word for your niece."

Benton made a quizzical face.

"Come on," Kate said. "Just try this."

Benton's fingers tapped the phone. And Kate tapped back in return.

Kate, would you mind putting a good word in for my niece?

Sorry. I don't work there anymore.

Ok, thanks.

Benton stared up at her. "I just don't get what we're doing here."

Kate pointed to the phone. "Try again. Send me the same text about your niece."

"The exact same one?"

Kate nodded.

Kate, would you mind putting a good word in for my niece?

Kate sent a row of laughing emojis.

Sorry, I don't work there anymore.

Ok, thanks.

Kate sent a row of dancing ladies.

Benton laughed at her screen.

"See?" Kate said. "Chloe is right."

"So she is. Thanks for the lesson, my friend." Benton got up and left, and Kate stayed for a moment to finish her coffee and then she headed out of the café.

Next door they were advertising "Manhattan Bagels," and the sign called out to her with a bit of connection and familiarity that she was vulnerable to in that moment. She was still hungry after her unsatisfying meeting with Benton, so she walked in hungrily and ordered a baker's dozen. The clerk looked at her with her head cocked sideways.

"A baker's dozen? So 12, right?"

Kate was about to mention that usually a baker's dozen included a freebie thrown in for good luck. But she bit her tongue quickly as she decided not to press her luck.

Manhattan bagels right here on the rural New Jersey block? What a lucky find!

Obviously, the owner traveled into the city at 4 am every morning to stock up on real New York bagels. The gas and tolls and surplus charges would be steep. It was unreasonable to expect an extra thirteenth bagel to be thrown into the bag without charge.

"Yes, please. 12. Four cinnamon raisin, four plain, and four everything. The girl behind the counter sorted through the trays and made up bags of bagels. Kate noticed she put the everything bagels in the same bag with the cinnamon raisin and yet, she stifled yet another criticism of the young employee. Instead Kate asked for an extra bag—hoping to re-bag her goodies herself in the car before the onion and sesame seeds overwhelmed the cinnamon.

Kate handed over her money and said, "Keep the change," with a loud high note in her words. As she turned to walk out of the shop, she was about to quash the question that was buzzing about in her head. Later, she wished she'd stifled it just like she had stifled the baker's dozen explanation and the incorrectly bagged bagels. She wished she had stifled it but she didn't.

Instead, Kate glanced over her shoulder and asked the young girl, who had returned to her phone to scroll through something hidden on the other side, "So who does the drive into Manhattan every day?"

"Sorry?"

"The bagels—they're from Manhattan, yes?"

"Sure."

Kate felt relief, and the coast was just about clear when the girl looked back down at her phone and mumbled. "Manhattan Bagel Store—we get them wholesale from their leftovers every other day. They make them inhouse—they're over by the railroad tracks in Secaucus." She gestured offhandedly.

"Secaucus? You mean the bagels are from New Jersey?

They just come from a place *called* Manhattan Bagels? And they are the leftovers?"

The cashier murmured distractedly while she scrolled through her phone, leaving Kate alone with her impostor bagels.

The bagels hadn't come from Manhattan. And her baker's dozen contained only twelve. And her everything bagels were in the same bag as her cinnamon raisin bagels.

Kate walked out of the shop and dumped all the bagels right in the garbage can outside on the sidewalk.

This new leg of the journey is going to be a lot harder than overdue coffee dates and emojis, she thought.

Ian

KATE WAS A SLAVE to her phone. In Mexico, he had a phone, but he wasn't nearly as dependent on it as the tourists who passed through the beach club day after day. In fact, he'd left his own phone behind in the Mexican cottage.

Ian watched Kate on her phone and he watched her frustration mount as she wasn't able to get in touch with Hope or Dee to tell them where they were.

"Is the service that bad in Carnegie Hall?" he asked. Kate shook her head over and over again. "Apparently. I can't seem to get in touch with those two."

He was almost glad she couldn't get in touch with Hope or Dee yet. While he was anxious to see Hope, he wasn't nearly as anxious to see Dee. Seeing Dee would mean confronting his misbeliefs about the last 18 years.

They had been hard years, difficult beyond belief. He'd distracted himself with war which seemed an insane thought, but also true.

He embraced his service with the passion of a man who had everything to live for and who had left it all behind. His first tour of duty turned into successive tours broken up by leaves in which he'd done everything he could to stay far away from New York, where Kate and Hope were forging a new life without him. The absence from them was painful but he knew that it was the right path for them.

He traveled back to the Okavango Delta and to parts of Africa he'd never been before. He traveled through Asia and even parts of the U.S. that were unfamiliar to him as well. He stayed off the grid, choosing his locales and connections wisely. He relished the breaks from war, but also found himself missing the comradery his service provided him. When he was away from war, he found himself directionless, and that scared him more than each tour of duty.

He checked in with Dee regularly.

He also checked in with Kate and Hope less regularly, his guilt overpowered by his knowing that he was doing everything he was meant to do. After all, wasn't that what Dee kept confirming each time they spoke?

They are doing well.

Kate and Hope are doing well.

Kate is living her best life. She's living her life in a way that would make you proud. It would give you relief to see her with her sons. Do not worry any longer about forgotten sons. She's found her way back to them.

You must know, everything you and Kate have been through— it has all been for something greater than you.

When he spoke to Hope, albeit erratically, he didn't ask her about half-brothers or her mother's husband. And Hope didn't volunteer any information. They talked instead about Hope. She had been boarding at school the last few years, and she loved it. She had plenty of stories about herself to fill the phone time. They left Kate out of the conversation.

And now, Ian wished he'd asked more questions. Everything Ian had learned in the last few days had overpowered him. Even though he'd agreed to come back for Hope's graduation, he was barely hanging on. His grief was overwhelming him.

And it was all because of Dee.

Dee had lied. She had convinced him that his leaving had been for something.

But as it turns out, he'd left for *nothing*.

chapter twelve

Rory

"HAS IAN REALLY been in the Army all this time?" Rory was still resisting an ending that had Ian not coming home from war. That seemed too brutal and gruesome to imagine. Even though she didn't know these people, spending the morning with Dee made her feel as though she did. And she was invested in a happy ending at this point.

"No, he signed up for several tours of duty. During times of leave, he traveled. He went back to Botswana and explored new countries in Africa, South America, and Central America. He even traveled in the western United States a bit."

"Why the west? Why didn't he come back east and be with his family?"

"He never did let go of the fear that he was holding Kate back in some way. That she needed to find her own destiny and her life outside of him. That decade of grief that they spent together marked him. All those years of uncertainty? He couldn't get past it. Even after Hope was born, he wasn't convinced that their destiny included the two of them together."

"That's sad."

"Every time he has reached out over the last 18 years, that theme has remained a constant for him. He has insisted that he needs to stay away to let Kate travel her own path."

"What has been your response?"

"Just listening. I've learned you can't make people hear the truth if they don't want to. I knew Ian would come back when he was ready. I never believed in trying to make him do otherwise."

"Will he ever be ready?"

"Well, a few years ago he retired from the military life for good, and settled in Mexico, largely off the grid."

"And he's coming back now?" Rory looked over her shoulder with the question.

"Well, we'll both see, won't we?"

Kate

WHILE THE CAB moved ever so slowly through the city, Kate opened her bag and found a half-full compact that she used to powder her nose. She was freckled and tan from her days in Mexico. Next to her red hair, her skin had a bronze glow to it. Yes, from the sun. But she knew there was more to it than that.

The cab stopped short and Kate's bag slid off the seat next to her. She reached down and started putting her things back into the bag. Her fingers found her lip gloss and a small sewing kit and her Rogers Fellowship Acceptance letter. She smiled with joy at the parchment. It had been a special recognition, and it had led to a new path. Ever since she found out the good news, she'd been traveling down a new road and she couldn't deny being very happy about it.

The day she found out about the Rogers Fellowship, the boys were gone, both at synchronized sleepovers. Rob would be picking them up the next morning for half of his scheduled weekend visitation. Work apparently prevented him from getting them for the whole weekend. Kate hated sleepovers (honestly, what could they possibly want to do after curfew hours except get into trouble?), but lately the only reprieve she got from parenting was when they had what she liked to call "teenage playdates." Since the separation, Rob was busier than ever, allegedly with work, and wasn't even able to take them reliably for his weekends. Kate suspected that the real reason he didn't show up on his weekends was that he just didn't want to deal with her, which was heartbreaking and exasperating all at once.

With the boys gone, Kate could whip through the house

and get it clean. The bathrooms stayed clean for a whole day in which no one would turn around and pee in them. She hustled through bedrooms, flipping beds, changing sheets, vacuuming corners, and washing dust boards relentlessly. She went from room to room, tidying and mopping, and gradually the entire house was clean, and she wasn't back-tracking at all. It was bliss. It was an entire thing finished and accomplished. It was unlike any other aspect of her life at that point. She reveled in the satisfaction.

As Kate put the cleaning supplies away that day, whistling even a little bit, she heard a timer on her phone go off and paused to check it. *Hot tub maintenance,* her phone reminder chimed. Every week, at this time, whether she was otherwise engaged in cleaning the house or not, she put a little chlorine and stabilizer and shock in the family hot tub, even though no one even used it. It was one of a hundred weekly chores that had become hers, long before the separation even, and she did them mostly grudgingly.

After silencing the phone chime, Kate headed outside, lifted the hot tub cover, hit the jets on and perched a meas-uring cup on the side of the hot tub while she twisted off the cap of the chlorine. As she measured and poured the chlorine into the churning waters, she found herself hyp-notized.

Why do we have this hot tub?

Why do we have half the things in this house we have never used?

Standing at the hot tub, Kate made a mental checklist as she did a tour of the house in her mind.

Hover boards for the boys purchased the Christmas before last. A ping pong table. A pool table with scratched felt and broken cue sticks. *A house full of toys,* Rob called it at the lawyer's table when they ironed out the final terms of the settlement agreement. *Those things have no worth,* he'd said, before his lawyer shushed him. Rob had been adamant that the value of everything was much less than Kate's lawyer was saying. But lawyers make the worst clients. His own lawyers had silenced him time and time again at the settlement table. *But it's not worth anything,* he'd say.

"He doesn't mean it. He just means, we haven't agreed to your valuation just yet." The lawyers tried to save their high commissions by keeping the numbers high, just redirected in Rob's favor instead of Kate's.

A house full of toys, Rob said again, as he sat back deep in his chair.

Kate had laughed out loud at Rob sitting in his seat in a gesture of defeat, and it had been her own lawyer's turn to shush Kate instead.

"He's not wrong," Kate stated when she stopped laughing. Both lawyers called an "adjournment," claiming their clients were tired and needed some rest before starting the next round of negotiations. It reminded Kate of the overtime playdates she'd stumbled into on occasion when the children were younger. Play sessions carefully scheduled at a neighbor's house and grown-up conversation over chicken salad were welcome outings until they spilled into the dinner hour. On those occasions, when all the children had missed naps and were gradually bubbling over with a tiredness that would cause massive explosions at any minute, the play sessions turned into nightmares. Someone would inevitably steal another's precious lovey, or push, or worst of all, bite, and then all children had to be quickly escorted from the hostess's playroom in a cloud of shame and regret coupled with loud promises of punishment and time-outs, which could never really materialize as the overtiredness was the fault of the neglectful mothers.

They'd let the playdates run too long. They'd let their selfish need for grown-up conversation and food that wasn't a dinosaur-shaped chicken nugget distract them from the brewing meltdowns in the next room.

They'd ignored the kids in some kind of collusive agreement to escape their ordinary lives for a few moments and the result was inevitable. They knew that, and even though they all knew that, they acted surprised anyway.

Kate thought about some of those expired playdates as Rob and she walked away from the negotiating table with their respective lawyers on several occasions. In a way, they were being put in time-out throughout the divorce proceedings, over and over again.

But after the "it's only a house full of toys" comment, Kate felt like a petulant child as her lawyer and she walked to their cars.

"He's not wrong."

"Come on, Kate. Don't talk like that. There's much more value to the property than he's trying to say."

"Ok, you're right. They are not toys. They are distractions. What could they possibly be worth at the end of the day?"

Kate's lawyer watched as she folded into her driver's seat; he closed the car door on her and let her drive away in one of her distractions.

Standing in the warm mist bubbling up over the hot tub as it frothed to metabolize the chemicals she'd just measured and poured in, Kate asked herself anew.

Why do we have a house full of distractions?

What are we trying to distract ourselves from?

Kate's answer nagged at her from the recesses of her memory, of course. Just the thought of Ian Campton could retrieve memories of love and warmth that lingered beneath the surface. Emotions she'd buried long ago came bubbling to the top.

But what about Rob? Kate fought back the memories of Ian as she considered this question.

What was Rob trying to distract himself from?

Or whom?

Still pondering and still in a trance somewhat from a day marked by alone time and adequate hydration, Kate decided to use the newly sanitized hot tub instead of just closing the top shut. She rummaged through a plastic bin in the back of the closet marked: "Seasonal clothes—Mom." While the kids' similarly marked bins had been turned over, cleaned out and replaced several times in the last few years, Kate's had been barely touched in many more, she realized, as she sifted through the contents.

Recent trips to water parks had seen Kate wearing warm-up pants and tank tops. She hadn't unpacked a bathing suit in years, as she hadn't been invited to join her kids on rides in quite some time. She had a couple of black bathing suits that had seen sufficient beach time in their day. They hadn't been to the beach in several years, and as Kate pulled the top suit out of the bin, she realized it was stretched and worn thin. It had last seen use when the kids were much younger, and she was still wearing baby weight—four, even five years post-partum—10, maybe even 20 pounds ago.

Kate held the suit up to her clothed body and wrinkled her nose. She didn't want to wear something so unflattering even to be by herself. She didn't need oversized bathing suits anymore. Pilates and the gym had made her body strong, even though it wasn't the body of a 25- or even a 35-year-old. She groaned at the old worn black bathing suit. She was tired of being embarrassed. Tired of hiding and covering things up.

Kate tossed the suit back into the bin, closed it shut, and grabbed a bath towel on the way out of the house. She dropped her clothes on the wooden steps leading up into the hot tub and lowered her naked self into the still frothing water.

Kate exhaled loudly, immediately and deliriously happy with her decision. A year or more of discontent washed off into the tub and she imagined it disappearing into the steam bubbles and floating up into the air—off toward the woods. She wouldn't need all the toys or any of the distractions soon enough. Rob could buy them or he didn't have to. She'd be moving on, and probably not even keeping the house. She couldn't imagine where she'd be moving to, but with the kids getting older, she couldn't imagine staying in the family home.

How would she greet Rob each week as he dropped the boys off in their formerly shared home and headed somewhere new?

No, Kate thought. *If I'm going to start over, I need to truly start over. I'll need my own space, and it will need to be practical—more practical than this place—distractions, or no.*

With the release of her tight hold on the past, Kate's eyes closed slowly.

I'm sleepy, she thought. The luxury of steam and heavy but light limbs combined to relax her. But still something deep down remained alert.

I can't fall asleep in the hot tub, she thought. *This is dangerous.*

Kate heard something in the background of her thoughts but dismissed the noise as her eyes stayed shut. *Probably just a fox or a raccoon in the waning daylight*, she thought. She didn't really want to see a critter. They'd be scared of her, she knew; but she also realized she'd be more scared of them.

She lifted her hands above the water line and clapped loudly, eyes still closed, hoping to scare away any critter that might be rushing through the yard, without having to actually see it.

"Well, thanks. I'm not sure applause is really necessary, but I'm grateful for the greeting."

Kate's eyes flew open, startled. "What the—"

Kate sat up abruptly, and then realizing what she was wearing—actually, *not* wearing—under the bubbles of the hot tub, she sank back down quickly.

"Mr. Dunn!"

"Oh! My apologies. I didn't realize—"

Kate saw him redden and realized he'd caught a glimpse of her and now they were both sort of stuck with what to do next.

"I'm sorry—I didn't mean to sneak up on you. I rang the bell, and then I thought maybe you don't use the front door—only the back. We used to only use the back door in the house I grew up in, and—"

He seemed flustered and Kate sank deeper into the water, sure the steam was reddening her already crimson face—not to mention the rest of her.

"No, it's fine. You're not sneaking around."

"I mean I saw right away you were alone in the hot tub so I didn't think I was interrupting anything. I thought it was still ok to be back here and I was having that awkward time of trying to figure out how to announce myself without scaring the bejesus out of you and then you started clapping and I thought you saw me. I mean, what *were* you clapping about?"

"Mr. Dunn—"

"Trey—please—I feel like this whole thing requires first names, don't you, Kate?" Dunn swirled his hand around the air confidently and coolly, but Kate noticed he was still red and he wasn't the one covered only in steam, so she did-n't think he was quite as cool as he was acting.

The hot tub was on a timer and suddenly it clicked off and the bubbles started dissipating, Kate realized that she'd soon be entirely visible to Trey Dunn, her sons' teacher, and now guest in her backyard. She eyed the button across the tub and calculated whether she could reach across the tub to reinstate the bubbles before they completely disappeared and without lifting her breasts out of the water. She took a risk and reached her hand out across the fiberglass until her middle finger reached the button, depressing it, leading to a quick swoosh and then the bubbles were back in action, jetting up to her neck which she lowered helplessly back into the water.

"I'm home alone and I was cleaning all day and then I realized it was the day to sanitize the hot tub, and I couldn't stand just filling my day with only chores, so I climbed in. But it turns out I don't have one single bathing suit that even fits me anymore."

Dunn cocked his head sideways and smirked.

"Not because I'm fat. I'm not being self-deprecating or anything," Kate continued rambling. "I'm actually in great shape."

More smirking. "I can see that."

"Oh my God, you can?" Kate slid down further and her toes popped up on the other side of the tub. Her hair got coated with water and bromine and splashed back into her mouth and she spit out the hot tub water ungracefully.

Dunn added to the confusion and awkwardness by laughing. Not a small chirping chuckle, but the kind of belly laugh that turns silent in spots.

That kind.

Kate leaned her head back against the hard built-in fiberglass pillow in the corner of the hot tub.

"Oh, dear God. This is mortifying on every level."

"For whom?"

"For both of us."

"I'm fine. Relax." Dunn turned a seat around at the patio furniture situated a stone's throw from the hot tub. He slid the weatherproof cover off the chair and had a seat in it. From this angle, Kate could only see his face bobbing above the bubbles, and she assumed that was the only view of her that he had as well. She relaxed a bit.

"So, you didn't come here for friendly banter while I sit in my hot tub, did you?"

"I did not. This is just a bonus."

"Please, do me a favor. Don't tell the boys about this. They will kill me. They wouldn't want to know their teacher saw their mother naked."

More belly laughing. "No. I promise. This will be our little secret. Cross my heart."

"Hope to die?" Kate laughed, but she looked upward so Dunn couldn't see her face and neck blushing more fiercely. And so she couldn't see if his were as well.

"I came to tell you the good news in person. You've been selected as a Rogers Fellow."

"Oh," Kate choked on a cry that felt equal parts rehearsed and primal. She wanted it. She wanted it so much, she'd been afraid to hope for it. But still she *had* hoped for it.

The Rogers Fellowship application had come home with the boys in a seemingly innocuous envelope. Alongside field trip permission forms and test papers, there had been an envelope containing a very interesting offer.

The boys' school was offering a fellowship opportunity to "lapsed educators"—lapsed being defined as those educators who had let their teaching credentials fall by the wayside while they started new careers or became caregivers to children or parents. The Fellowship was an attempt to draw more educators into a new program started by the family of the late Morris Rogers—a benefactor of the school who believed that all educators should be multilingual to accommodate an ever-growing multilingual population. The Fellowship was a one-year paid opportunity to reactivate the teaching credentials of the recipient, a subsidized internship, and access to an intensive language immersion program. Applications were open to all schools in the country, but it had been advertised widely at the boys' school as Morris Rogers was an alumnus. It was expected that several Fellows would be named around the country, but that at least one would come from the boys' school, in light of the Rogers connection. It was just what Kate needed in light of the separation and impending divorce. It was the promise of financial security and independence while she transitioned to her new life. She was afraid to hope too hard for it. But still she wanted it.

She'd forgotten that the handsome Trey Dunn was the program coordinator, and a close friend to the Rogers family.

From his seat, Trey held out an envelope looking much like the one the original application had come home in.

"I'm here to bring you your official acceptance letter. But maybe I'll just leave it here for when you dry off." Kate saw Trey smile and wink over the steam as he placed the envelope on the patio table. She sunk down a little lower.

"Yes, that sounds like a good plan."

"Anyway, the ceremony will be in Quintana Roo, Mexico, in just a few weeks, and if you can get away, all your expenses will be paid. I'll be your escort. I mean, you know what I mean. Not an escort. Your guide, really. Well not for just you. For you and all the recipients. Man, maybe now I *am* feeling a little mortified." Trey made an exaggerated motion of adjusting his shirt collar.

Kate scooted up in her seat and looked at Trey over the bubbles and steam, forgetting that her breasts were dancing dangerously close to the water line. She tried to assess Dunn's face and expression; he appeared sincere.

"I mean we don't have to travel together or hang out together or anything. I just have to get you there and back safely. This is your week, and I don't want anything to distract from that simple fact."

Distractions—a house of distractions.

A life of distractions.

Kate sank back down in the bubbles of air and heat.

"It's wonderful news. You didn't have to come here in person, but I really appreciate it. I'd be happy to accompany you to Mexico. Thank you."

Trey nodded from his seat. "I think it's wonderful that you're revisiting your education career. It's no small feat, so kudos to you."

"Thanks. I just hope it's not a move backward."

"Backward? How so?"

"Just that—it's what I did in the past. My whole life has changed so much in the last few years, I don't want to get stuck in the past. I really want to—"

"Find your way to a new future."

He interrupted her by finishing her sentence for her.

"Oh!" Kate was startled. "You read my essay in support of my application."

"Indeed. I was on the Review Committee. As per Morris' instructions," Trey sounded sad.

"I'm sorry. I remember reading that you two were good friends."

"The best. He was a friend and mentor, and we lost him far too young. I'm thrilled to be carrying out his last wishes and helping foster his legacy through this Fellowship. And I think you are exactly the kind of person he created it for. I don't think your application or its sentiment reflects being stuck in the past at all."

"Thank you," Kate said solemnly.

They both sat in a comfortable silence for a few moments, before Kate piped up. "Hey, Trey. If you don't mind, I need to get out of here before I prune. Would you mind?"

"Sure, I'm leaving. Have a great night."

Trey stood and tapped the envelope he'd left on the patio table. "If you have any questions about the paperwork here, you just let me know, ok?"

"Right-o."

As Dunn turned to leave, Kate slid back down in the water.

Right-o?

And then she let the news sink in.

Mexico. Was she really going to Mexico?

She sunk down lower, this time submerging even her head and screamed out loud under the water. She let out low guttural screams that swam to the top, perched on the surface of steam bubbles, and then floated to the tree line at the edge of the property that Kate once shared with Rob and now shared with no one.

Ian

THROUGH THE OPEN window, Ian heard the sounds and yells of the city.

He closed his eyes and took them in.

He thought he heard his own name being yelled out but realized quickly it was just a memory of his many days back in Mexico.

"*Ian!*" The manager seemed to know little English, but he knew Ian's name, and he yelled it often. He'd yelled it a little differently three days ago.

Everything changed three days ago.

Kate had arrived in Mexico three days ago.

Was it only three days? Ian thought as he looked through the open cab window in New York City. He knew his perception of time was skewed. But still, he knew when Kate had arrived and turned his world upside down yet again.

That day, Ian had felt a difference in the air when he arrived at work in the morning a few minutes late. "*Ian!*" His boss had yelled his name familiarly but there was nothing familiar about his next words.

"There was an American woman here looking for you this morning. I told her to come back at the end of the day. When you are off duty." The boss winked.

"Was she alone?" Ian asked.

His boss nodded.

"What was her name?" Ian asked unnecessarily. He knew who it was. He'd been expecting her or Hope all year.

"Kate. And she was beautiful. Much too beautiful for you, *mi amigo.* Now get to work."

Ian finished his day with a looming heaviness of the anticipated reunion with Kate. What would they say to each other? Their conversations over the last 18 years had been merely perfunctory and limited. Mostly by email and only a few short phone calls. He sent money for Hope and while

Kate told him it was unnecessary, she also agreed to keep it and deposit it for Hope's future. The Manhattan boarding school was largely subsidized by an endowment that covered her schooling and room and board. Hope's education was mostly free, but she would need the money in the future, Kate told Ian. Kate shared little of her life, and his conversations with Hope continued to revolve solely around Hope.

Hope was happy. She loved boarding at school. She was proud of her father and his service to their country. She loved him. These were her recurring messages when they spoke infrequently and he held onto them like tiny life preservers as he tried not to drown in his life and his choices.

But as her graduation date loomed ahead, she grew insistent that he come home for it. "You're retired now," Hope would insist when they spoke. "Why can't you come?"

"It's not that easy," Ian protested without basis.

"Yes, it is. It is exactly that easy. Just come."

So, when his boss said Kate had arrived, Ian wasn't exactly surprised. He figured Kate had obviously come to make good on Hope's threats.

Ian spent the day setting up and cleaning up from a wedding ceremony on the beach. While he generally enjoyed his work at the beach club, wedding days were the worst for Ian. Happy, smiling couples with their lives and love laid out for everyone to see, filled him with rage. He'd set up and clean up, but always found a way to make himself absent from the ceremonies themselves.

On that day, three days earlier, Ian had placed chairs at the water line around a framed mirror that reflected the receding tide. He tied ribbons around each chair with the mechanical movements of someone who had done this all many times before. He stood out of earshot during the ceremony.

Then when it was all over (always so quickly!) he moved in and untied the ribbons and stacked the chairs away from the tide to await their turn for another day.

At the end of his work day, Ian collapsed into a chaise lounge in the sand with a bucket of beers and waited. It wasn't long before he heard her. He turned in his seat to look back and see her profile at the bar. She was sitting and talking and laughing with another woman and Ian knew he must be drunk already because it looked like Kate was talking to herself on the next barstool over. He turned back in his seat and drank another beer. He'd need to be good and drunk for this meeting. That much and that much only he knew.

Ian waited by the ocean. He drifted in and out of dreams while he waited for Kate to finish talking to herself and come down and rescue him from that chaise lounge by the mirror.

"Ian."

She looked like an angel framed in the moonlight as he opened his eyes and looked up at her.

"I've been waiting for you," he whispered.

"I can see that," she replied, nodding her head in the direction of the bucket of empty beer bottles.

Ian shook off the beer and the sleep and pushed up to a sitting position in the chaise lounge. He swung his legs over the side to sit sideways on the chair and gestured for Kate to sit across from him on the empty chaise lounge to his left.

She complied and they sat in silence for a while. Ian looked around and tried to see the scene from her point of view. He rarely stayed at the beach past dark and it did look different to him through Kate's eyes. If not for the framed mirror perched on the sand reflecting the twilight, Ian might not have recognized it at all. The chairs that had been set up for the afternoon wedding were gone from the beach and with them all evidence that something joyful had occurred there. The beach now looked dark and empty and foreboding. Behind Ian and Kate, torches lit the perimeter of the straw hut, and the wedding guests had moved under it using the matching glassware and napkins he'd helped set up earlier. The bride and groom were at the center of the hut. They looked happy from afar. He could see them from his spot and knew Kate could too. Ian stared at them longingly.

Were they happy on the inside? Had they found the one?

Ian found his cynicism fighting its way out. He was tempted to march up to the hut and warn them.

You don't know what you don't know. Don't get too settled in this happiness. It might not last.

As he sat in silence with Kate, he tried to quash the thoughts like old memories. He looked down at his dirty work shorts and white tee. He certainly wasn't dressed for this occasion, but Kate was. She was wearing a long white sleeveless dress with cherry blossoms decorating her from neckline to toe. She could have been a guest at the wedding.

She could even have been the bride.

Ian looked away quickly with the thought.

Kate was the first one to break the silence.

"Ian. Look at me."

He tried. He did. But his eyes filled up with tears when they met hers, and he had to look away. He looked up at the stars and then he stood up.

Kate seemed confused. She said, "Ian, please don't leave." But he wasn't going anywhere. He stood over her and summoned her to stand up with just a gesture.

Kate sat and stared up at him, looking unsure. He continued looking at her deliberately. Eventually, she rose from the chair like a physical pull propelled her to her feet. Ian had worried that when they found each other again they wouldn't recognize each other. They stood there frozen for a few minutes separated by a foot or so, and then Ian cocked his head, subtly to the left, beckoning her. She walked toward him and stepped in between his legs and let him wrap all the way around her. Their bodies remembered each other instantly. Even though they were two people with nearly two decades of memories without each other, those decades dissipated to a small pebble that barely separated them.

They stood there for a few seconds, her head on his chest, her arms loosely around his lower back. His hands moved up and down her back familiarly, and then he reached for her hair.

There was something so gratifying in the familiarity as he moved his hand along the back of her head. The shape of her head and the texture of her hair were all the same. He felt a thin metal necklace at her neckline and then he moved his fingers lower to find the skin at the top of her dress below the edge of her hair and it felt new and fresh. Even though she was nearly 20 years older than the last time they'd touched, her skin felt fresh and new. Like it was not used to being touched there.

Ian relished the thought for a moment. The one that let him believe that Kate remained in the place where he left her 18 years earlier. He ignored what that would mean. What sadnesses that would mean for Kate. He ignored the thought that the Kate he left behind was angry and grieving and didn't even comprehend all that she had lost. A dark thought crept into his mind, but he pushed it out because it had no place there with the woman with the smooth young skin below her soft hair.

He stood like that for a few more moments with his hands stuck in that place between her shoulders and her hair, and then Ian put his hands on Kate's shoulders and pushed her out at arms' length. "I was hoping you wouldn't still be so damn beautiful," he said, his voice gravelly with beer and age and life.

She stared at him, studying his face. He knew what she

saw. Eighteen years showed more on his face than it showed on hers. He had lines and wrinkles and a small scar over his eyebrow that wasn't there before. She reached up and touched it with her finger and he let her.

"It's been a long time, Ian."

He only nodded, while a broken jagged piece of his heart answered silently. A lifetime. *Our lifetime.*

"Are you surprised to see me?" Ian asked.

"I came looking for you."

"I know. But are you surprised to see me?"

"Yes," she answered.

Ian reached down with one hand and grabbed the last bottle of beer that had anything left in it. He took a sip of his beer while still holding her with the other arm.

"It looks like you've been drinking for quite a while, Ian. Don't you think that's enough?"

"I've been drinking for nearly 20 years, Kate, and it still isn't enough."

Kate pulled away from his embrace and pushed down into her chaise lounge. She pointed to his chair too as a command.

"Please don't do this," she said as he joined her face to face.

"Do what?"

"Patronize me. Don't pretend you have a right to act this way."

There was a silence then. The kind of silence that would have been comfortable a few decades earlier. Time had changed everything—even the silences. Ian refrained from his gnawing temptation to fill it.

Kate didn't. "This is where you spend your days?"

"Yep. I have a bungalow not too far from here."

"Do you live there alone?"

Ian smirked. At the time he still thought it was a hypocritical question. He still believed that Kate did not live alone.

"Indeed."

"So, here's where we've both landed."

"Yes, it is."

"Both of us alone with a grown daughter and a lifetime of catching up to do. Isn't it about time we do that?"

Ian narrowed his eyes to look at her.

"What do you mean alone? You're not married?"

Kate looked at him with a peculiar expression.

"No. Don't you think you'd know if I was?"

"I thought I did." Ian tried to put the pieces together in his drunken haze.

Had Dee told him she actually married Rob? Maybe not. Maybe they just got together and had the boys and never married? He was confused. He looked down at the empty beers and suddenly regretted his lack of clarity. He should have prepared better for this meeting with Kate, he realized.

Kate seemed to attribute his confusion to the beer. Or the time.

"It's been a long 18 years, Ian."

"Yes, it has."

"Do you have regrets about leaving or have you made peace with your decision? Because I'll tell you—I've made peace with it all. It took some time, but I did. I understand why you needed to leave."

"You do?" He looked at her, eyebrows matted into one over questioning eyes. He felt some relief at her acceptance. She seemed to get it, so he jumped in. "You needed me gone. I had to give you your space to reconnect with Rob. So, you could have the life you were supposed to have."

Kate should her head violently.

"Jesus, Ian. What are you talking about? I am not sorry I chose you over Rob. I came to peace with that decision as well. Those past struggles are only a memory for me. I wish they could be for you too. After I got pregnant with Hope, I realized that everything worked out the way it was supposed to. If I had stayed with Rob Sutton back then, I wouldn't have had Hope."

Ian rubbed his temples trying hard to wrap his brain around what Kate was saying.

"I understood why you felt you had to leave. I was there too on 9/11, don't forget. I came to understand that the way it affected us both was very different. Although, I confess, that I struggled for a long time, wondering how it was so *easy* for you to leave."

Ian's head shot up and met Kate's gaze. "Easy? How dare you. It wasn't easy. It was hard. The hardest thing I've ever had to do. But I did it for you."

"Please. That's bullshit. It shouldn't have been hard. It should have been impossible."

"But if it was impossible, I wouldn't have left."

"Exactly."

After a moment, Kate whispered, "I'm sorry. Maybe I haven't quite reached the level of peace I would like to reach. It's been a long time getting to this point. And I've traveled the road alone with just Hope by my side. Willingly alone, but still. I'm working on true peace and forgiveness. Maybe I'm not quite there, but I'm getting there. I promise."

Ian tried wrapping his head around the words she was saying.

"Kate, you never married and you never had other children?"

"Oh, Ian. You must be drunker than you look."

Ian felt the world spinning. *Had Dee lied to him? Was it all for nothing then? This time apart had been for nothing? Kate never found her way back to her boys?*

And then another thought occurred to him. *Kate must be lying.*

She knows I don't want to come back to see her happily married to Rob.

She's lying to get me to come back for Hope.

Kate brought him out of his thoughts by taking his hands in hers.

"Ian. What's important now is that Hope needs you. You need to come back with me. Now."

Ian shook his head. "No, she doesn't. You've raised her without me. I deserted you both. And maybe for nothing, as it turns out."

"Ian, that's not what you did, and I know it. And so does Hope. You had something you had to do. But you've done it. And now you have to come home again. It's time."

Ian stared at her trying to understand. He felt a little dizzy and he wanted to get away from the beach.

"Can I take you back to my place?" he asked.

Kate nodded and they headed to the resort parking lot, where Ian found a driver friend, slipped him some money and the three of them headed away from the beach and the reflection of the sea in the beachside mirror, and directly into the night.

They arrived in a residential neighborhood about 15 minutes away from *Playa del Espejo*. Small cottages lined up next to each other and perpendicular with the ocean—with small pebble-lined yards side by side. The driver stopped outside of a small terra cotta-hued cottage after three left turns in the neighborhood.

"Where are we?" Kate asked.

"Home. Come on." Ian grabbed her arm and they left the driver and headed inside. Ian opened the front door, and as he had on the beach, he suddenly saw his surroundings through Kate's eyes instead of his own for the first time.

Across from the open door, there was a couch covered with a floral slipcover that reminded Ian of his own parents' living room in the 1980s. In front of the couch was a chipped and weathered dark-stained wooden coffee table, and next to it a small round wooden table with photographs standing humbly in tarnished frames. There was a white table pushed into a corner of the room with three mismatched chairs flanking the table. There was a round rug under the table but little else in terms of furnishings on the walls or floor.

Kate walked over to the wooden table and picked up the photographs one by one. She would have known two of the three photographs, as she and/or Hope had sent them. One was a photograph of Hope and Kate when Hope was a baby no more than six or seven months old. A more recent photo was of Hope alone laughing toward the camera. And a third photo was a green tarnished framed photograph of a woman and two small children. It was that one that Kate held out to Ian after examining it.

"Who is she?" Kate had asked.

And Ian hesitated before sharing the truth.

The cab driver slammed down on his brakes at the tail-lights fluttering in front of him on New York City's West Side Highway, sending Ian's carry-on bag flying off the seat onto the floor below with a thud. He left it on the floor, but reached in gently to feel for the framed photo. Reassured that it was there and still intact, he zipped up his carry-on and sat back in the seat. Ian had brought the green framed photograph of the woman and her children from his home in Mexico, and not much else. He didn't tell Kate that. He got the sense she thought he should be letting her go.

But, how could he?

"Who is she, Ian?" Kate stared at him holding out the framed photo toward Ian who was still standing in the door-way of the cottage. "Why is she sitting here in a place of honor beside Hope and me?" Kate was direct and Ian was starting to believe that Kate really was still single and on her own back in America. She seemed genuinely concerned to be sharing his heart with an unfamiliar woman. Surely, she couldn't be that hypocritical? Maybe there really was no Rob, or any other man, at home waiting for her.

Had Kate really waited for him all along?

Had his leaving been in vain then?

Had Dee lied?

Ian shook his head sadly at Kate and the outstretched frame. "I was working border control near Afghanistan when I met her. She was fleeing God knows where. And I let her pass against orders. I had a camera on me, and I asked her to let me take the picture as a condition of going past. I wanted to keep the memory forever. I never saw her again after that day."

Ian saw the mix of confusion and relief on Kate's face. "You took this photograph to remember violating the rules?"

Ian shook his head. That wasn't it at all.

"When I first saw her, she was running at me. She couldn't have been much more than 20 or 21 years old. She wasn't much older than Hope is now. And she was running at me with a baby in her arms. She had a toddler—maybe two years old—running behind her, and she was using her baby as a shield to protect them all. I was horrified. I wasn't going to shoot her or her baby. I was going to stop them from passing, but she actually thought I might shoot them. I could see the fear and the desperation in her face. She was trying to save the 2-year-old by offering me the baby."

"Oh, Ian." Kate sat down on the couch and caught her breath. Her voice got choked up. "What a horror. Why would you want to remember that?"

"I needed to reassure myself that I would never do it again. That I would never make anyone choose again." Ian sat on the floor of the bungalow in front of Kate, choking on thick sobs. "I never wanted anyone to choose again because of me. God knows, I never wanted you to choose, Kate."

"Ian." Kate was across the room with one fluid motion, the green-framed photograph of the woman still in her hands. "Ian, I chose you because I wanted to. I chose you because I needed to. Hope needed me to. Hope wouldn't be here if I didn't choose you. How can you question that?"

Ian sobbed loudly into Kate's shoulder because if she was telling the truth, then she didn't seem to remember what choosing him and Hope had cost her. He was the only one who seemed to remember. And it was too big a burden to bear alone much longer.

Ian stopped crying after a few minutes and got up self-consciously and walked to the kitchen sink for a glass of water.

Out of the corner of his eyes, he saw Kate pick up an item from the coffee table. A small bound book. He called out to her from the kitchen sink. "Please don't. It's my journal. I—you can't."

Kate nodded and replaced it on the table.

"Ok. So, let's catch up here. This is where you live when you're not working at the resort?"

Ian nodded.

"And you send us money each month, but you're still able to get by here? You're pretty off the grid, you know."

Ian nodded and wiped his tears. "It's not as hard as you might think. The owner of the club pays me in cash and his sister owns this place. I come home and pay her some of the cash he gives me during the day. It's not technically a hand-out that way. I keep a little for food and supplies, and I send the rest to you guys."

Ian walked over to the corner of the kitchen where a small and outdated Frigidaire creaked open. He retrieved two beers. "Want one?" When Kate said no, he shrugged, but still opened them both and placed them down on the coffee table. He took a seat on the floor in front of Kate.

"You live with the sister?"

"No. I live alone. I find your jealousy endearing but still irritating, Kate."

Kate looked chastised. "That's not what I meant. I'm just catching up."

"Kate, I've wanted to hold onto you for my own since the day I met you. But you were never mine, were you, Kate? Never mine." Ian chugged his beer and looked away from Kate's judgmental glare.

Ian noticed Kate eyeing the door. It occurred to him that she might just give up and leave. He wasn't sure he was ready for that. He said the only thing he knew that could keep her there for a while longer.

"Hope is really graduating this week?

Kate nodded. "She's extraordinary. She's headed upstate after graduation. Cornell."

"Ah, so that's what she finally decided. She'll overlook the cold after all."

"Apparently. "

"Not really my kid after all, is she?

Kate laughed, but Ian shuddered at the ominous tone that accompanied his words; he hadn't intended that.

"She is indeed your kid, after all, Ian. The way she thinks and talks and moves through life. More than anything, she's *your* kid."

A long silence followed.

Kate walked the perimeter of the small cottage. There wasn't much more to see, but Ian decided to let her figure that out for herself.

"She's the Valedictorian of the class. She's giving the commencement speech."

Ian's head lolled in her direction. "What?"

"Hope is giving the commencement speech."

"You're kidding? Why didn't she tell me that?"

"Why should she have to? Shouldn't it be enough that she wants you there? Why do you need accolades to make you proud of her? Why do you need her to give a speech for you to agree to come home for her?"

"You know that's not me, Kate."

She shrugged. "Yes, I do. That's why I'm here and not Hope. Because I know you need help getting there and I accept that. Hope thinks you should just step back into your life and your family and that you shouldn't need any prodding or convincing to do so. I know Hope's being a little unrealistic but I don't want her to settle or compromise her idealism just yet. So, when it turned out I was the one coming here, I told her I wouldn't tell you a thing about the commencement speech."

"Ah, so we're all liars now."

"Ian, stop. She needs you there. That's why I'm here and that's why I'm telling you the truth." Ian got up and walked to the empty couch.

Kate took his place on the floor watching him settle back into the couch. She leaned forward toward him but still a comfortable distance what with the coffee table separating them. She exhaled loudly and dramatically. "Ian, what are *you* lying about?"

Ian glared at her. "What's that supposed to mean?"

"You said 'we're all liars now.' You said it yourself. What did you mean?"

Ian shook his head and leaned back into the couch. "Nothing. I meant nothing at all."

"Oh, Ian. I swore to myself, I wouldn't do this, but I can't help it. Why did you do it? Please help me understand."

"Do what, Kate? You're going to have to be a bit more specific than that."

chapter thirteen

Rory

"IT'S A TRAGEDY, this story," Rory said with realization.

"How so?"

"Well, theirs was a once-in-a-lifetime love, no?"

"Yes."

"But it didn't last forever."

"Well, forever hasn't happened yet."

Rory shook off Dee's words. "So, what's the point? I mean, if it was once in a lifetime, and yet clearly not meant to last—because she had to find her way back to Rob and the boys and her other life—what's the point of a once-in-a-lifetime love?"

"The, I'm sorry—what did you say? The point?" Dee seemed to be struggling with Rory's English for the first time all day.

"Yes, the point. If you can't have it again? What's the point?"

"A once-in-a-lifetime love just signals something special. But each one is a once-in-a-lifetime love, if you think about it."

"Ah. Clever."

"Yes, life is so very clever. But we are not. Running around chasing after love that's long over, trying to wring the life out of it and marring the memories of all that came before, is not clever at all. Better to accept when something is over and something is due to begin anew."

"So, once you've had a once-in-a-lifetime love, what then?"

"True loves are like snowflakes. Beautiful and unique. No two are ever the same. But there are more. Where there is one, there are more." Dee reached her hand out to the sky as if touching an invisible blizzard in May. Rory found herself tricked into glancing up at the blue, sun-filled sky.

"There are more, my dear. Always more where that one came from."

Rory wondered if that was the truth for her and Marcos.

More where that one came from.

"Marcos says that about my work. He says there will be more stories and more work in Miami. I don't want to leave New York. But he says my fears are unfounded."

Dee nodded. "Tell me something, Rory. What would you have been writing about today if you hadn't stumbled upon this story?"

"The story that found me," Rory murmured.

"What did you say?"

"Oh, nothing. It's just that Marcos says I need to stop hunting down stories, and tell the stories that find me instead. I always thought that was sort of nonsensical. Until today. This story definitely found me. I was on my way to the immigration protest at City Hall, but look at me now."

Dee's brow furrowed. "Ah, that's right. I believe you mentioned the protest earlier. Is it still happening?"

"I'm not sure. It seems everyone in the city is here instead. Even though I heard nothing about this event before today, it's certainly become the story *du jour*." Rory waved her hand generally toward the press representatives in the front of the room and continued on. "Actually, the protest was just one little part of the story I was working on. I'm following this trial—of a man who immigrated from Central America a few years ago and is now on trial for murder."

"Oh my. That sounds terrible."

"It is, frankly. But Marcos says I'm focused on the wrong things here. That by turning it into a political piece about immigration policies and lax media attitudes, I've turned this whole trial into something it's not. Maybe this 9/11 survivor story would make a better immigration piece instead."

Dee smiled at her. "You want to make this day into an immigration story? That's a heavy cloak to drape over an event that is meant to be full of joy. Sometimes things are as simple as they appear."

"Can I ask you a question? You've traveled a lot. What do you think of America?"

"In what way?" Dee looked positively confused.

Rory tried again. "Is it a place people still want to come to?"

Dee smiled. "It is. In my experience."

Rory harrumphed as if vindicated. It was so loud she might have easily missed Dee's next words. But she didn't.

"But it's also still a place that some people want to leave."

The next sound Rory heard in her ears was her own disappointed groan. "Oh man, maybe Marcos is right. Maybe I have this all wrong. What a great time to have an aha moment." Rory looked over each shoulder as if there was a magic rabbit waiting to come out of a hat.

"I think the problem with your piece—perhaps the problem that Marcos is trying to identify for you—kindly, mind you—is that the people who do these terrible and bad things—they don't want to come to America and live here. They hate this country.

"They love where they came from—and they want to destroy America as a misguided love letter to the place where they hail from. They do not want to live here.

"That's the difference between a terrorist and an immigrant. Terrorists are not fleeing *to* this country. They are trying to destroy it. And immigrants aren't inherently dangerous. No more so than the large majority of American citizens already living here. Who are all descendants of immigrants, mind you."

Rory caught the eye of the Native American woman across the aisle and shuddered with the burden of history and of hundreds of years of genocide. How very naïve she'd been recently. Possibly racist as well.

"Marcos wants me to come to Miami with him for six months and maybe a year. That will mean leaving my job. I can't cover breaking stories in New York remotely. I might be able to cover some lifestyle pieces. I might even be able to pitch to my editor some regular stories about Cuban-Americans in Miami who have some link to New York. But what business do I have writing those stories? It will reek of appropriation. I'm certain if he's doing his job, he'll tell me so."

Rory was doing her brainstorming and her naysaying all at once for herself.

Dee nodded in agreement with her conclusions.

"If you feel that way, you should find your own story to tell. Not someone else's story."

"My story? But there's nothing interesting about me or my story."

"I think you're selling yourself short. What about your story with Marcos? It's about a man and a woman trying to find their voice together in a faraway place. Why isn't that a good enough story?"

"Because anyone could write that story. Aren't we all just trying to find our voice? What's so special about that? No, I need to find something to really sink my teeth into. That's why I'm here. I feel certain that the universe directed me here. Otherwise, I wouldn't be here. I wouldn't have met you."

"Yes, the universe did send you. On that, we can agree."

"The thing is, the museum in Miami is struggling and I'm not sure I'm willing to just give up everything to follow

Marcos to Miami when it might not even work out." Rory wasn't ignoring Dee's "universe sent you" theme, but she was trying to inject some pragmatism into the conversation, before they both got too carried away.

"Struggling in what way?"

"Good question."

"Struggling in what way?" Rory had asked Marcos that same question just a week or so ago.

"Well, the exhibit was funded with grant money to celebrate Cuban exile art."

"Wait, but you're not an exile, Marcos. You're an American citizen."

"Because my parents had to flee our homeland. You're being naïve if you think just because I was born on this soil doesn't mean I haven't been exiled too."

Rory hadn't thought about it that way. She said so.

"Of course you hadn't. And neither have lots of other Americans. This is why my voice is so important down there. This is why I can actually do some good there. I really want my work to be part of the exhibit. But they are struggling. They have very little budget for installation and transportation and promotion coupled with a history of corruption at the administration level. Going all in here means going down there ahead of time and helping promote and then staying with my exhibit and supporting the museum. I'll be there for a year at least."

"A year! Can't you hang the art and come back to New York?"

"Why would I want to be here when my art is there?"

Rory looked at him and bit back the words she wanted to say.

Because I'm here.

But why was she here in New York? It was her birthplace

just as it was Marcos's. But he didn't feel eternally connected to this place. Why did she? Was she waiting in New York for something big to happen? Was she waiting for a father to show up? For her mother to grow her own wings? What was she waiting for and why was she so sure it was in New York City?

Maybe she *was* meant to be somewhere else. But unlike Marcos, she had no idea where she belonged.

"I don't understand," Rory conceded.

"That's fair. I don't understand *your* work. But I support your doing it. If it's really feeding your soul, that is. For example, I don't understand this trial that you're following."

Marcos proceeded gently. "And to be honest, I am supporting your coverage of the trial even though sometimes it feels like a slap in the face to my deceased parents."

"But it has nothing to do with what happened to you or your parents," Rory replied indignantly. "I'm working on an article about a man who broke laws in this country and is on trial and is going back to his country because of that."

"But you're inflaming them. You're inflaming the emotions of the readers."

"I don't have that kind of power."

"Words have power. Just the same way art has power. Why else would you do what you do if you didn't believe in its power?"

"So, you're saying I shouldn't stay on this assignment? Even though it could mean the difference between me having a career and not having one?"

"I'm saying you should only take assignments that feed your soul. Does this one do that?" Marcos turned back to his canvas with swift angry, albeit small, strokes.

"Marcos, that's terribly romantic. But let's not forget something important here. Your art doesn't feed anyone around here."

"That was mean, *Bella*."

"I know. I'm sorry. It's just—you know what, Marcos? I'm obviously grateful that your parents came here and brought you here. But we can't be sleepy about our immigration policies. This lax sort of ideologic view of America as the great melting pot is arguably how 9/11 happened in the first place.

"Lapsed visas. Less than ideal border control. This is how they got here. This is how they got us. We weren't having the conversation about responsible border control. We took our eye off the ball and that's how 9/11 happened. On our own soil."

"Spoken like a true American patriot. Next you'll be voting for Trump to be re-elected."

"Don't make me sound ridiculous, Marcos. You know I'm *for* immigration. I love you. I'm grateful for you and the sacrifices your parents made, but they were—no doubt about it—sacrifices. They also obeyed the law at the time. Dry Foot was the policy. And they got here. Yes, they risked their lives to escape poverty on a raft across the ocean that you wouldn't even use to cross the Hudson River. And still, they made it here."

"Nothing dry about their feet, I assure you. One doesn't get over the memory of that in a lifetime."

"Marcos, you don't remember it. You were in utero at the time."

He stared at her for a beat too long.

"It's imprinted in my identity, Rory. Please don't ask me to disclaim my very existence."

They stared at each other for a long time.

"Come with me to Miami, *Bella*."

"You just want me to stop working on this article."

"It's doing something to you. Something I don't like. Something that's not you. Come with me, *Bella*. Cover the art exhibit. Cover the Cuban diaspora. Cover something that will feed your soul. Use your talent alongside me, and not against me."

Rory grabbed her laptop and shook her head and headed out to the corner coffee shop where she would continue to work on her article while not drinking any coffee and not understanding Marcos.

"The museum is just struggling," Rory responded belatedly to Dee in the middle of Carnegie Hall, the exasperation hard to hide at this point. "And I just think Marcos is asking too much of me lately."

"Too much?"

"Well, at first, he actually wanted to go to Cuba. Can you imagine? Then he downgraded to Miami. But, my God. It's just too much to ask."

Dee nodded, "Sometimes when we think people are asking too much of us, it's because they really aren't asking enough."

Rory stared at her not comprehending, but desperately wanting to.

Kate

NEW YORK CITY is far too crowded.

As the cab stalled a few feet beyond its previous stop, Kate read the billboard above them.

New York City is far too crowded. Be part of the solution. Solution Storage Space.

It seemed everyone in New York City was storing their belongings. Advertisements for storage space could be seen on nearly every corner of 11th Avenue. Kate had never noticed these signs before, but now that they were stopped dead alongside the Hudson River, she could do little else but stare above her.

What were all those storage spaces filled with? Kate couldn't help but wonder. *What would a person hold onto so dearly that they'd be willing to pay to have it hidden in the dark across town if they couldn't fit it into their own living space?* The possibilities were few, in Kate's opinion.

Your dead parents' ugly furniture.

Your Size 4 dresses from college.

Old love letters.

Housewarming gifts

A few months ago, she'd been invited to a housewarming party in Manhattan. Lex had told her to go.

"It will do you good," she said without explaining why. "Call them and tell them you'll come. Bring them a houseplant. You'll see."

"See what?"

"It's just an expression, Kate. RSVP yes to the party for heaven's sake."

Kate had been opening mail while Lex was over for coffee; otherwise the housewarming invitation would never have been disclosed to anyone. Kate had no plans of going. It was for an old colleague from the university. A fellow teacher she hadn't really seen in years, but whom she'd kept in touch with largely through social media posts, so not in any real way.

The teacher was retiring and moving from the Bronx into a studio in SoHo. It seemed an odd move for a retired teacher, as if she'd suddenly come into money or won the lottery or something. *Who retired in SoHo?* Kate was mildly curious to see the new digs, but not curious enough to agree to attend a party where houseplants and other items that would soon end up in storage, were prerequisites.

"Kate, you need to start doing things again. You need to re-enter the world. God knows Rob isn't sitting around turning into a recluse."

"Gee, thanks."

"Tough love works, my dear."

Kate rolled her eyes and put the housewarming invitation on top of a pile of bills.

Lex kept bothering her to RSVP, but Kate noticed something on the invitation and held it up to Lex to examine.

"Hunh," Kate grunted.

"What?"

"Oh, it's just one of those invitations that kind of makes me crazy."

"What do you mean?"

"It says 'Regrets Only.'"

"Kate, you have to be the only person in the world who minds that kind of invitation. They're kind of standard these days. No one wants to field a bunch of calls from people they're going to see shortly anyway."

"That makes no sense to me. *Only call me if you're not coming?* Then when I run into the hostess, I feel so weird. Do I mention, 'hey I can't wait to come to your party next week?' Or do I just stay silent, because who knows who else has been invited, and I don't want to offend anyone who's nearby, and plus, I want to follow directions.

"And then I keep wanting to pick up the phone and say, 'thank you for inviting me! Absolutely, I'll be there.' But it feels totally disingenuous to ignore such a clear directive: Regrets only. Only call me with regrets."

"Kate, clearly you've given way too much thought to this. I promise you no one else has."

"So, you don't sit around thinking, God, I *really* want to call and RSVP yes but that feels totally crazy and they'll think I didn't read the invitation, or worse yet, that I read it and I'm ignoring it?"

"Nope."

"And wouldn't they want to hear from me, rather than wondering if my silence means I'm still trying to get a babysitter, or the invitation got lost in the mail, or something else? Wouldn't they be living in sort of a constant state of confusion unless and until they hear from me unequivocally?"

"No, they would not."

"But how do you know? Also, for the record, I never once held a party in which the RSVP methodology was Regrets Only, so I feel like karma should not have served me up so many of these damn invitations in one lifetime."

Kate flicked the invitation in the air as if to dry it and Lex reached up and took it from her. "Here, I'll RSVP for you. No need to get yourself hot and bothered."

Lex picked up an imaginary phone and pretended to tap out numbers. "Hi, how are you? Yes, so I'll be coming to your party. Don't be worried that you haven't heard from me. Don't worry that it means the invitation got lost in the mail. Or that I'm not coming. I am indeed coming. Can't wait! I'm so excited to come to the party in fact, that I'm ignoring your asinine directions in the invitation and I'm responding with a big fat yes. How's that for Regrets Only? See you next Friday!"

Kate laughed at Lex's pretend phone call until tears rolled out of her eyes, and then she stopped. "Wait. Did you say next Friday? Is the party next Friday?"

Lex nodded.

"Oh, forget it. I can't make it."

"What?"

"I can't make it. I have a conflict that night. Opening night of the boys' art show at school. I promised them."

"So why are you making me crazy with the philosophical discussion about whether or not you should have to call or not? You're a regret. A legitimate regret. You can call with your regrets. In fact, you're in the only class of invitees who is indeed allowed to call. Go to it." Kate took the imaginary phone held up by Lex. And then pretended to throw it on the ground.

"I'll call for real. I'll give my regrets. Leave me alone."

With Lex still shaking her head, Kate said, "I hate this system for RSVP'ing, but in life that's a totally different thing. I have no problem with setting up a system whereby the only feedback you give are regrets. *Regrets only.*"

Stuck under the Solutions Storage sign, Kate was thinking about houseplants and storage and regrets and also the fact that Benton was leaving New York City.

It was hard to imagine New York City without Benton, but Kate would soon have to.

Things had changed very dramatically in the last few months for both of them.

On the eve of the adoption proceedings scheduled a few weeks ago, Chloe's biological father had showed up. After 14 years, he'd been located. From the minute he was found, he made it clear that he wasn't willing to take on Chloe as his to raise, but that he also wasn't willing to terminate his parental rights, a necessary step for Benton to go through with her adoption plans. Chloe's mother had succumbed to heroin addiction several years earlier. It seemed this long absent father was the only real parent Chloe had.

"Well, him and me, that is," Benton said sadly when she delivered the news to Kate. Benton had agreed to help facilitate meetings between Chloe and her father. Benton said she needed to be prepared for the worst (or the best, depending on perspective). There was a very real possibility that Chloe would want to continue a part-time relationship with her father, and still want Benton to stay on as her foster mother. Benton needed to steel herself. "It might mean that I won't be able to adopt her and be her forever mom. Just when I was starting to really get used to the idea."

Kate felt sorry for Benton who had become a real mother to Chloe, so much so that she was willing to sacrifice her own happiness for Chloe's.

"I may never get to adopt her now. She might just age out of the foster system despite all my best efforts," Benton said in the same conversation she told Kate about finding Chloe's father. "It's like all the work and none of the reward."

Kate had laughed dryly. "Welcome to motherhood, Benton."

Ian

BACK IN New York City, three days after Kate first arrived at *Playa del Espejo* in Mexico, Ian watched Kate's profile pressed against the cab window, her phone in her lap, and sadness overtook him.

He looked away and caught his breath. After all she'd revealed to him in Mexico, he'd need to accept that while things hadn't worked out the way he'd hoped, this was their present now. He'd have to find a way to make peace with it.

I'll have to re-examine the decisions of the past under a new lens of the present.

Ian glanced over at Kate again. A long pendant hung from her neck. A bright star glittered and bounced as the cab driver sped up and slowed down over the New York City roads.

Ian was tempted to reach over and touch the star. But he refrained.

He recognized the necklace. Dee had given it as a gift to Kate. After Hope's birth, she'd presented it to Kate when she got home from the hospital. Ian assumed it must have been something Dee brought with her from the Bahamas, because Ian couldn't imagine she had time to shop for something so special while they were at the hospital having a baby and the world was collapsing all around them.

Dee had placed it down on the table in front of Kate and then reached out with both hands to take Hope from her. Kate had handed their daughter over and then gingerly opened the box.

"Oh, Dee, it's beautiful."

"They are the same stars, you know. Through all these journeys and in all these distant places, still the same stars shine over us. For millions, sometimes billions of years. They are a constant. I wanted you to have a constant. I know it is challenging to have so much change in your life. You weather it with grace, Kate. But still, I know it is challenging."

Ian watched Kate nod and seem to understand Dee on a level he wasn't sure he shared. While Dee held Hope, Kate turned her back to Ian and put the pendant around her neck and asked him to help her fasten it. He'd clasped that star around her neck over 18 years ago.

Ian watched the pendant bounce with the New York City potholes—another constant.

Dee was the one who had given Kate that pendant, and Dee was the one who had made him believe his decision to leave was the right one. Over the years, she'd told him to be at peace. That Kate had found her way to the boys and the destiny she was meant to have. "Come home when you're ready, Ian. But don't stay away because you think you need to," she'd said again and again.

But with Kate settled into a relationship with Rob, Ian couldn't bear to be a witness. He'd accept it from afar. He signed on to multiple tours of duty, never coming home while on leave, but traveling aimlessly around the world instead. Eventually, he made enough friends and connections to have a place to stay in Mexico after his last tour of duty.

He'd made some peace with his wandering and loneliness. Kate had found her way to her own destiny, so this must be his.

But in Mexico, Kate had told him a different story than Dee had told him all these years.

She said she never married.

She said she never had other children.

She said she'd focused on raising Hope and she'd forgiven him for leaving.

Ian had to accept something that up until three days ago, he hadn't even entertained could be a possibility.

Either Dee or Kate was a liar.

As he stared at the pendant around her neck, Ian

wondered: Did Kate really keep that star around her neck the whole time he was gone? Or was it just for show? Had she put that necklace and its meaning away in a box only to bring it out just in time to summon him home from Mexico? Was it possible Kate was putting on an elaborate show for Ian? And if so, what could be her motive?

Other than revenge?

chapter fourteen

Rory

IN THEIR SEATS inside Carnegie Hall, Dee changed the subject again. "Your mother. She's a teacher?"

Rory turned quickly. "How did you know that?"

"You mentioned it, no?"

"I don't think I did."

"Hm. Maybe it was what you Americans call a lucky guess." Dee laughed a small laugh that grew as Rory stared at her.

Finally, Rory answered her. "Well, she *was* a teacher. She retired this year."

"She's been teaching all your life?"

"Well, not exactly. She had to leave her first teaching job almost before she started. All because of me. Turns out the university world wasn't quite as progressive as you might think 23 years ago. Single mothers scared them." Rory made spidery gestures with her hands and whirred a low spooky serenade to provide background music to her tale.

"Really? That's terrible," Dee replied.

"Oh, it's no big deal. Academia was different back then. They were afraid of impressionable minds. No one's afraid of *those* anymore." Rory winked at Dee. "The university asked her to give up her class and work in the registrar's office."

"The registrar? But she was a professor?"

"I know. I actually think it was their idea of not discriminating against a pregnant woman. Giving her a job completely irrelevant to her actual degree and training made them feel good about themselves. Go figure."

Dee's eyes widened slightly.

"Anyway, she couldn't exactly turn it down, what with a baby on the way and everything. And she supplemented her income with, well other things."

"What other things?" Dee looked stumped.

"Tutoring royal children."

"Really?" Dee clapped her hands. "How resourceful!"

Rory nodded. "I know. Turns out there were plenty of children of dignitaries staying in New York back then. She tutored them a few hours a week all throughout my childhood and made more money than she ever could have at her professorial gig. Later she went back to teaching, but she never gave up her side jobs. They gave her the financial freedom to stay single, something she has always sworn she did by choice."

"You don't believe that?"

"No, it's just that, I've started to see my mother differently lately. I always saw her as such a fierce and independent woman, and now I'm worried that maybe all that time I thought her aloneness was badass, maybe it was really just *lonely*."

"Why do you think it never occurred to you before that your mother might be lonely?"

"Well, she just always seemed so *busy*. I mean, every year she would take on a new challenge. She'd learn something new or take up something new. She'd give herself a year to learn a new skill or hobby and she'd pursue it relentlessly. Then every year on her birthday, she would pick a new thing."

"What kinds of things?"

"She learned Russian one year. And one year, she learned how to play poker. And one year, she took up the sport of jet-blading."

"Jet-blading?

"Indeed."

"What has she moved onto now?"

"Just recovering from all those years. I think mostly what she was trying to do with those annual challenges was stave off a midlife crisis."

"Did it work?"

"Hard to know."

"Your mother," Dee said. It was a statement and not a question. And not an incomplete one.

Rory nodded. "I know."

"I mean, she's extraordinary."

"Yes, that's what I meant when I said *I know.*"

Kate

BENTON WAS DESPERATE for Kate and Chloe to meet. They made several lunch dates but Benton had to cancel each one at the last minute for visits with the biological dad that kept getting rescheduled.

"I understand, Benton," Kate said each time Benton canceled. And she did.

And then after the last cancellation, Kate had said, "I think it will have to be after I get back from Mexico, now. I hope you understand."

"I do," Benton said, without the same conviction Kate had when the shoe was on the other foot.

Of course, the trip to Mexico had not gone according to plan. But then again Kate wasn't sure exactly what she *had* planned.

The first thing that happened when they met up at the airport was that Trey noticed Kate had overpacked for the trip.

"Whoa. Is all that just for you? Or have you packed for me too?"

Kate laughed and then covered her mouth. There was a comfortable air about this man. She was going to enjoy spending a few days in a beautiful place away from home. She was going to enjoy a few days in a beautiful place with *him*.

Kate tried to push the thought from her mind, but it was too late.

When her friend, Pam, had come over to help her pack for the trip, Kate had looked at her open suitcase with embarrassment. "I feel like now that I'm divorced, I'm evaluating every man I meet as a potential love interest. It's juvenile, really.

"It's not juvenile at all. It's natural. You're a beautiful, desirable woman, Kate. You're not dead, you're just divorced. When single men find out *you're* single, they are going to give you a different level of attention than they have in the past. You're free to examine whether that attention is comfortable or not. You're also free to examine whether you want to reciprocate it or not."

Kate had reluctantly accepted the advice, but in the airport getting ready to board a plane to Mexico with the handsome Trey Dunn, she still found herself unsure about just how much attention she wanted to reciprocate.

"I haven't flown since 9/11," Kate said to Trey as he waited for her to put her shoes back on after security so they could head to their gate. "Things really have changed."

Trey nodded solemnly. "Indeed."

Seated on the plane after Trey had helped her wrestle her carry-on bag into submission in the overhead bin, Trey turned to her. "So, got anything you want to do or see in Mexico?"

Kate grew silent. There was something of course, but she didn't know how to bring it up to Trey Dunn.

"I'd be happy to show you around. I've traveled extensively throughout Mexico and it is an extraordinary country," he said kindly.

Kate studied his expression. She tried to think about how to approach this request. She got an idea.

"I have something silly I keep thinking about."

"What?"

"I read this book last year called *Girls' Night Out* by Liz Fenton and Lisa Steinke and there's a huge plot thread that revolves around the cenotes—"

Trey laughed.

"See, I told you it was silly."

"No, it's not. I'm sorry. I shouldn't have laughed. It's just that it's pronounced "sin -o – tees" not c-notes. You said the word like you meant hundred-dollar bills."

"Oh! How embarrassing. I was reading the word wrong every single time in my head."

"Don't be embarrassed. Keep going. Tell me about the cenotes."

"Well, the concept of a sinkhole that you can swim in sounds fascinating and mystical. I'd love to see one in person."

"Then you shall." Trey settled back into his seat and closed his eyes and they didn't speak for the duration of the flight, but Kate didn't mind.

Ian

IAN PICKED LINT off his new linen pants and flicked it out the cab window.

At his bungalow the night Kate found him in Mexico, Ian agreed to come back to New York with Kate, but he told her he'd need to make things right with his boss and landlord before he left. He spent two days finishing up some work around the bungalow and at the resort and said goodbye to the friends who had been so good to him for so long.

He wasn't sure how Kate spent those two days as he left her each morning and returned each evening at dark, but she claimed to have spent the time on her phone trying to get them both on a last-minute flight in time to make it to Carnegie Hall. She'd been relieved to know he still had a valid (barely!) passport. But there'd been no time to shop for suitable clothes. Later, they'd stop in an airport shop and Kate would pick out a beige linen suit for Ian.

But first, in Mexico, Kate had let Ian take care of what he needed to for two days, and then they had stayed up all night together before they boarded a plane to New York City.

She'd drunk a little tequila.

Ok, more than a lot.

"What do you miss about your 20s?" she'd slurred around 1 am, a few hours before their plane was set to depart.

They were both lying on the floor staring up at the ceiling. There was a comfortableness in having her close by. A comfortableness that had evaporated now that they were back in New York City, Ian noticed.

"I miss *you*," he'd responded with an absence of self-consciousness. Another thing that had evaporated on New York City soil.

"Ian." She'd looked at him clear-eyed for a moment.

"How about you?" he interrupted the moment reluctantly.

"I miss inexpensive and leisurely travel. I miss down time. Long afternoons with literally nothing to do but waste the day."

"You sound like you've given a lot of thought to this," Ian said.

"I have. Oh, and I miss kissing."

Ian turned up on his elbow and looked at her. "Does no one kiss you anymore, Kate?"

"Kissing is not the same as it was in the 20s. The urgency. The novelty. It's all used up by your 40s, no?"

Ian shrugged and was about to settle back down off his elbow, when she added, "But no. No one kisses me anymore. I—"

He didn't give her time to finish whatever it was she was going to say. His lips were on hers in an instant and she was gasping for breath—literally—until she found his breath and stole it for her own.

Kate was being kissed.

And so was Ian.

Urgently.

It was magical.

No, it was better than magic. It was like a first kiss all over again.

"You can't just give up, Kate."

"On what?"

"On kissing. After all, it's just this one wild and precious life. What will you do with it?"

"Oh, Ian." Tears ran down Kate's face, and Ian thought he'd made a mistake. Perhaps the zealous bungalow floor kissing had been an overstep? He apologized.

"No," Kate insisted. "Don't apologize. It's just—God, when she was about four or five, Hope used to wake me up every morning with all this crazy enthusiasm. Head first into her day. That was how she always moved. She generally left me struggling to catch up.

"I'd be sitting on the bed drinking coffee and she'd be having none of it. It was just two speeds. Asleep and awake. And it could be exhausting but also exhilarating. She was always ready for what the day held. I envied that about her. That and so much more, of course.

"One day, I found Mary Oliver's *A Summer Day* in the grocery store aisle. Next to buckets and shovels in the seasonal aisle was a framed ode to life and nature. I bought it on a whim."

"Doesn't everything die at last, and too soon?"

"The words had gutted me as I picked it up. It had gutted me too to see Mary Oliver's words treated so carelessly, plastered on a cheap wood background behind an acrylic frame for someone to hang up as a decoration rather than a warning.

"I placed it gingerly in my cart alongside cheerios and tampons and string cheese. Originally, I have to be honest, I thought I'd hang it in my own room to read and study each day as a lesson in awe and patience. But as I unpacked the groceries, I heard our daughter playing in the next room with her dolls."

Tears were streaming down Ian's own face now too. It was hard and good to hear Kate sharing these stories of Hope. He'd missed so much. He thought he'd come to accept that, but here was Kate telling him stories and calling her "our daughter" in a way he both craved and didn't deserve.

"What did you hear that made you change your mind about Mary Oliver's poem and where it would hang?"

"In Hope's singsong voice, one of her dolls was telling another one who later responded in a forced baritone—"

Kate acted out the words and the scene: "We can't play that game today. I want to have tea and play school today. We'll play that other game in another life."

"Oh."

"Yes, oh."

Ian watched as Kate's head turned back to the ceiling. He wished they'd started this evening outside so they could be looking up at the stars. But it was too late to move now.

"I was afraid for her, Ian. Afraid that maybe she'd believe and maybe cause me to start believing as well, that there would be more lives for us. More do-overs. More times around the sun than there really are. Because maybe it's only this one life left. And I didn't want Hope squandering one minute of it."

Ian nodded. Of course, he understood everything she was saying.

"Anyway—every night since she was about four or five, Hope has slept under Mary Oliver's words like a prayer and woke with the exuberance of a girl who was convinced by them."

"Tell me what is it you plan to do with your one wild and precious life?" Ian whispered.

The cab stalled at another light on the West Side Highway, and Ian asked: "Could I get out here?"

Kate looked at him sharply across the taxi seat.

"Ian, what are you doing? We've come too far for you to give up on this day now."

"No, I just want to grab a newspaper. I—"

In an instant, he was out of the cab and jogging across the street. He needn't have hurried. They weren't going anywhere. He headed across the street to the newsstand kiosk and grabbed a bunch of newspapers and laid them on the counter.

"Seven dollars, Sir."

Ian reached in his pocket and laid pesos on the counter. "Will you take these?"

The kiosk owner looked at him strangely and then

agreed. Ian counted out his Mexican money and jogged back to the cab with his papers in hand.

When he got back into the cab, Kate asked him, "Did you really need to read the news all of a sudden? Are you craving current events that much?"

He pointed to the top of each paper in his stack.

"I just needed to make sure. I needed to make sure of the date and the year."

Kate nodded with sad eyes. "Ian, it's been a very long time. We haven't gone back in a very long time. I think the loop is over. For good or for bad."

Ian nodded. But still he ran his finger over the dates across each of the papers as if needing to reassure himself.

May 5, 2020.

Proof of today.

Proof of life.

Time to decide what to do with this one wild and precious life.

chapter fifteen

Rory

THE LITTLE GIRL with the sundress and her mother spotted some people they apparently knew in another row, and exited the area to join them, leaving the seats in front of Rory and Dee open. Rory found herself wondering who would fill them. The universe seemed to have plans for the day that kept surprising Rory.

This morning she'd left mad. But just a few weeks ago she would never have thought of leaving Marcos while mad. How quickly things could change. That might have been one of the themes of Dee's storytelling, Rory realized.

Lately they'd been disconnected and out of sync. The last time Marcos and Rory had woken up together had been a few weeks earlier. Rory remembered they made love in the morning half asleep and then she closed her eyes willing time to stop but of course it didn't. Marcos wrestled his leg free.

"Come on *Bella*, I have to get to work."

"Work" was the warehouse work he did in the meat-packing district under the table. He loved the physicality of the work. He said it was better than a gym membership, and more affordable. She loved how resourceful he was, but he stank when he came home. So, she held onto him for extra time that morning before he left, knowing she wouldn't want to go near him when he returned.

She often loved holding onto him until the very last second, but that meant this. That meant there was a moment when she overstayed her welcome and she'd feel sad when he left instead of feeling satisfied. Someone might argue that hardly seemed worth it. But for Rory, it was.

Marcos walked away from her toward the shower and she sprawled out in the sheets, stretching her arms and legs to the four corners of the bed and back again. It was a silly game of hers. One time he'd caught her and laughed and the sound he'd made had been heavenly. Pure delight. Pure magic.

"Are you making bed angels?" he'd crowed as he laughed.

She'd closed her eyes and smiled.

Every time he left her, she pulled back on that memory and it comforted her. She ran her arms and legs across the sheets making her customary bed angels. The last time they woke up together, she made bed angels and waited for him to come back out and see her. She waited for the sweet sound of his laugh, but instead she heard the groan from the pipes as he turned the water on in the bathroom on the other side of the bed.

It's ok that he's leaving, Rory thought. *He'll be back soon enough,* she thought.

But then he told her about Miami.

And it seemed no amount of bed angels was going to make Marcos change his mind.

Kate

AS IT TURNS OUT, Kate got her trip to the Mexican cenote.

They drove for what seemed hours but when she checked her watch it had only been thirty-five minutes. The trip took them down a long curving dust-filled road marked with potholes every 10 feet. Their driver, Luis, had to slow at each pothole then turn the truck nearly off the path to avoid getting caught in the potholes. The road wound and curved so much that you couldn't see the end, and the incessant pattern of stopping and swerving and driving was making Kate a little nauseated but also curious. She stared ahead which helped alleviate both.

Trey sat next to her and their bare knees bounced against each other comfortably in the van and the intimacy both surprised and satisfied her. A few times she thought to herself that this felt like a day she was meant to have with Rob or Ian, but since she knew better than to dwell in that place, she stopped the thoughts and pushed them away at each pothole.

Luis stopped suddenly at a gate that appeared on the road to the right of the van. In front of them the road appeared to curve on and on, but to the right the road ran in a straight line at a right angle to where they were stopped. Luis backed up and maneuvered onto the new path, which seemed to be free of potholes but still marked by the same dusty covering. They passed a small lean-to shelter. Four or five children emerged and swarmed the van and Kate caught her breath loudly, afraid for the children's proximity to the moving (albeit slowly) vehicle. Luis turned and smiled at her warmly, and then stopped the van. He grabbed a handful of bananas from a cooler next to the driver's side bucket seat, hopped out and handed them all to one lucky boy who ran off with his bounty raised high in the air in triumph. The other children followed after him and away from the truck. Kate smiled at Trey and Luis, relieved.

Onward they traveled. A small animal darted in front of the truck. Luis slammed on his brakes and yelled something to it in Spanish through an open window, dust kicking up all over them as the animal stilled. "Damn coatis," Luis mumbled. "Going to get themselves killed."

Luis flicked his hand out the window and the coati left, running back into the woods. Kate marveled at the way Luis had seemingly communicated with the animal with words and gestures. She stared out the open window. Dust and clean air merged together and she breathed both in deeply.

They continued on their course, past a row of toilets that had been installed in the middle of the jungle with no covering or shelter, toward a small stand marked "gift shop" that seemed to sell only brightly colored bracelets. Luis parked near the bracelets and then opened the side door, motioning to Kate and Trey, and extending his hand to Kate.

"*Vamos.* Let's go."

Kate stretched her leg out of the van and took Luis's hand. His hand closed around hers warmly for a moment before releasing it and she felt embarrassed as if she'd done something disloyal to Trey. Trey was meant to be her guide, her protector on this trip. The thought both offended her feminist sensibilities and delighted her at the same time. Outside the van, Trey appeared beside her and she reached for his hand. It was his turn to look surprised and satisfied.

"*Donde estamos*?" Kate finally asked. "Where are we? Is this a park owned by the government?"

Luis shook his head forcefully. "No. A Mayan community owns this land. This is Mayan land and the government would have no business owning it."

Kate felt chided. Scolded. She wanted to make up her gaffe to Luis, so she spread her arms out and continued in her broken resort Spanish.

"*Es muy bonita. Gracias. Gracias.*"

Luis smiled and Kate felt forgiven somewhat.

"Can I buy one?" She pointed to the bracelets.

"Later. Right now, we are on time."

Kate sorted through his words.

On time? For what?

"*Vamos.* Transform yourself," Luis said.

Kate looked up at him, confused by his English. "Transform?"

"*Si,* your bathing suit. Transform is not right? How do you say?"

Trey spoke then. He had been silent for so long, she'd almost forgotten the low tone of his voice until it cut through the forest air. "Is it time to change, *Senor?*"

Luis nodded again. "Yes, sorry. Change. That is what I meant." He looked chastised, and remembering how it felt just a short moment ago, Kate wanted to comfort him. But she also meant it so firmly when she said, "No. Please don't feel badly. I like your way better—time to transform ourselves."

She and Trey took turns changing into bathing suits in the truck. Luis pointed up the way to the barely-shrouded toilets in the forest, but Kate's modesty got the better of her and she decided to wait for another stop to use a bathroom.

Next they headed behind Luis on foot, down yet another dust-covered path to a clearing in the woods. There were shower faucets out in the open and a wooden stick hanging between two trees, supplying a makeshift hanging rod for a row of lifejackets.

"Wash yourself. We must keep all the chemicals out of the water in the cenote. You will see it is pure and clean. You will be able to see to the bottom, and we must keep it this way. Go wash yourself." Kate and Trey stood under side-by-side shower faucets. She couldn't figure out how to turn it on, so Trey turned his on and reached across the stream of water to help her. She tensed up as his cold arm brushed against hers. "I'm sorry," he said.

"Don't be," she replied, and laid her hand on his cold arm as an apology of sorts.

The water Trey turned on for her came down in a slow stream on Kate's neck and she looked up into it, welcoming it. She rubbed her arms and legs free of sunscreen and the day's pollutants. She watched out of the corner of her eye as Trey did the same. She had an urge to reach over and help him, but she refrained. After a few moments, she turned the water off and walked over to Luis, dripping and shivering. "*Estas listo*?" he asked.

"*Si*. I am ready. And transformed," she winked.

Luis helped her into a lifejacket and handed one to Trey. The three of them walked in a single file line toward a dark cave near the shower faucets. At the mouth of the cave, they followed behind Luis down steep and winding wooden steps that looked unsafe. The only light came from a bulb attached to Luis's helmet. Kate looked behind her at Trey for reassurance. He nodded so she continued on behind Luis to the bottom of the cave.

When they reached the bottom, there was a platform in semi-darkness, with steps leading into the water. The platform looked man-made, but it was the only thing that did. A pool of water stretched out in front of them with mineral formations covering the ceiling and rainbow-colored walls surrounding them. Small lights were perched around the platform and shone directly inside the water, lighting up the bottom which was indeed visible from the top. Kate sat and lowered herself from the wooden platform into the water with a small yell as the cold water lapped her skin.

"*Hace frio?*"

"*Si*. Very cold." Luis smiled and Kate ducked her head down and popped up, her body used to the cold already.

"*Tiene cuidado*." Luis looked at her sternly. "Be careful. No free diving under the water. Heads up. Keep your heads up at all times and stay with me. You never know—when you go under the water, you might come up right below one of these." He pointed to the rock formations jutting down from the ceiling. "Pain. Hurt. Hospital. *Si? Comprende?*"

Kate looked around, understanding, and nodded. Towers of minerals grew up from the water and dropped down from the roof of the cave in opposing directions—coming close to each other but leaving small openings that one could swim through. But if you didn't know these waters, and she didn't, they could surely be dangerous. She sensed from Luis's sternness that even if you knew these waters, they could still be dangerous.

Kate and Trey swam through the caverns for a few moments in silence, following Luis at all times, but stopping to look up as he pointed soundlessly at crystalline formations in each room, one more beautiful than the next. They arrived in a place where the crystal formed huge columns down the middle of the cavern.

Kate eyed one, wanting desperately to touch it as it was so close to her, and so beautiful, but knowing she shouldn't. Luis read her mind. "The cenote is a beautiful place, but we must be respectful of it. Do not touch. These ones coming from the top, they are stalagtites. Do you know how much they grow in a year?"

"A centimeter?"

Luis shook his head with a smile.

"A half a centimeter?"

"A quarter of a centimeter?"

"No, no."

More shaking. Luis held his pruned hand up from under the water. "See my thumbnail? This much in one hundred years. That is how much they grow."

"Oh!" Kate and Trey said in unison.

"So you see, they have been growing for thousands, maybe millions of years. We can't touch."

"And the bottom ones? How do they grow up through the water?"

"They are formed from the ones up top. When they—
como se dice—how do you say like this?" The guide made a
dripping motion with his hands. Kate was about to say
"drip" when Trey said something better: "overflow." The
guide nodded vigorously.

"Yes, flow over. The top ones flow over to the bottom
ones. They are separated at first—and then over time each
grows to the other. They meet eventually—*mira*? See?" The
guide pointed to one solid column around the bend.

"Like lovers." Kate exhaled the word in the cave in spite
of herself. She closed her mouth with her wet hand, embarrassed from her relaxed intimacy with Trey. Trey reached
over and took her hand away from her mouth and he
laughed. "Lovers? I'm not sure that's the best analogy for
this."

Kate tried to stifle an insistence.

He heard it and responded anyway. "Well, sure. If lovers
take several lifetimes to make their way to each other."

Kate swam away from Trey because she didn't want him
to know just how true his words were in her case.

After the swim, they crawled back out of the same hole
they'd descended into. It was as dangerous and open as the
water they'd just come out of.

Later Kate was able to get a real shower, indoors, at their
hotel. She was just toweling dry her hair while wrapped in
a bathrobe when she heard a knock on her door, and
opened it to see Trey standing there. He had lines on his
face she didn't remember seeing that morning. She had to
keep herself from reaching up and tracing them with her
finger. He seemed taller than before. She pulled her
bathrobe closer, less out of modesty, and more out of a need
to do something with her hands so she didn't reach out to

him. She knew this feeling. It was loneliness and vulnerability. It couldn't be trusted. It was the feeling that had pushed her to Rob for comfort after Ian left all those years ago. Now that Rob was gone, Kate didn't want to keep running away to someone else.

"Tomorrow the festivities will be starting and there will be lots of official meals and events. Tonight is our only free night before we travel back home together. Do you want to join me for dinner, Kate?"

"Sure."

"There's a great beach club near here, *Playa del Espejo*—Mirror Beach. How about if you get dressed and meet me down in the lobby in a half hour? I'll take you there for dinner."

Kate nodded, and just before she closed the door on Trey, she pulled her robe closed even tighter. Of course, she had no way of knowing at that moment that she wouldn't be going home with Trey Dunn after all.

Ian

WITH THE NEWSPAPERS still folded in his lap, date-side up, the cab turned a bend in the highway, and the Freedom Tower appeared on the horizon like a ghost. And not a friendly one.

"Oh!" Ian exclaimed out loud at the sight of the singular structure rising up in front of them. And then the cab came to a screeching halt at the next red light for emphasis.

"Ian, I'm sorry," Kate said. "I should have prepared you."

Ian shook his head and tried to catch his breath. Where once the majestic Twin Towers stood, there was a new structure—a replacement.

It's not good enough. The thought crystallized before he had time to stop it.

Certainly, he would need to accept that in the 18 years he'd been gone, times had changed. Things had gone away and other things had replaced them.

He remembered recently reading an article about the innovations post-9/11. Twitter and smartphones. Meetup and Uber. Ramped up airport security and drones.

But these things had appeared in Mexico too, so these things he'd experienced with less startling transition.

New York City was another story altogether.

The stories he'd read over the years had astonished him. He was amazed to hear how a city had come together to build a memorial to the victims. Granted, it had taken years and fights and court battles. But it had been done. In his daughter's lifetime. In his own lifetime.

Trapped at the red light, he stared at the looming structure ahead. It looked smaller than he thought it would. He'd read that the Freedom Tower was exactly the same height as the original of the Twin Towers: One World Trade Center, the first.

Maybe the fact that the Twin Towers once held the status as the tallest buildings in the World (before they were surpassed by Sears and others), made them loom taller in his memory. Freedom Tower had never and would never claim the same status. Of course, watching the towers collapse while he was trying to get Kate to a hospital in time to give birth made them loom much taller in his memory as well.

Still, this new One World Trade Center had a quiet elegance to it. It stood straight and tall as if to say—*I'm not trying to be anything but what I am.*

I'm not trying to be the tallest or the same.

I'm trying to be respectful and new.

Ian glanced at other new construction peeking around the bend on 11th Avenue. Scaffolds and construction signs and dumpsters along the Hudson River hinted at plenty more nearby construction sites. New York City had been growing and building and reconstructing far away from him. He would need to accept this. He would need to wrap his head around it.

For the first time since Kate had arrived at *Playa del Espejo* with her story, he found himself softening even toward Dee who had lied to him for who knows how many years now.

Maybe it had pained Dee to lie to Ian. After all, she had been an incredible truth-teller since the moment he met her.

Their first meeting was in Botswana.

He'd trusted her instantly.

It was 1997 and Ian had just left Kate back in New York City after realizing she was probably the great love of his life, and he'd found Dee while drowning his loneliness in a dusty Botswanan bar.

"I'm here to write a story about time travel." He ignored the possibility that she'd think he was crazy. It was too late for him to worry about such things anymore.

"I am here to bury my mother," she had responded.

"Oh I'm so sorry."

"Well, she is not gone yet."

"Oh, I misunderstood."

"No. She is soon gone, though. And I need to be here at the last. At the very last moment."

"I understand," he nodded. "Closure. I get it."

Dee shook her head and chastised him. "Such odd English phrases you have. Closure? I'm closing nothing. I am opening everything."

And then, "Tell me about Kate."

Ian had shared Kate with Dee from the moment they met. Later when Kate and Dee got to meet, it was just the natural evolution of a relationship they already had.

And over the years, when Ian checked in with Dee, she'd told him that Kate and Hope were all right. Dee told him that Kate had found what he left her to find. Maybe that was true in a different way than he'd heard it.

Kate had grown and evolved into the beautiful, strong woman now sitting next to him in the car. The daughter he left at 8 weeks was 18 years old now, giving the commencement address and headed off to Cornell. Erratic Facetime "visits" and airmail were a poor substitute for watching your daughter grow up. Even he knew that. She'd be changed and evolved in ways he had never bargained on. She'd be a brand new person essentially.

As would Hope's mother.

The cab started moving again, taking them directly toward the new World Trade Center. And a shift occurred in Ian as he studied it with Kate at his side.

Maybe the new Freedom Tower *was* good enough after all.

And maybe Dee had her reasons for lying all this time.

chapter sixteen

Rory

AS RORY AND DEE sat in their chairs in Carnegie Hall ticking away at time, there was silence. It was a comfortable silence finally. Rory didn't feel the need to fill it.

Until she did.

She blurted out, "I wrote a note to my therapist last week."

"A note?"

"I do that. I subscribe to a therapy app. You know, on my phone." Rory tapped the phone that was sitting on her lap.

Dee threw her head back and laughed the kind of laugh that both embarrassed and warmed Rory in the same exhale.

"Tell me more, child. I want to understand why you don't want to tell your fears to someone face-to-face."

"It's not that—it's just that I have access to her all the time. In the morning, in the middle of the night. I can write down what's bothering me. What I'm fearing. What I'm dreaming about."

"Like a journal."

"Yes, like a journal, only someone is reading it and analyzing it."

"Interesting. Does she give you good feedback on this journal of yours?"

"Sometimes. But sometimes she just asks me questions

that I can tell are on some kind of a checklist because she's asked them before. I see us circling back to the same issues and questions like there's a sort of pattern to my madness."

"Do you think you're mad?"

"Like the kind where they lock you up in a soft room kind of mad? No. But in the you-sure-don't know-what-you-want-in-life kind of mad, yes."

"Do you think that's unusual?"

"How do you mean?"

"Do you think it's unusual for someone to not know exactly what they want out of this life?"

"Yes, I mean, in my life—everyone I've known in school and in life—everyone was focused on something tangible, and I've often had trouble finding that one singular thing to focus on."

"You're still looking for your thing."

"I guess so. My mother was focused on me. My father was focused on whatever it was that he left my mother for. But me? I didn't have a focus. At least, I thought I didn't. But then I found Marcos."

"I see. So this note?" Dee brought Rory's focus back around gently to the thing she'd actually brought up on her own. Rory wasn't at all sure why she'd blurted this information out.

"So, in the therapy app, I usually talk around things. I lay things out and I use the space for pros and cons and to babble and ramble, and I never ask at the end—what should I do? Because I don't want her to tell me what to do. I don't want to have to tell her, 'Oh, I'm sorry, I really can't do that,' because I don't want to disappoint anyone, least of all the therapist in my app that I never see and will likely never meet. But recently I did something I never do. Sometimes she says, 'Do you want my advice? You're free to disregard it, but do you want to hear my professional opinion?' And I always say no. I always do."

"So—your note?"

"Right, see? Unfocused." Rory tapped on her brain like it needed rebooting. "So this time I said, 'Marcos is going. He's leaving for Miami with his small art and his big dreams for maybe a year, and he wants me to come and leave my job and my small dreams and my mother behind. And I need real answers. I need you to tell me what to do. None of that mumbo jumbo therapy stuff. I need you to tell me which one is the right answer.'"

"Bold. Assertive."

"Right. And she said, 'So you want my advice?' And I said, 'Yes.'"

"And?"

Rory liked that she finally had a story that had Dee on the edge of *her* seat.

"Well, she responded right away. Like five minutes later, I saw a notification light up that I had a new message from her. She's always responsive, but this takes the cake even for her."

"And what did she say?"

"I don't know. I've let that message stay unread for seven straight days. It's like a bomb of truth I cannot trust myself to open."

"Will you ever open it?"

"Honestly?"

"Always."

"I really don't know."

Kate

WILL YOU BE bringing him?

Benton sent Kate a message through Instagram while she was still in Mexico. She commented on Kate's photos: a few obligatory shots of the scenery and water around the hotel where she and Trey were staying.

She had left her phone in the van at the cenote so she had nothing but her memories to document that part of the trip. She was certain that would be enough. Those weren't for public consumption anyway. She measured her words and information, posting only enough to vaguely brag about the Fellowship and the recognition. She didn't mention Trey by name, but she posted a picture of the group at the Award dinner, and as luck would have it, she was the one standing next to Trey in the picture with her arm around him and his arm around her, and the goofiest smile she'd ever made.

No matter, she posted it anyway, figuring no one would possibly suspect a thing.

Benton did and she messaged Kate within minutes of the posting.

Who's the tall drink of water with you?

My guide. Don't be cute.

Your guide, hunh? I haven't seen a smile on your face like that one in a long time. Looks like he helped you find something.

Winking face emoji.

Clever. You're using emojis and everything. I'm impressed.

Right? So, will you be bringing him?

Bringing him where?

Chloe's adoption proceeding.

Benton!

Yes, her dad has agreed to terminate his parental rights. He finally understands what's best for Chloe. The hearing is scheduled for the day after tomorrow. Please come.

I'll have to get an earlier flight home. I'll do whatever I can to make it happen.

Thank you, Kate.

Does this mean you're not moving out of the city?

No. I'm still moving. I will want Chloe to be able to see him easily if she wants. Even if it kills me.

Ah, Benton. Sacrificing your happiness for hers. You're a mother already.

Three dots appeared and disappeared. And then—

So are you bringing him?

No. It's not the time or the place. I don't even know if he's going to be around for the long term.

When you know, you know, Kate. Isn't that what you always said?

True.

Like me and Chloe.

Kate paused before she typed, *Yes, like you and Chloe.*

Just remember, every today is a memory for some tomorrow, Kate. Make this a good one. Make this the best memory you can.

Whoa. That's really beautiful. Did you make that up?

God, no. I read it in a meme or something.

Laughing crying emoji.

But it's true, no?

Yes, it's true all right.

Kate? I need to tell you something.

I'm waiting.

A long time of three dots, then blank, then three dots, then:

I want Ian and Rob at the adoption proceeding too. But I want your blessing for them to be there.

You have it, Benton.

Thank you, Kate. Will you bring the boys too?

Of course.

Wouldn't it be amazing if we could all be there filling up the room in a show of support for her?

Yes.

And then a string of emojis followed including, for reasons unknown, a pineapple, a bee, a flower bloom, and a single sneaker.

Ian

"WE HAVE TO RE-ROUTE completely," the driver said as he headed east suddenly. Kate nodded.

By 17th Street, Kate was wiping tears from her eyes.

"Kate?"

"It's just a lot. I'm sorry. And we still have so far to go."

"Sorry Ma'am. I'm doing my best here." The driver interrupted Kate as he looked up at her through the rear view window.

"No, I know. I'm not blaming you. It's just that it's our daughter's graduation day, and we're missing it."

Ian stared up above Kate's head at people walking above the city on an elevated path.

"What's that?"

She followed his point.

"What? Oh the High Line. Yes, that's new. Well, relatively speaking, I guess. I think it opened in about 2009. Hope and I used to walk it a lot. Great views."

Ian looked over at Kate wiping her tears and he watched the star pendant dangle around her neck and he wondered how long he could keep pretending that there was some ending here that didn't have Kate waking up and realizing what she'd given up for him, and then walking away from Ian forever.

chapter seventeen

Rory

A NEW FAMILY came and moved into the seats in front of Dee and Rory. They didn't take all the chairs, though. There were still two left. Rory watched as the new faces got settled into their seats. Her clock told her that the hour delay had almost expired.

"So back to Hope's parents. Ian left, and her mother moved on?"

"Moved on. Such an odd English phrase. What Hope's mother did had little to do with movement and everything to do with staying still. She let her mind and soul be at peace, at rest, for a moment, and then more. I left and went home when the baby was about three months old, and Kate stayed in the moment with Hope. She fed her and loved her and bathed her and stayed with her."

"But she had no choice?"

"Well of course she did. Time is simply a series of choices strung together. The time passed while she chose to be the best possible mother to Hope that she could be."

"She stayed single?"

"She stayed herself."

"Did she love again?"

"She loved still."

Rory exhaled impatiently. "Well, for heaven's sake, what's the difference?"

"There is a big difference." Dee left it at that.

Rory flipped through her notepad studying her scribbles and trying to make sense of them. "Interesting to think that everything in this story—indeed the reason Hope is even preparing to get up here and speak—is because Hope's mother chose Ian on the Beatrice all those years ago."

Dee nodded. "Well, she chose him *that* time."

"What do you mean? That time?"

"Well, those bad dreams that she had? Those questions she had? And the sons she thought she remembered after she chose Ian? They may have been based on something. Some reality, somewhere. Some *other time.*"

Rory shook her head. "That doesn't make sense. You're suggesting that there were some sort of parallel universes? In one, Kate ended up with Ian? Who then left her and Hope? And in one she ended up with Rob and had her boys?"

Dee just smiled at her. "You never know."

"No, I guess we won't." Rory's brow furrowed and she studied Dee, wondering if she even believed her own spun tales.

Rory's phone lit up with Marcos's number and it startled her. She'd left him this morning while she was still angry and since he hadn't called her all day, she assumed he'd sensed it. Or maybe he was angry at her too.

She hit decline to stop the humming noise of her vibrating phone and whispered to Dee, "I'm going to go take this call outside."

Dee nodded. "Unless they somehow collided."

"Sorry?"

"We'd never know whether there were parallel universes unless somehow those worlds collided."

"Um hum. Ok. Well, I'm just going to go grab this."

She passed by the usher on her way out. "Still no word on a starting time?"

"Not yet, Miss."

Outside on the curb, Rory hit Call Back.

"*Bella*. I've missed you. How's the protest?"

"I didn't go."

"Hunh? So where've you been all day?"

"Oh, it's kind of a long story, actually. I'll fill you in later. I met the most interesting woman. My cab got rear-ended and—"

"*Bella*! Are you ok?"

"Yes, yes, I'm fine. Only I never made it to the protest and I landed at Carnegie Hall instead. There's this commencement ceremony scheduled today and I've been waiting all morning and now into the afternoon for it to start. A group of students whose mothers were all pregnant on 9/11. They are literally the first survivors of 9/11."

"Oh what a beautiful story to find you, *Bella*."

"I know, it's like you said. You were right, of course."

There was a pause and then, "Marcos?"

"Yes?"

"I don't think you should go to Miami."

Marcos sighed loudly.

"*Bella*, I know how you feel and all your reservations. I don't want to discuss this on the phone."

"No. I mean, I don't think you should go to Miami, because I think we should figure out how to get you a passport and you should go to Cuba. I'll go with you. We'll go for a few months, or however long it takes. We'll take your parents' ashes and your art and we'll try to get someone in Cuba to show your art. I really think you should try to take a risk on your art. But it should be in Cuba."

"*Bella*." It was a whisper.

"I mean it, Marcos. Think about it. I know there are logistical issues, and I have no idea how to get you a passport, but still, we can figure it out together."

"I have to make a confession."

Rory's heart stuck in her throat for a moment waiting for the confession and when it came, it was nothing she expected.

"I have a passport. I found all my paperwork among my mother's files in storage just before we got married. I applied for a passport and I got one. *Mi mama*—she was pretty disorganized, but even she must have known I'd need everything in order one day. I never had any doubt I'd find them."

"But, Marcos, why did you say you didn't have anything? You made me believe you were really worried about your legal status, and well, everything."

Rory twirled the lanyard with her married name around and around while she processed this news.

Marcos has a passport.

He had no ulterior motives for wanting her to spend the rest of her life with him.

Her mother was wrong.

She was relieved but also disappointed to find among her feelings—*surprise.* Because she must have believed there was a possibility that he was lying to her too.

But wait. He *was* lying. He told her he didn't have a birth certificate or a passport or any proof of his legal status. Why would he do that?

He was answering her inner questions on the other end of the phone while she was still arguing with herself. She tried to quiet her thoughts so she could hear him.

"It started as just this mental exercise with myself. I was trying to understand the fear my parents must have felt when they first moved here and so I put all the paperwork in storage and didn't even bother looking through it, just to see if I could try to trick my brain for a moment. You know, the way you do when you set your alarm forward or backward and you know it but you still sort of trick yourself and you're able to simulate the fear of being late or the relief of being on time?"

"Ok, very odd analogy. But I actually sort of understand it, strangely enough. But Marcos, why did you keep it up?"

"Well, I guess I didn't want you to think I was a liar. But that sort of backfired, didn't it?

"And then I started to develop this crazy fear that maybe the only reason you actually agreed to marry me was that you were afraid I wasn't a citizen after all. I guess I wasn't exactly afraid of telling you the truth. I was afraid of *learning* the truth."

"Oh, Marcos. What a mess we've made of things. This is no way for married people to behave."

"No, it's not. I guess I'm just learning how to be married. Will you forgive me?"

"Yes, I will."

Rory looked over her shoulder. "I can't wait to tell you about my day."

"I can't wait to show you Cuba."

"I love you, Marcos."

"I love you too. Now go. Finish your assignment and come home to me."

"Ok. See you soon."

Just as she was turning to head back into Carnegie Hall, there was a loud crash beyond the traffic barriers. Rory turned around quickly and saw a police officer on his radio as he started sprinting into action. She heard him say into the radio, "Send backup. There's been a terrible accident outside Carnegie Hall."

Rory looked up to see six or seven cars collided, but that's not what made her gasp out loud.

What kept her frozen in her spot staring, gawking, and re-evaluating the story she'd heard all day in a brand new way, was the sight of two women emerging from two of the collided cars. They were turned away from each other and didn't seem to see each other, but Rory saw them.

One striking red-haired woman with a golden dress emerged from one of the cars aided by two teen-age boys, and one striking woman with a blonde bob emerged from one of the cars aided by a handsome man in a beige linen suit who looked like he wore the weight of a lot of regrets on his back.

Rory stared at the women who were focused only on their travel companions. Despite the differences in hair styles, they looked so alike. And even more bizarrely, they looked so *familiar*.

It couldn't be. It can't be.

Rory felt light-headed. She backed away slowly. She thought about calling Marcos back but had no idea what she'd say to him.

She looked over her shoulder and thought about going back in and dragging Dee outside for an explanation.

It can't be. She repeated to herself. *I'm only dreaming this all up because of this completely bizarre story Dee told me.*

Snap out of it!

Rory dug her fingernails into her palms, hoping to wake up or shake out of this dream she seemed stuck in.

There are no parallel worlds. Rory kept repeating to herself until her thoughts became low audible whispers, repeated with passion. *There are no parallel worlds. There are no parallel worlds.*

But how would we know? She stopped and asked herself a question that suddenly became quite serious.

How would we know?

We wouldn't, Dee had conceded: *Unless they somehow collided.*

Something important occurred to Rory just then. She looked over her shoulder, toward Carnegie Hall, where Dee was sitting inside, and she wondered something for the first time all day.

What was Hope's mother's name?

Dee had never told Rory the name of Hope's mother.

The entire day, Rory suddenly realized, she'd never known Hope's mother's name.

But now she did. Suddenly she did.

Kate

THE CAB HAD been winding through a detour for what felt like forever when the driver hit the brakes again and Kate's bag went flying. She reached down to collect everything, including the tossed Rogers Fellowship parchment, and she felt her head hit the seat in front of her.

She heard some expletives from the driver as she massaged her head.

"What just happened?"

"We've been hit from behind. Are you ok, Ma'am?"

Kate felt a little woozy. "I think I just need some aspirin. I'm going to run into that bodega over there."

"No, Ma'am. Don't go anywhere. You sit here. It looks like a lot of cars were involved. Let me see what's going on. We're going to call the police and get you checked out. Sit here, please."

Michael and David started wrestling in the third row of the car. Kate groaned loudly. It seemed to Kate that her life had become a series of mediations in recent years. Mediating the relationship between her two sons. Mediating the relationship between the boys and their father. Mediating the relationship between herself and their father too. She was tired. She leaned her head against the car window.

"Mom!" David yelled. His voice reverberated against the window Kate's head was leaning against and made her head rattle. "Are you seeing this! Are you seeing what he's doing?"

Kate turned around in her seat and intervened.

"Stop it! You two, just stop it right now. If you think I'm going to spend the day screaming at you two and keeping you from embarrassing me, you are out of your minds. You are way too old to be acting like toddlers. Knock it off."

"Ok, ok, calm down, Mamacita."

The driver made a laughing sound from the front seat.

Michael reached over and patted her shoulder like she

was a golden lab. She shook him off. "Cut it out."

"Oh, come on mom, you love me. You can't stay mad at me. Come on."

David started in on the chorus from the back seat, too.

"You look so pretty mom. Come on. Don't put that face on, or you'll look all wrinkly by the time we get there. Don't worry."

"Oh, you two. They each had a hand on one of her shoulders by now. Kate grabbed each of the boys' hands in her own and clasped them hard. She adored these two. They were a handful. No doubt about it. But they held her heart in their hands. She leaned her head back against the window and closed her eyes again.

My sons. Thank God for my sons.

"Just wait here, you three," the driver said as he got out of the car.

Kate nodded, and dialed a familiar number on her phone.

"Rob? Our cab was in an accident outside Carnegie Hall. Yes, we're fine. Don't worry. We're all fine. Are you there yet? Can you detour in this direction and come pick us up? Ok, call when you're close."

Kate hung up the phone, and then she opened the cab door, summoning the boys to come with her.

"Come on. I need to get some air and some aspirin. You can grab a Starbucks if you like. Meet me right back here in 15 minutes. Your father is on his way to help us out." The boys followed her out of the car and then they split directions with Kate who headed for the closest bodega. The boys headed for a Starbucks sign on the next corner.

Across from the bodega, Kate saw the looming structure ahead of her. Carnegie Hall. An old corny joke ran through her head that Rob used to tell often as if he'd invented it.

Sir, how do you get to Carnegie Hall?

Practice, practice, practice.

Kate pulled the bodega door handle, feeling the heaviness of the door as she exhaled with the day's weight. She took a deep breath and then she heard it.

It was the sound of a cry. Of a child's cry. Kate let the door slam shut and turned to walk toward the sound.

The sound was coming from a girl. Not a child, but a teenager. She was maybe a few years older than Michael but not too many more. She was sitting on the curb outside a back entrance to Carnegie Hall and she was wearing a half-zipped graduation gown that was twisted around her as she cried into her long legs that were pulled up to her chest.

The girl looked up and gasped at Kate.

Kate grew more concerned by the gasp than the crying. "Are you ok? Do you need me to call someone?" Kate felt panic at the girl's reaction to her and to the odd feeling she had creeping up her neck at the sight of the girl.

"God, I'm sorry. You just startled me. I didn't know anyone was there, and I was just so angry and then there you were and I thought you were my mother for a moment, but oh ..." The girl leaned back into her legs.

Kate looked over her shoulder, wondering if there was a person responsible for this girl.

While Kate paused, someone came out of the bodega Kate had been about to go into, and headed in the opposite direction. Kate felt conspicuously alone with the crying girl in the alley. Kate sat down next to the her, and reached in her purse for a tissue. "Here."

"Thanks."

"You're graduating?"

"I am. This was supposed to be the best day of my life. It's turning out to be the worst."

Kate laughed.

"Thanks a lot."

"No, I'm not laughing at you—I get it. I've had plenty of those days as well. And this day has definitely not been the greatest for me either."

"Oh, sorry." The girl blew into the tissue long and

loudly. It made Kate laugh again. The girl laughed along with her this time. "I know, I have the worst nose blow. My mom always makes fun of me for it."

Kate handed the girl another tissue and the girl used it to wipe her eyes and nose and studied Kate carefully. "God, I'm telling you—the weird thing is—the reason you startled me so much—is that you could be my mom's sister. You look a lot like her."

"Do I?" Kate felt an unnamed emotion that mirrored something like misplaced pride. She puffed up a bit.

"Yeah, definitely. Like her older sister. Seriously."

She instantly deflated. "Well, I can't be *that* much older than your mom."

This time it was the girl's turn to laugh at Kate. "Oh, sorry. No offense."

"You're like my sons. I always have to remind them that just because they *say* no offense, doesn't mean they haven't offended."

The girl blew again loudly. "Sorry," she apologized again and tried handing the tissue back to Kate.

Kate waved it away. "Oh no you don't, that one is all yours now."

The girl pointed to Kate's forearm. "Cool tattoo. What does it mean?"

"Mayan Goddess Warrior," Kate lied.

"Wow," the girl reached over and traced it reverently. "I love it."

"Thank you. It's new. So, is it a boy?"

"Hunh?"

"The reason you're out here making this horn-blowing sound with your nose while the rest of your class is in there graduating? The reason your best day is now your worst? Is it a boy?"

The soon-to-be-graduate shook her head. "No, it's a long story."

Kate smiled. She wanted to tell the girl that she was late

for something herself, but she didn't want to make her uncomfortable. "So how about you give me the abridged version?"

"It's my dad."

Kate nodded.

"So I was right, it *is* a boy." She winked and the girl chuckled before continuing on. "My mom—she promised she'd bring my dad back in time for today. For this." She waved toward the hall. "I'm giving the commencement speech. It's kind of a big deal."

"You are? That's a huge deal. Congratulations."

"Yeah, well, my dad should be here. And my mom promised he'd be here. And she went to bring him here. And now neither of them are here. So I'm alone, and I don't think I can do this. And I am *always* the girl that can do this. You know what I mean? Like I'm unflappable. This should be no big deal for me. I'm always telling my mom that things she thinks are a big deal are not, and now I feel like such a hypocrite, because this should be no big deal. This should be precisely the thing I tell her is no big deal. And yet, here I am, freaking out."

Kate felt out of breath and was certain the girl had stopped breathing. "Ok. Ok. Deep breath." Kate reached over and put her hands on the girls' shoulders and pressed down gently. "You need to calm down."

Kate took a deep inhale and nodded at the girl to follow her lead. They took several deep breaths together. "Now listen, I know you don't know me. And by the way, don't be so trusting of strangers you meet in the alley, young lady. Sheesh."

The girl smiled up through her tear-streaked face and kept breathing in and out slowly.

"But still, even though you don't know me, I'm a mom. I have two teen-age boys. And I can tell you, that we do, hand-on-heart, honest-to-God, every single day, the absolute best we can. Like the literal best we can do. And yet, we parents, we moms especially, we are broken and complicated people who fail at sometimes the simplest things while simultaneously triumphing at the most ridiculously hard things. We are, I promise you, completely surprising and paradoxical, and not always in a good way."

The girl looked at her rapt, so Kate kept going.

"And listen, I have a feeling that if you are giving the commencement speech in Carnegie Hall, then you have two parents who most likely want to see that speech as badly as you want them to see it. But sometimes timing is everything. Sometimes timing is just, well, off. So, you need to go out there and give it your absolute best. That speech you're giving? It's not for them, is it? It's supposed to be inspiring an entire room full of graduates. And what is more inspiring than a girl who picks herself up on her worst day ever and inspires her graduating class that they can do the same?"

"Oh wow. That's not bad. You're pretty good at this Mom thing."

"Not always," Kate laughed.

The girl reached into a pocket in her graduation gown and pulled out a little notecard and pen and jotted some words on it.

Kate looked at her incredulously.

"What?"

"They have pockets in graduation gowns, now?"

"I know! Aren't pockets the best?"

"Oh my God. If I could never wear a pocketless dress the rest of my life, I'd be the happiest woman ever."

"I feel the same way!"

The girl held out the notecard to Kate. "Do you want to hear part of my speech?"

"Absolutely! Lay it on me."

The girl took a deep breath and then began: "We try to outrun time. We try to outsmart it. We try to squeeze more time into every day. It's all in vain, of course, because time has a funny way of catching up on itself."

There was a pause and Kate leaned in to her. "Why did you stop?"

"I want to know what you think of it so far."

"I think it's perfect. Is that the opening?"

"Actually, no. It's the middle. Don't ask me why that's the part I decided to sample for you."

Kate laughed.

The girl shook her head and stood up. "I'm late. I better get back inside. Listen, sorry you had to stumble upon me just then. This is so embarrassing. But you really helped. I hope your day turns into something good; you really helped with mine."

"Thanks. And congratulations." Kate pulled herself up and turned in the direction of the bodega before realizing her nagging headache had actually dissipated.

She turned back around for one last wave and saw the girl was doing the same as she ducked into the back door of Carnegie Hall. With her head peeking out and the rest of her body already moving inside, the girl called out, "Oh and Ma'am. You're obviously a really, really great mom."

Kate waved and felt her eyes well up before she could stop them.

Kate, get a hold of yourself. She's just a stranger in an alley. What does she know?

At the end of the alley she turned the corner only to bump into a young woman with a press badge holding a phone and staring at her not unlike the way the girl in the alley had stared a few moments earlier. "Oh my God. I'm so sorry." Kate glanced down at the press badge and saw her name. She added it for emphasis, because the young woman looked dazed and she hadn't even bumped into her that hard. "*Rory*. I'm so sorry, Rory."

Rory shook her head like she'd seen a red-headed ghost and Kate tried not to let it bother her. She headed back toward Starbucks to find her boys.

Ian

THE COLLISION WAS hard and unexpected. They were just a block from Carnegie Hall, and were actually high fiving each other in relief because they'd made it.

Or so they thought.

The car lurched with a jerk and sent them both into the seatbacks in front of them.

"Ian!" Kate yelled.

"Kate, are you ok?"

"I am." She massaged her head. "Oh, Ian, you cut your forehead."

Ian reached up and felt a wet spot, just before he watched some drops of blood trickle down onto his beige linen pants. The suit had felt somewhat impractical when they picked it out in the airport, but Kate had convinced him to just put it on, and "let's go!"

Now that he was about to see his daughter looking like a crime scene victim, he felt even more embarrassed.

The driver jumped out of the car and so did Ian. The driver reached Kate's door before Ian did, so they both competed to help Kate out of the door, and the driver said "Come, sit here. We will wait for the police and the ambulance. I'm sure someone has called them."

But Kate got out of the car and pulled away from the driver moving closer to Ian. "No, no. We're fine. We have to get to Carnegie Hall. Right over there. See? It's our daughter's graduation day."

"Ma'am, you have to wait. The police—they will want to talk to you, take statements," the driver insisted.

"Oh, no, we absolutely do not have time for that right now." Kate peeled some bills out of her wallet, handed them to the driver, and pulled Ian's arm. "We only have one daughter. And she only has one graduation day. Ian, come on." Ian knew there was no talking Kate out of getting into

Carnegie Hall. He apologized to the driver, as they hurried away from the accident scene leaving him looking flustered and frustrated. Ian felt his pain.

Kate raced over to the door at Carnegie Hall, but security stopped her. "Whoa. Hold on there. This is a ticketed event."

"Yes, I have—Oh God, I forgot the tickets." Kate looked at Ian panic-stricken.

The security guard looked at them skeptically.

"Have we missed everything?" Kate said.

"Actually, the ceremony has been delayed. It hasn't even started yet and it's not expected to start for another hour or so. You have time to go home and your tickets." He smiled.

Kate looked at the security guard incredulously. "Are you kidding me? Do you know what we've been through to get here?"

"Looks like quite a bit, actually," the security guard pointed to Ian's bloody forehead.

"Oh Ian," Kate said. "Ok, let's go get you cleaned up and I'll try to get in touch with Hope. She'll send someone to the door for us. It will all be fine."

Ian looked around and spotted the Starbucks sign up ahead. "Let's head over there and I'll use the restroom and get a shot of espresso or something to calm my nerves. And then we'll get to graduation."

In Starbucks, Ian washed up his forehead. It turned out to be a very small cut and he washed the trickled blood out of his suit the best he could and stood under the blow dryer for a few seconds before joining Kate in the barista line where she was waiting for him. As he walked toward her, he saw two boys clowning around in front of her bumping into each other as they waited in line.

When Ian joined Kate in line, she squeezed his hand. "You look much better. Good job." The pinballing boys in front of them suddenly bumped into Kate and not just themselves, and they turned around together to apologize. Ian noticed the taller one do a double take when he saw Kate.

The taller boy hit his companion in the arm who nodded and turned his head to the side. "Wow, you look like—" the shorter boy looked over at his brother as he cut off his sentence. He looked a little embarrassed, but his brother finished for him. "You look like a younger version of our mom. You could be her little sister, seriously."

"Gee thanks, I'll take that as a compliment. You guys waiting to get into Carnegie Hall?"

"Hunh?" the shorter one said eloquently. Kate pointed with exaggeration. "The graduation. Over there across the street? We're heading over there, but I'm not quite sure how to get in. We forgot our tickets. I've been texting my daughter to find out how to get in, but I can't get any signal. I haven't been able to get any signal since we left the airport a few hours ago." The boys stared at Kate and Ian blankly.

"Uh, no. We're not going to any graduation or anything. We just got in a little collision out there. We were headed with our Mom to City Hall to her friend's adoption hearing. We're really late, but luckily it got delayed because of some big protest across town. We're just killing time. Our dad is trying to make his way over to help us out. He was already at the adoption hearing. Don't ask us how he was able to make it through the traffic when we've been stuck in traffic all day."

"Oh. That's nice. I mean about the adoption and your dad trying to help you guys out, not the collision. We were in that collision too, as it turns out. The city seems to be a bit of a hot mess today. We've literally just gotten in from Mexico. Only a few days away from this traffic, and I'd already gotten used to life without it." The boys looked at themselves back and forth like maybe they were dealing with a nutcase.

Ian wanted to tell Kate to dial it back a little. She was a stranger and these boys were strangers, and here she was giving her life story out in the line at the Starbucks.

"Funny," the short one said. "Our mom just got back from an award thing-y in Mexico."

"You didn't go with her?" Kate asked.

"Nah. We stayed with our dad. It's lacrosse season, and we didn't want to miss. She caught an early flight to make it to her friend's adoption hearing. You guys were probably on the same flight."

Kate nodded. "Small world."

"Anyway, it would have been a riot if you two had bumped into each other. You could have switched places or something. Come back and tricked us all. Like they do in the movies."

Kate laughed. "Yes, that would have been a riot, indeed."

"She just went to get some aspirin. She should be back any minute. You can see for yourself."

"Well, all right then," Kate said, and Ian watched her tap on her phone.

She held it up to Ian. The message kept reading non-delivered.

"I'm trying to text Hope, but I just can't get through. How are we ever going to get inside?"

"You still on Airplane mode, Ma'am?"

"Sorry?"

The tall boy looked at Ian and Kate, blushing. "I'm not spying or anything. I just see you keep trying to send a text and I heard you saying it wasn't going through, and I was just thinking maybe you're still on Airplane mode. Didn't you say you just got in from Mexico?"

Ian felt a tingling feeling in his arms and legs. The boy reached over to Kate.

"Can I?" Ian watched Kate hand over her phone to the tall boy and after a few taps he handed it back to Kate.

Ian watched as she typed the message again. He heard the swoosh of a delivered message and she held it up to all of them.

"Message Delivered! Finally!"

The tall boy smiled sheepishly and looked down at the ground.

Kate touched his arm gently. "I feel like such an idiot. Thank you."

"Oh, you're not an idiot. That's something my Mom would do. You probably have a million things going on. Don't beat yourself up."

Ian watched Kate and the boys interacting. The tall boy looked at her with such warmth and the smaller boy had a goofy smile on his face. Ian's heart hurt as it did every minute of this trip since learning there had never been any sons for Kate.

The younger boy nodded along. "Yeah, lady. It's not a big deal. Aren't you glad you ended up behind us? You'd have been trying to send that message for the rest of your life with no luck."

Kate laughed at the entertaining and sweet boys they'd been lucky enough to get stuck behind in the latte line.

"Next!" The barista called out, and the boys headed up to the register and ordered two caramel apple spices. Then the tall boy turned around and looked at Kate and Ian. "How about you guys? Our treat."

Ian watched the boys regard Kate. They both looked her in the eye as they asked for her order. Even though she was a potential nutcase who couldn't figure out how to work her smartphone, still they were looking her in the eye and treating her with respect.

"Um, what was that you just ordered? I scanned the menu but I couldn't find it." Kate stared up at the menu board.

The short one stage whispered. "It's a secret menu item. You have to know about it. Now you do. You want one too?"

"Really?" Kate laughed and winked. "Yeah, I'll take one of those." Ian shook his head. He'd decided against the espresso after all. He was already feeling too jittery.

The tall boy turned back to the barista. "Make it three please." He pulled out a bunch of bills and counted them out and paid for the three drinks.

"That's really generous of you. Thank you."

The younger boy piped up. "They're from both of us. He owed me. Don't think I'm a mooch or anything. But I did three of his lawns last week so he could go to the movies with Lisa."

The younger boy said Lisa like it was a funny word and the tall boy punched him in the shoulder for it.

Kate nodded enthusiastically. "No, I didn't think anything at all. That's nice. You work hard and you treat yourselves and you're generous with each other. And with strangers. You're really good kids. Tell your parents they should be very proud of you."

They both shrugged in a teenager-y way. They all stood awkwardly for a few moments until the drinks came up. The boys waved and headed out the door ahead of them, drinks in hand, and Kate and Ian looked at each other, pausing and taking a breath before they headed over to Carnegie Hall. "Well, hope you guys have a great day. Thanks for the drink and the secret menu tip." Kate smiled and waved to the boys as they walked out.

Ian heard them as they left. "God, didn't she look like Mom? Like Mom would look without the grey and the lines under her eyes. Well, I mean, now she has this crazy new red hair, but still, didn't she look *just like Mom*?"

"Yeah, man, she really did."

Kate held up her phone to show Ian: MOM! YOU'RE HERE! AND DAD TOO?

Kate called Hope and put it on speaker.

"Yes, honey. We're here. I told you."

"Hi sweetheart."

"Dad! I thought you weren't going to make it."

She sounded out of breath.

"Relax, honey. Deep breaths," Kate told her.

"Funny. I just ran into a lady who told me the same thing."

"Smart lady."

"Yeah, she was. She looked like you. But older. And with red hair. It was the weirdest thing."

"Ah," Kate and Ian shared a smile over the speaker phone. "Yes, I think I just met her boys in Starbucks. Apparently I have a doppelganger out there. They were telling me we could be sisters."

"Oh, how funny! Isn't the world small?"

Ian laughed. It didn't feel all that small to him, really. But he felt more relaxed than he had since he started this trip. Just hearing Hope's uncontained excitement through the phone line was rejuvenating.

"Ok, you two, get inside. From backstage, I can see Aunt Dee sitting near the front and she's saved a bunch of seats."

"Sweetie, don't kill me, but in all the excitement and chaos of flying to Mexico and getting here, I forgot the tickets."

"Mom!"

"Honey, I said don't kill me. Any ideas?"

"Sure, I'll send Miss Corbin out to meet you at the door. She'll get you in."

"Ok, honey. See you soon. Break a leg!"

Kate pressed End.

Ian reached for her hand and squeezed it.

"God, I've missed you, Ian."

Ian pulled her in for a hug. He held her head and breathed her in.

"We did it," she whispered.

"You did this, Kate. You did it all. You raised Hope. And

you did it all alone. And you gave up so much to do it. And I—"

Kate pulled away.

"No. Stop. We're not doing this. I didn't give up a thing. Let's go see our daughter."

They walked hand-in-hand back to Carnegie Hall and somehow found the door they were supposed to use. Tanya Corbin was waving to them to get their attention near the security guard and they headed to her, past a pretty girl standing in the doorway, staring at them in confusion, with a dazed expression and a press lanyard twirling around and around in her hands.

chapter eighteen

Rory

RORY TRIED HARD to catch her breath after watching Kate—*this* Kate—walk hand-in-hand into Carnegie Hall with Ian Campton. She'd just seen her red-headed twin comfort Hope in the back alley. Both women were so startlingly similar—even more so, because—

Rory stopped herself. She couldn't even go there.

The worlds have collided.

Did Dee know?

What would she say?

Did she know everything?

Rory followed behind Kate and Ian soundlessly. Kate looked so proud and happy, while Ian looked tired and worn. They headed toward Dee who was facing all of them with open arms. Dee wrapped Kate in a warm hug and looked at Ian over Kate's shoulder. "You're home, finally. You're where you should be." She pointed them to the seats in front of her. They settled into their seats, and Rory slid back into the seat next to Dee.

Rory couldn't resist. She leaned in, and whispered everything she'd seen to Dee.

Dee nodded. There was no trace of surprise on her face.

"Just now?" she asked.

Rory nodded.

"How much longer?" Dee leaned over Rory and asked the usher.

"It'll be another 15-20 minutes until we get started." Dee nodded and leaned forward to Ian and Kate.

"Kate, you stay here. Promise me you'll stay here. Ian, come with me."

Ian stood up without hesitation. Kate looked alarmed.

"But Dee? Ian? You can't be late."

"We won't be, darling." Dee sang out to Kate. She bent down and whispered to Rory, "You too. I want you out there as well." Ian and Rory regarded each other slowly, and then followed Dee out of Carnegie Hall in silence. As they walked obediently, Rory wondered how this day had taken such a dramatic turn. Again and again.

When they got out to the curb, Ian broke his silence.

"Dee, you told me she reconnected with Rob. That she found her boys. That it all worked out. That it was all for something."

Dee nodded.

Ian looked distraught and Rory was uncomfortable watching him unravel in front of her.

Dee took his hand and pointed with the other.

He didn't look. He just kept lamenting.

"I left for nothing. There was no other life. There were no other children. She told me in Mexico that she never married. And she never had any children other than Hope. It was all for nothing. And you made me believe I hadn't left in vain."

"Stop it right now."

"Dee, please. Either you're lying to me, or she is. And I don't know which one is going to destroy me more."

"Ian. Stop. Look." Rory followed her glance. A beautiful redhead was corralling boys with Starbucks cups into a sedan, driven by a man Rory couldn't quite make out.

Rory could hear the gentleness of her voice as she called out, "Boys, come on. Let's try to salvage this day. Move it. Your father is holding up traffic. Let's get in."

The boys bumped into each other purposefully making

the process of herding them into the car both entertaining and frustrating. Apparently it was both for the woman as well. She scolded them with a smile on her face. "Boys, move it. Come on."

"Aw, mom, do you love me? Say you'll never ever leave from beside me." The tall boy started singing his own words to a familiar song and the younger boy joined in. The woman smiled and they kissed her head fiercely, aggravating her and making amends in one fell swoop.

"I met those boys," Ian said. "They were extraordinary." Ian's legs gave out and he sat down on the curb.

Dee sat down next to him. Rory remained standing. She watched the redhead and her boys climb into the car and head off through the crowded city streets.

"But how?" Ian held his head in his hands.

"You can't change things that are meant to be, Ian. It's egotistical to think you can," Dee responded. "On one path, she left the ship and chose you, and struggled and fought, and then found Hope. But, there was another course altogether. On that path, Kate left the ship and chose Rob. She had her boys. There was no Hope."

Ian stood and watched the car in the distance. "Did she stay with Rob?"

"No. They divorced eventually. But she found more love. A kind man who loved her as he found her later on."

"How did all of this happen?"

"I think there was a collision of sorts."

"Here? Outside? Kate and I were in that collision too."

"Well, yes. But in Mexico, too. I think they were both in Mexico at the same time. And well, there must have been a shift in time. Another storm, if you will. It brought you here. But it brought her here too."

"This is a lot. It's a relief in so many ways, but also a lot to take in and believe."

"Kate found you in Mexico and brought you back here like she was meant to. You and Kate had a daughter that lived and thrived and saved and inspired."

Rory watched the same car speed away that Ian was watching. He asked hopefully, "And in another time and place Kate had her boys?"

"Everything works out the way it's supposed to. Maybe not at the same time. But it does. You have to trust. You have to believe. It's like I always told you again and again, ever since we met in Botswana that first day. You have to trust that it all works out in the end."

Dee pulled Ian up off the curb.

"Come. It's time. But first, I need to introduce the two of you." She turned to Rory who had been standing on the curb unsure of her place in the current scene.

"Rory Monroe Garcia. Meet Ian Campton."

Rory shook Ian's hand, and she couldn't exactly understand the way he was looking at her. But it made her feel something she hadn't felt in a long time.

Whole.

Kate

KATE PULLED THE passenger side door closed and ordered Michael and David to put their seatbelts on in the back seat. Rob got behind the wheel, and glanced over his shoulder at Kate.

"We can still make it. Benton says the proceedings were delayed, and the protestors are starting to disburse. It will mean so much if you can get there. She wants a room full of support for Chloe."

Kate nodded.

"By the way, I like your hair."

Kate smiled her thanks. She was pulling her own seatbelt across her when she saw them. Only their profiles were visible but it looked like Dee and Ian. And a young woman who looked so much like Ian, it was uncanny.

But wait. If Ian was on this side of town, he couldn't be—

"Did Ian make it to City Hall?" Kate asked Rob.

Rob looked a little disappointed as he answered, "Yes. Benton said he made it in time. I know you're anxious to see him."

"No, it's not that. I thought I just saw him over there. But that's crazy. Why would Ian be at Carnegie Hall?"

Rob shrugged.

Kate looked over her shoulder at the boys in the back. "Boys, stop wrestling. Please."

She stared at the trio walking back into Carnegie Hall. She could only see their backs.

"Rob, can you stop the car? I need to get out a minute."

"Kate!" Rob yelled as he slowed the car while Kate had her hand on the door handle. "You're not getting out, are you?"

The boys leaned forward suddenly from the rear seat.

"Come on, Mom," Michael said.

"Don't be mad, Mom. Don't get out of the car." David said.

Kate took her hand off the door handle and exhaled.

In her lap, her phone buzzed with a message from Trey.

Just got into town on the later flight. Dinner tomorrow at 6? I'm cooking.

Kate smiled at the phone, and tapped out a reply.

Perfect. Can't wait.

Then aloud to Rob and the boys, she said, "I'm sorry. I'm just torn between worlds a bit. Ok, let's get to City Hall."

Ian

IAN FOLLOWED DEE and Rory into the auditorium with the shell-shocked expression of a man who had been in battle and survived.

He wasn't sure what to make of any of it.

The long journey to this point had weathered and eroded him, but suddenly he felt light. Lighter than he had in years.

He was anxious to begin the next leg of his journey. He was so anxious to see how it would turn out. He made it back inside just in time for his daughter, Hope, to come on the stage and begin her speech:

"Dear Faculty, Staff, Families, Friends, and Fellow Students, Welcome.

To my peers and friends in the graduating class of 2020: I join you as we come to this stage with all the idealism and hopes and dreams and ambitions that we will certainly conquer the world. To those of you a little older than our 18 years, I know what you're thinking. You're thinking you already know how this ends. And maybe you do. But I'd challenge you to rethink that notion.

And to my fellow graduates, I'd challenge you as well to keep writing and rewriting your story as many times as it takes."

Ian took a seat between Kate and Rory, and he applauded. Loudly.

epilogue

WHILE HOPE CAMPTON delivered her commencement address, her father and mother and Dee and a familiar-looking young woman with a press badge were all sitting in her view. They gave her strength as she delivered her five to seven minutes of inspiration.

If Hope would have known the entire story (*which she could not, of course, because who can ever know the whole story?*) she would have known that the young woman sitting with her family on Commencement Day was Rory Garcia. She would also have known that Rory Garcia was born Rory Monroe to a single mother, Kate Monroe, in 1997, after a whirlwind love affair with a man who'd left her for Botswana and time travel and marula oil. A man named Ian Campton who had insisted when he left that he was not interested in settling down and not interested in having a family, and Kate had taken his insistence at face value.

Kate Monroe raised Rory alone without resentment and without help, but with a quiet confidence that she'd made sacrifices, yes, but also choices that needed to be made.

Kate tried to find Ian over the years, but he'd evaded her. She heard he was in the army. She heard he might be in the Middle East. Or maybe in Mexico.

After a lifetime of no travel, with a grown daughter, Kate Monroe went to Mexico for a yoga retreat in the spring of 2020. And maybe, she had to admit to herself, with some far-fetched idea that the universe would reunite her with Ian Campton.

Rory's mother, Kate Monroe, was in Mexico, as it turns out, at the same time that Michael and David's mother was there with Trey Dunn to receive her Rogers Fellowship recognition, and at the same time that Hope's mother was there to finally bring Ian home, creating a perfect storm of sorts. Three lifetimes converging in one place. And at one time.

On a break from the yoga retreat, Kate Monroe took a cab to a nearby beach resort, *Playa del Espejo* one night. It was there she ran into a woman at the bar sitting on a stool not far from a mirror that reflected the sea. The woman might have been Kate's sister in another lifetime. She held out her hand and said, "Nice to meet you. I'm Kate." And Kate Monroe laughed and laughed because that was her name too.

And what were the odds?

It's a very popular name, they both agreed.

Neither one of them noticed the handsome couple dining nearby in the same beach resort at a table for two, one half of which was a woman in a bright red sundress with hair the same color. Because neither of the women noticed the couple, they also didn't notice that the woman in the bright red sundress looked like Kate and Kate at the bar. Neither of them noticed that the red-headed woman had a warrior tattoo and a new friend named Trey, and they didn't notice that the red-headed woman and Trey ordered fish tacos and sangria.

Likewise the red-headed woman and Trey didn't notice the striking women at the bar, both of whom were named Kate, one with a blonde bob, and one with a long grey ponytail, who looked alike but for their hair color. They didn't notice the man seated at the chaise lounge nearby, drowning his sorrows in a bucket of beer.

The blonde woman at the beach bar told Kate Monroe she was looking for a man named Ian Campton who was working at the beach resort by day and living nearby at night. She intended to bring him home for their daughter's graduation. Ian Campton, it seems, who had always been so adamant he wanted to remain free and childless, had decided he did want a child after all. And then he didn't. He'd left the woman and her daughter behind as he enlisted in the Army, and he'd lived his life in exile and regret. In the dark beach bar, Kate Monroe had a realization. While she was tempted to go find Ian Campton herself, she recognized that this woman needed him more in that moment.

Someday, though, Kate Monroe resolved then and there, she'd help her daughter, Rory, find her father, when she was confident that he would embrace and not reject her. In the meantime, Kate Monroe paid her tab, left *Playa del Espejo*, and headed back to the yoga retreat, where she made a decision to extend her trip for another week, maybe more.

Kate Monroe's daughter, Rory, was intrigued to learn that her mother was finally making good on those long ago promises to travel. In reality, Kate Monroe was reluctant to chance another collision with Kate (and now Ian and Hope) in New York City.

When Kate Monroe returned to her yoga retreat, she put aside the encounter she'd just had, until the following week, when a new guest joined them from the Bahamas. Kate Monroe felt quite close to the new guest—quickly and inexplicably, and confided in her about the woman named Kate that she'd met at the beach with the sea reflected in the framed plane of glass. The new guest said, "The choices we make in this lifetime. They are for this lifetime alone. Make them and then own them. Move forward with confidence, one step, one choice *at a time.*"

And it was then, that Kate realized something powerful. It was time, Kate knew, to let her daughter go. Time for Rory to go to Cuba or Miami or wherever she and Marcos decided to go. It was time for Kate to move forward with her own life.

After all, she thought, *we only get one lifetime.*

Or at least, as her new friend at the yoga retreat named Dee, had pointed out: we only get one lifetime—*at a time.*

Acknowledgments

THE THING IS, THIS NOVEL WAS NOT GOING TO BE.

I did not anticipate writing a follow-up to my debut novel, *Lemongrass Hope*, originally published in 2014. In fact, for years when Book Clubs asked if I was planning on writing another chapter for Kate and Ian and Rob and Dee, I emphatically stated: *no.* As more and more readers found the story contained in the pages of *Lemongrass Hope,* and made it their own, I became bolder in my denial. There were so many interpretations of what might have happened to these characters after the last pages of *Lemongrass Hope*, I was certain that I had nothing left to add.

And besides, I would think quietly at the Book Clubs and Book Events over the years, when readers would ask if I was going to write another story about these characters: *I'm just not sure how it ends.*

I kept resisting. I wrote some notes. I thought a lot about *Hope.* I wrote other books. I kept telling Book Clubs and readers and friends the same thing over and over again. *No.*

But as Marcos tells Rory over and over again in these pages, *sometimes, you have to tell the story that finds you.*

And as I wrote, secretly and late into the night, much like *Lemongrass Hope* was written, I discovered the truth. I discovered *I Know How This Ends.* And suddenly the book that was never to be became the book I absolutely couldn't wait to share with you.

The launch of this, my fifth novel, and sixth book, into the world coincides with a decade anniversary since I left my former career as a corporate litigator. *Lemongrass Hope* and *I Know How This Ends* are now bookends for this period of my life, and the books I've written this decade, including *Lawyer Interrupted, Secrets of Worry Dolls, The Truth About Thea,* and *Why We Lie,* set end to end, create a memoir of sorts of this leg of the journey. These stories, while not strictly autobiographical, explore all the things I have been personally exploring this decade: crossroads, authenticity, my origin story, love, heartbreak, second chances, my place in the #metoo movement, legacy, regrets, and destiny.

I am so very grateful to every reader who not only found my stories, but reached out to tell me your own story. Without these connections, I would not have found the courage to keep putting my words out into the world. So thank you, first and foremost, to all my readers, past and present.

Thank you to the book bloggers, and bookstagrammers, and book groups who support authors with their #booklove every single day, including Barbara Bos's Women Writers, Women's Books, The Pulpwood Queens, Bolo Books, Readers Coffeehouse, Books & Margaritas Readers Lounge, The Back Booth, Sue's Booking Agency, Bookworms Anonymous, A Novel Bee, Jamie Rosenblit, Chris Moore, Carol Doscher, Novel Gossip, Holly's Little Book Reviews, Marisa G Books, Kate Rock, Jaymi Couch, Rebecca's Book Reviews, Suzy Approved Book Reviews, Jenny Ellis, KT Book Reviews, 832 Book Reviews, Miss W Book Reviews, Reading is my Remedy, Midwest Ladies Who Lit, Live To Read 89, Michelle Dunton, just to name a few!

A big thank you to Maria Gothie for donating to the Tall Poppy Writer fundraiser for Room to Read, for the chance to have a character named after her beloved mother, Nancy Gothie. What a privilege to honor your mother's memory in these pages while at the same time raising money for girls' literacy programs all over the world!

Thank you to my agent, Bob Diforio, for your zealous representation of my art.

Thank you to Paul, for motivating me in ways you probably don't even realize.

Thank you to my friend, Jane Ubell-Meyer, for inviting me to be part of her amazing Bedside Reading program. Thank you also, to the hotels who have featured this and others of my books, including Acqualina Resort and Spa, Baron's Cove, Indigo East End, White Fences Inn, and more!

Thank you to Ann Garvin and all the Tall Poppy Writers without whom this whole releasing-books-into-the-world thing wouldn't be nearly as much fun.

Thank you to the BLOOM community who raises up my sisterhood of Tall Poppy Writers and rewards the female storytelling community with so much loyalty it makes my heart full. (www.areyouinbloom.com)

Thank you to Nancy Cleary of Wyatt-MacKenzie Publishing who has taught me so much about the world of publishing, and who has embraced my stories from the start with such care and zeal that I have the rare experience of having loved not only the art of writing, but the business of publishing. May we continue to find new ways to avoid (together!) the cynicism and snark so prevalent elsewhere in this industry! Cheers!

Thank you to my friends and family for all your love and unconditional support, with a special shout out to my parents: Kathy and Mike Shelley; my siblings and siblings-in-law: Megan, Kate, Carli, Patrick, Joe, and my adopted sister, Kelly Wasielevski, for all you do from showing up at book events, to reading early drafts, to buying my books for full retail price when you don't have to, for recommending them to your friends, and for never ever making me feel foolish for pursuing this dream of mine.

And finally, to Paul, Luke, and Grace. You are the beginning, middle, and end of my story. I thank you and I love you.

book club
discussion guide

Dear Book Clubs,

Thank you for your vibrant discussions of *Lemongrass Hope*. You pushed and inspired me to explore another chapter for these characters, and I couldn't be more grateful. I hope your Book Club discussions about *I Know How This Ends* are just as rich. Here are some questions to get you started.

xo
Amy

1. "Commencement means beginning." How many graduation speeches have begun this way? The fact that a ceremony to mark the *"end"* of an era is named *"beginning"* is a paradox that I wanted to capitalize on in this story. What advice would *you* have for these very special graduating seniors in *I Know How This Ends*—as they experience both an *ending* and a *beginning?*

2. What do you think of Rory and Marcos's relationship? Do you think Rory was right to disregard her mother's caution and warnings?

3. This story is told from three points of view: Rory, Kate, and Ian. In *Lemongrass Hope*, we didn't get Ian's point of view. Now that you are able to get inside Ian's head for the first time, are there any surprises?

4. How did you feel about Ian and Kate's relationship at the end of *Lemongrass Hope*? How about now?

5. Rory learns much of Kate and Ian's story through Dee's story-telling inside and out of Carnegie Hall. Do you think Dee is an impartial or biased narrator of this tale?

6. What do you think of Kate's friendship with Benton? It's clearly undergone an evolution as the two women have aged. Do you think they will remain friends after this story is over or not?

7. If you read *Lemongrass Hope*, you might have noticed echoes in the two stories. For example both stories have a pivotal coffee shop encounter near the end. What other echoes did you pick up on?

8. How did you feel about Ian staying away for so long? When Kate finds the photograph he took at the Afghanistan border, did that change or validate your feelings?

9. Did you at any point say to yourself—*I Know How this Ends*? Were you right?